"This is abou  was left before us. the buttes, the can just appear and understand it all. Once you're rooted, it flows through you; it speaks to you; it lives in you. You will never get that because you're not part of that. You work up there on that butte with someone who couldn't care less about what we are, who we are, and you think you have it all figured out. I feel bad for you, Cal, tumble weeding along. You're just dry roots, rot, dust in the wind. We don't need you anymore. Get out!" Tommy yelled.

The bar was silent, every face turned toward Tommy and Cal. He could see Cal's eyes starting to water, red flushing her cheeks, a slight shake of her hands as she removed them from her glass. Noise returned to the bar, but Tommy's eyes were once again unmoving.

"If it's really more than that," Cal said, her voice quivering, "then you deal with your own mess. I'm out." Cal stood up and walked away.

"Hey, Cal!" Des shouted. "Wait up."

The words fell hard on Tommy, much harder than he anticipated. There was a weight that he hadn't felt in a long time: responsibility. It was time to take matters into his own hands.

Praise for Kerry Fryar Freeman and Sedona

Sedona was long-listed for the Santa Fe Writers Project Literary Award in 2022.

~*~

"…magical and mystical as its namesake…very real characters [are] woven together in an intricate storyline that pits family members one against another…the writing is smooth, the dialogue crisp and the characters distinct and memorable. Ms. Freeman proves that Sedona really is a state of mind that can be experienced in the pages of her excellent book."

~Amazon Bestseller Tom McCaffrey, author,
The Claire Trilogy

~*~

"…an immersive and intriguing trip through the dark side of a tourist paradise…if you've been waiting for a modern and diverse take on the Phyllis A. Whitney school of southwestern suspense, this is it…"

~Award-winning Radio News Anchor and Mystery Author, Nikki Knight.

Sedona

by

Kerry Fryar Freeman

Sedona

Cover Art by *Tina Lynn Stout*

The Wild Rose Press, Inc.
PO Box 708
Adams Basin, NY 14410-0708
Visit us at www.thewildrosepress.com

Publishing History
First Edition, 2023
Trade Paperback ISBN 978-1-5092-5097-4
Digital ISBN 978-1-5092-5098-1

Published in the United States of America

Dedication

To Barrett for being my courage, heart, and home, no matter where our adventures lead.

Acknowledgments

Writing might be a lonely business, but it takes the support and love of people to make it possible. First and foremost, I want to thank my husband, who is my biggest fan. Without him, life would be lacking in laughter and inspiration. He is my motivator, my heart, and my best friend. I love you, Barrett.

To my kids, whose patience and understanding are a blessing each day, especially when I'm writing. To my mom and dad, who encouraged me to get lost in books as a child. To Tom and Mary Elizabeth for being my spirit squad! To my brother and sisters who inspired me at every turn. To my friends, Randi and Emily, who are the Cals in my life.

To my Books and Bevies family, who share my passion for libations and see their value in literature. Because of you, I get to be a part of your journeys and help readers find your amazing stories. To the #WritingCommunity and #Bookstagram friends for being a positive force in social media and selflessly liking, commenting, and sharing posts that help authors. To the great Kaycee John, editor extraordinaire, for loving Sedona enough to give it a chance and make it what it is today.

Last, I want to thank the readers. You breathe life into the words we write, giving them that little bit of magic they need to survive.

"No matter where in the world I'm coming back from, in Sedona I always feel a sense of safety and peace, as if I've returned to the home of my soul, into the arms of Mother Earth the red land that always welcomes me with open arms."

~IIchi Lee

Forward

Sedona, Arizona. Population 10,377.

Known for its majestic red-rock landscape, towering buttes, devastating views, mystical vortexes, spiritual experiences, magical crystals, tribal lore, and a sky the color of turquoise. But behind the veil of tourism is a hum, a vibration that reverberates in those who truly live there, who tune in with their ears and their souls. Visitors hear the tales of healing and spread their own stories of hope and deliverance from coast to coast, from continent to continent, bringing Sedona to life.

Chapter One

Sitting in the doctor's office in rural North Carolina, Cal Novak and her grandmother awaited the test results. Deep down, they knew the answer before the doctor said it: "Cancer, and it has started to spread."

Cal had driven all night from Atlanta to make this appointment; she felt the heaviness of her eyelids as she tried desperately to focus on his words. She clicked the heels of her red high-tops together, a childhood habit that appeared whenever she was anxious, which was often.

"What does that mean?" she asked, keeping her voice strong and steady.

It had only been a couple of years since her grandfather had died from cancer, and it was as if someone had hit the replay button in her life. The familiar smell of the office and the ticking of the clock above the door overwhelmed her senses as her grandmother gave her hand a reassuring squeeze.

"It means that we'll need to talk about some next steps, chemotherapy, for example," the doctor said, keeping his focus on Grandma Ruth.

Grandma Ruth smiled. "No, we won't be doing that, Doctor, but thank you."

Cal understood what she meant and knew it was futile to argue with her. They had both watched her grandfather waste away to nothing from the treatment, and Grandma Ruth had said many times that her guilt was too much to bear. She wouldn't allow that to happen again.

"Ms. Ruth, I understand your hesitation, but we must be proactive. You're already showing signs of—"

"No thank you," Grandma Ruth interrupted as she stood. "We'll be in touch."

Cal watched as her grandmother walked out of the room, waiting until the footsteps disappeared down the hallway before turning to the doctor to say, "How long does she have?"

The doctor took a deep breath and folded his hands as if the answer were buried somewhere deep within, and he had to dive to retrieve it. "It's hard to say, Cal." He shook his head, then answered grimly, "At this stage and without treatment, it's not a matter of when; it's about being comfortable."

"Thank you, Doctor." Cal shook his hand and left.

There was so much she wanted to say after the two got into the car, both silent and spacey, but Grandma Ruth spoke first. "Cally?" Her voice was quiet and confident.

"Yes?" Cal looked over to find her grandmother staring into her eyes.

Grandma Ruth smiled, "Sedona."

That was all she had to say. Cal knew what it meant. She spent the next month selling furniture, packing what she could, then quit her job. Her whole life fit into a Rent-A-Truck trailer, and the two set out for the healing powers of Sedona. It was a promise, the most important promise she had ever made.

****

Eight months later, Cal stood before Crystal Blue Publishing, repeating the phrase "you can do this" repeatedly. The promise that once fueled her great adventure out West had now sunk into her stomach and formed an ulcer. Grandma Ruth's health had deteriorated, and though her Southern spunk was going strong, Cal felt that time was not on her side.

She had managed to pick up some contract work editing for Crystal Blue, but her bills were stacking up like the buttes in Sedona, and not much was coming in. Her grandmother had some money; most of it was going toward a nurse, Alice, who came in a few days a week to help take care of her. Cal knew they would have to consider more than just the dry air of Sedona to help her grandmother. Right now, she had more pressing worries. Today she either needed a raise, or she needed to get another job—and the prospect of all that simply exhausted her.

She took a deep breath, flung open the door, pushed her sunglasses onto her head, and said, "I need more money!"

It came out louder than anticipated, and her boss, Jack Miller didn't seem impressed. He slowly lifted his head, nodded, and responded, "Is this a hold-up?"

Cal rolled her eyes and plopped down on the chair opposite his, the large desk between them. "Do you ever take me seriously?" she asked, feeling a bead of sweat trickle down her back. Cal hadn't realized how warm it was already, and it was only spring.

"I try not to take anyone seriously who comes in demanding things of me," Jack said with a smirk.

Cal could tell that, at some point, Jack had been polished and clean because it looked like he stood in front of the mirror in the morning, teetering between hippie and professional. He could have coined that look with his messy-but-clean hair, leather necklace with tiny crystals, a collared shirt untucked with a pair of loose khakis and sandals. His skin lied about his age, with premature wrinkles—courtesy of the Sedona sun—and the black-rimmed glasses almost looked like fakes, but Cal had never seen him without them. She guessed he was in his late forties but wasn't one hundred percent sure.

"I've worked my tail off for you ever since I started, hitting every deadline you've given me. What's my incentive for staying?" Cal's last line was a joke, seeing as there was little work anywhere during the off-season in Sedona. She hoped he wouldn't call her bluff.

Jack rummaged around in his desk drawer, brought out a wrinkled collection of bills, and slapped them on the desk. "Here, here's your raise."

Cal scoffed loudly. "This is like three bucks, maybe four—this isn't going to help me."

"Yeah, well, it's more than three bucks; drop the drama. You know, I don't have to give you anything extra. You already got your paycheck." Jack shifted in his chair and adjusted the fan on his desk, so the air blasted into his face.

Cal imagined reaching over and aiming it at herself with a smile, yearning to escape the heat. "How am I going to make rent?" she fired back.

"Well, it's tight around here, as you know. Look, Cal, if I could pay you more, you know I would. You finished both of your contract jobs for this month. It's all I have right now."

"What am I supposed to do then?"

She didn't expect an answer, at least not from her boss. It was a question she had asked herself for months.

Jack seemed uncomfortable, possibly even irritated by her presence, but they had become close since he'd hired her. He was like many of the past publishers Cal had worked with, brilliant, quirky, too caffeinated for their own good. Plus, she respected him.

In the end, that is what made today so tricky. It's one thing to ask for money from someone you don't like, but Jack was one of the few people in her new hometown who felt like a friend. She could feel the desperation oozing from her mouth with that last question. Why couldn't she get a break, just this once? Cal took a deep breath and met his eyes.

There was an awkward cough and shift before Jack responded. "I know that. Trust me, I know. My mother, God rest her soul, was more expensive dying than she was alive, but there was nothing I wouldn't do for her. The truth is that we do what we can. I saw the ranch down by Sunset Valley is hiring. Maybe you can pick up some odd jobs?"

"This is an odd job, Jack. Look at me. I'm a contract editor for a small publication specializing in magic stones and—"

"Crystals!" Jack's voice boomed, more serious, a nerve that Cal knew better than to pinch.

"Yeah, yeah, crystals. I was supposed to be someone, you know, a big-time editor for a publishing house dripping in books. How did I get here?"

"I like to think you followed your spirit to us."

"That's cute."

"How 'bout Sunset Ranch? I know a guy."

"You know lots of guys. I'm a city girl. The closest I've been to a horse was the merry-go-round at an amusement park, and even then, I wasn't a big fan. I'm

5

pretty sure I puked, so no, no thanks."

"I'm sure they aren't looking for someone to ride the imaginary horses. If they are, let me know after your interview because that sounds like something I might enjoy. Just give them a call. Who knows? In the meantime, I'll see if any other places around here are looking for a sarcastic, somewhat lazy female to look for grammatical errors."

"Thanks, Jack. You're a real…gem."

Cal grabbed her bag, threw it over her shoulder, flung the glass door open, and nodded quickly, making her sunglasses slide onto her nose. The wad of money was damp in her hand, drenched in embarrassment and annoyance. Since settling in Sedona, the time had dragged on slowly; it felt like it had stopped. And even on days when time did pass, it felt like a song on continuous replay.

Sedona crawled with peculiar people. The tourists weren't nearly as bad as the locals. Cal was amazed by how many people had moved to Sedona to experience the healing powers of the weather and rocks. Even her grandmother had been suckered into the mystery. Cal stopped by The Vortex, a local bar, and a total hole-in-the-wall complete with a literal hole in the wall where there was once a door.

The owner, Lucio, thought the hole had more charm than the door after a delivery truck backed into the front of the bar one day. "I feel that it captures the spirit of the place," he claimed and even got it in the papers.

She waved to the bartender, who stood at the end of the bar, cleaning copper mugs. "Bourbon on the rocks."

"You got it, Cal," he yelled back.

Des Adams was the first "normal" person she had

met in Sedona. His family had lived there his whole life, working at the Red Rock Resort. He was tall, black, and slender with an afro that he usually kept pulled back.

"Hey, do you know if Lucio is hiring?"

"Not sure. Why? You trying to work at a bar now?" With a laugh, he slid the bourbon-filled glass to her.

Cal nodded without smiling. "There isn't enough work at the magazine, though I can't imagine why."

"It's not tourist season yet. It'll pick up. Once the car and RV loads of people come flocking in, you'll see. Money'll start flowing through those rocks again. It's tough living in a tourist town. Save-Mart's always hiring."

"Yep, they were not impressed with my retail résumé. Can I just say that no one else would have done anything differently if a kid had thrown up all over aisle five." Cal laughed, recalling the one week she survived working at a grocery store. Who would have thought there were so many rules for retail employment?

"You don't have the sunny disposition for Save-Mart. I can ask Lucio, but he doesn't have the money. No one does until—"

"Tourist season. Yeah, I've heard that one.

"You can start saving money by not drinking at the bar. You know, there's this place called a liquor store, and they sell this stuff for much cheaper."

"I don't come here for the booze, Des. I come here for the conversation," she said while shuffling the empty glass back in his direction. "I could strip. Strippers always seem to have a lot of money."

Des's head didn't stop shaking. "Nope, no way…that would not work for you."

"I'll take that as you feel that my character and

moral standards are much too high for such a low road."

"No, I wasn't gonna say all that. I was going to say you're much too hotheaded. You wouldn't last a night before you punched someone and got arrested. Can you imagine good ol' boy Drunk Tommy grabbin' at your ruby slippers?"

"Seriously? Why would you bring him up? This was such a clean conversation until then."

Drunk Tommy was a thorn in Cal's side. Since she stepped foot in The Vortex the first time, he had made it his life's mission to hit on her until she punched him, and he was gross, really gross. With just a patch of hair on his face and tattoos on his head, he looked like a commercial for how not to use hair restoration products. He was always in a dirty white t-shirt and jeans and often started conversations with "Tell me something."

There wasn't much to "tell" Drunk Tommy other than "sit down" or "leave me the heck alone," but that didn't stop him from saying it. He owned a tourist trap that gave tours where ancient pines could cure everything from memory loss to arthritis.

"Maybe he has a point."

"Wait, that was just one bourbon, right? I did just serve you one. Did you just say that Drunk Tommy has a point?"

"Yeah. Think about it! He owns his own business and a house, and how many people can say that?"

"Not sure what made you say any of that. It's a trailer and barely a business. There's no way you can be this desperate! I'll help you find a job. Maybe my mom and dad know of something at the resort. Sometimes there's turnover."

"You're the best, Des. Give me a call if you hear of

anything." Cal slapped a ten on the bar and waited for the change but decided the tip was worth it if she got a job from it.

She didn't want to go home. The nurse, Alice, would be there with her grandma, either bathing her or taking her around outside, and she couldn't take the overly optimistic aura. Her grandmother had been the most critical person in the world to her after her parents died. But now, after leaving her life in Atlanta and moving to Sedona, she felt the love for her grandmother shift to a feeling of responsibility, and she hated it. She figured that she could be an editor from anywhere in the world since most jobs were online, but with her résumé more of a bulleted list of small internships, there wasn't much to show. If she were going to work, it would have to be from the ground up, the red-rock ground up.

It wasn't too bad at first. The magazine paid well, there were many people in the town, and she felt the energy of Sedona buzzing around her. As the tourists left, and the wind picked up, she became the "tumbleweed" for which she always felt sorry in all the Westerns she used to watch with her grandfather.

Then the money dried up.

"Well, well, if it isn't Cal Ripken Jr. walking the streets of Sedona. Are you lost?"

"Officer Sanchez. No, sir, just on cruise control today. It's nice out."

"Hot as hell out here. What're you really up to?"

"How can you drive that car and talk to me with your head turned that way? Aren't you afraid you're going to hit a pedestrian? I heard a rumor it was a police cruiser that made that hole in The Vortex all those years ago."

"Ha! We all know that's a lie. Lucio probably

9

started that rumor."

It was likely he did. Lucio and Officer Sanchez were brothers and not the good kind. They hadn't spoken since Bush was president, the first Bush. Apparently, there were wives involved, but Cal didn't ask questions.

"Is there something I can help you with, Officer?"

"Nah, just saw you walking."

"You wouldn't happen to need a deputy, would you? I might be hitting the open market."

"The only market you need to be hitting is the one selling me my groceries. And it just so happens that Jenny is about to have an opening. Her son is graduating and going to college. I'm not sure why anyone would want to leave Sedona. It's heaven on Earth here."

"Thanks for the tip, and yeah, she's a real 'butte,'" Cal said, using her fingers as air quotes.

"Butte, I like that. Take care, and tell your grandma I said hello, will you?" he yelled, driving off.

Cal rolled her eyes and adjusted the bag across her body. The heat was getting more unbearable, indicating that summer was approaching. She couldn't wait that long for business to pick up, though she wished she could. The heat didn't inspire work.

Chapter Two

"Is that you, Cally?"

Cal dropped her head and took a deep breath—back to reality. She put on her best Southern charm and yelled, "Yes, Grandma, it's me. I have some work to do, so I'm going to get to it."

"Oh, come on in and talk to her first," Alice said, appearing in the hallway. She was smiling and frowning simultaneously as if gravity had played a cruel trick on her face.

"Okay." Cal trailed her and shuffled into the hole of a living room.

"Now, Cally, tell us all about your day." Grandma Ruth leaned forward in her chair, beaming with pride. "Did you get any new articles? I'm just so proud of her, Alice. My little writer."

"Grandma, I told you. I don't write; I edit. You know, look for mistakes? Add periods? Things like that."

"Right, right. Well, she's going to be famous one day. You need to eat something, Cally. You're nothing but skin and bones. What would your folks think of me?"

Cal's parents had been dead for years, and their mention made her uneasy. "They would probably think you're doing great, Grandma. In fact, how about I go fix you a little something before I head to my room."

"Aren't you just a peach! A real Georgia peach!"

Cal disappeared into the hallway and through

another door into a small kitchenette. The house wasn't much. Her grandma stayed in the living room, and Cal took the one bedroom. There was a bathroom, kitchen, front porch, and back stoop. The house was on a flat, weed-ridden lot with the red rocks of Sedona rising behind it like a sunset that never went away. She felt the glow of red against everything in the house: the walls, furniture, floor, and clothes. Cal was in a constant state of light red as if someone had washed her world with a red sock. She took a plastic container from the refrigerator and popped it into the microwave.

Alice's voice broke through the drone of the machine. "Your grandma had a rough morning."

"Yeah, how so?" Cal asked, opening a water bottle and leaning against the fridge.

"She's talking more nonsense than she did before. You need to start considering a healthcare facility."

"That's why you're here, to facilitate health care. The doctor said she could live on her own. She's walking okay and eating well. She can hold a conversation—"

"I'm not talking about that. I'm talking about the quality of life. I only come here a few days a week, and you're out of the house. She spends a good amount of time alone. She'd have constant care and interaction with others if she were in a facility. Cal, she's talking to herself now. I heard it on and off all day. You must want more than that for her."

"You know I want more. I'm here because I want more, but I can do nothing. I can't afford a home. I can't afford this place. All the money I had saved after my parents died and my grandmother's savings, which wasn't a lot, has been sunk into our home here. I'm trying to get another job and still applying to some online

12

stuff, but there's nothing. Sending her somewhere feels like losing her, and I can't lose her, too."

Alice walked forward and placed her hand on Cal's shoulder. Cal fought the urge to shrug it off. Her hand held the weight of judgment like Cal was a child again, getting in trouble for talking too much in class. "Believe me; you're taking the easy way out right now. It doesn't feel like it, but you are. You're selfish, Cal, young and selfish. I've been young and selfish, but I didn't have someone to care for. You do."

The microwave beeped loudly, sending the smell of BBQ through the air. She shoved past Alice, grabbed a fork off the counter, snatched the plate from the microwave, and took it to her grandmother without rebuttal. If she had less restraint, she could have exploded with "I gave up my life to be here for her" or "Do you have any clue what it's like to watch the person you love most in the world drift away, little by little, knowing there's nothing you can do to stop it?"

But Sedona had taught her that patience is survival, much like a rattlesnake coiled and waiting to strike its prey at the right moment. Not that Cal was a snake—though deep inside, she felt the shaking and rattling, warning the outside world that she was wound tightly.

"I'm leaving now, Ms. Ruth. I'll see you in a couple of days," Alice said, smiling as she popped her head into the room.

"I'll behave until then," Cal's grandmother answered with a smile.

Cal's contempt for Alice was heavy in the room. Even her breathing was labored as the words echoed in her ears. How could she accuse Cal of being selfish? "She doesn't know anything," Cal mumbled.

"Do you hear it, Cal?"

Her grandmother's words were soft. Cal almost didn't catch what she said. Then she whispered again, "Do you hear it? I do. Sometimes, when I'm still, it touches me. It starts here, on that knuckle, and it slides slowly up my arm, ever so slowly, until it reaches my collarbone. And then it dances up my neck and up to my cheek. Then?"

Grandma Ruth laughed loudly, a shocking sound after such a whisper. She stopped as suddenly as she had started and looked into Cal's eyes. "Then, it rolls back down slowly, each little hair moved by its weight until it disappears in the groove of my fingers. It touches me, and my body responds. It's real, Cally. It's real."

Cal was both perplexed and nervous by the ramble. Alice had warned about this, but Cal hadn't heard it before. It was off, for sure, but not too concerning. Cal stifled a chill that began to creep down her spine. She had seen too many horror movies to think maniacal laughs were funny. She kept her eyes on her grandmother while she ate and traced the trail Grandma Ruth described from her knuckles to her cheek.

She noticed something for the first time. There was a faint green line, a vein, that had appeared. It went from her knuckle to her cheek in a slightly meandering line. Cal didn't know much about veins, but she did think it was odd that it would be so prominent from its origin to its end. The afternoon sun drenched the room even redder than before, casting a glow against her grandmother, making her look more like the rising rocks than a person.

She turned and smiled at her. "I'm finished now. Thank you, Cally."

Cal took the container back into the kitchen and grabbed another water. The heat was getting to her again. There was no air conditioner in the house, just fans she had bought before moving in. She tried to keep the living room cool, but the sun was unbearable as it was setting.

There was only one window in the bedroom, and Cal had covered it with a black curtain to keep out the red glare. The small twin bed was pushed against one wall with a desk and dresser on the other. Cal kicked her red high-tops off into the corner and opened her computer. The house didn't have internet, so she used her phone as a hotspot as she visited the usual suspects. There were a couple of hits on her résumé, and she took a job editing travel brochures for twenty-five bucks. It would take her a couple of hours—it was worth the money. She scanned social media, but it was the usual: political warfare, virus talk, indirect bragging, and sob story competitions.

Her phone buzzed, alerting her a text message was coming in from Des.

—*Hey, girl, you at home?*—

—*Yeah, doing work. Why? What's up?*—

—*Heard about a job! My mom just told me ...*—

She quickly typed— *Going the suspense route, eh?*—

—*Not everyone types a million words a minute.*— he responded, then continued.

—*Mom said there is nothing at the resort, but a new tour company is opening near Belle Butte ...looking for people.*—

Cal asked –*People? What kind of people?*—

—*Do you want me to call them and ask? Better yet, should I go and interview for you?*—

—*Fine ... I'll look it up myself.*—

—*You are so welcome! Glad to help!*—

Cal ended with —*THANK YOU and stop whining.*—

—*Hahaha! You love me!*—

Cal put her phone down and typed Belle Butte Touring Company into her browser. It came up immediately, showing a picture of a slew of people doing yoga along a ledge overlooking the canyons. Above them, instead of stars, were crystals of all shapes and sizes glowing in the sky.

Creative, she thought, scoffing at an incorrect apostrophe on the page. *Maybe they're hiring a website editor.* The "Job Openings" page did not list an editor, but there were multiple tour advisor openings. The description sounded like tour guides. "Not exactly brain surgery. I could talk to people about rocks."

Before she could make an excuse, Cal opened the application, filled it out, and sent it. Two hours later, she finished editing the travel brochures and found herself lying in bed. She had no concept of time with the blackout curtains fastened tightly to the window and didn't care. There wasn't anything else to do, and sleep sounded better than being conscious.

Chapter Three

"Your jeep may not make it up there," Des said, leaning against it as Cal frantically pushed the buttons on the gas pump.

"How is it that we live in the twenty-first century and these stupid gas pumps look like they were here when the dinosaurs were?" Cal slammed the palm of her hand against the machine until she heard the familiar rush-whoosh-whine as gas began filling her tank. "I'm sure the tourists love these things. Vintage!"

"You're funny. Really! You nervous?"

"No. It's probably not even a job I'll have for long. The magazine will pick back up when the season starts, and I'll likely quit. I can't leave my grandmother for this long every day. It's already going to be a stretch."

"I don't mind checking on her when I go to work. That nurse scares me, though. She's super nice to your grandma and super mean to me, like that day I dropped off that cable for you?"

Cal knew what he meant. It was a random weekday that she got stuck working the desk at the magazine because Jack was running late. Des had to drop off an HDMI cable at her house, so he planned to leave it at the doorstep. However, Alice on seeing a young man with an afro standing on the front porch with a cable in his hand, came out of the house screeching and screaming about no soliciting, then accused him of being a robber.

Des said that the sheer volume of her voice sent him backward off the porch and into his car before he could explain. Cal apologized profusely, but Des wouldn't hear it; instead, he made a joke that "of course, the one black guy in Sedona would get thrown off of someone's porch for being a solicitor and a robber at the same time." Another story in the months they knew each other solidified their friendship.

"Our vicious common enemy. Whatever, she's good to my grandma, and that's what counts. I worry when she isn't there. Maybe I shouldn't do this."

"Cal, you have to. As you said, there's nothing else, and it's what, like, thirty minutes away? And, a nod to the twenty-first century, phone reception is everywhere, so if she needs you or you need her, boom, done. No more excuses. Go get yourself a job!"

Cal leaned against the jeep on the other side of the pump and looked at Des, nodding. She knew it was the right thing to do, and if the pay listed were true, it would be enough to sustain them for a while without the stress of wondering what she would do for money.

Des hopped into his car and leaned out the open window. "You should have worn different shoes, though. Those things have seen better days, don't you think?"

Cal looked down at her trusty high-tops and noticed the whites were more orange and the shoelaces were going gray but the red was still radiant. She shrugged and responded, "They still have some magic left." Des laughed and sped off toward town.

The drive was a welcome distraction. Green patches of flora covered parts of the ground and climbed up the rocks. She passed the sign for Drunk Tommy's

Whispering Pines, and her eyes immediately rolled. How did a guy like that get such a break in life? Where's the justice in the world?

The first time she'd met Tommy was a couple of weeks into her new life in Sedona, and he was at The Vortex playing a rowdy game of pool with a couple of locals. A tourist came over to the table and said he wanted the next round, with a slur that sounded more like "sly wants shenex run." Tommy was more than happy to accept.

A half-hour later, he displayed a fan of cash and victoriously offered to buy the next round of drinks for the bar while the inebriated opponent was doubled over in the can.

Cal had turned to Des and asked, "Who is that guy?"

The answer still echoed in her ears. "That's Drunk Tommy."

At first, he didn't seem so drunk, but as the night wore on, he lived up to his name. Now, recalling that first introduction, Cal felt jealous and hated herself. She would give anything to have a life of freedom, for Grandma Ruth to be well and her cancer healed, and for her life back in Atlanta, editing by day and going out by night. It was a constant internal battle between guilt and claustrophobia, like living on a ledge debating whether she should jump into the vast openness. Of course she did the right thing because that was the only way she could sleep at night; she wondered how Tommy slept at night. I mean, his life couldn't be that great.

Chapter Four

Drunk Tommy sat, chair on two legs leaning against his trailer wall, eyes half shut, swatting at a fly. There wasn't much to do, and even if there were, the cooler of beer on his pathetic attempt at a porch wouldn't drink itself. Tourist season would be here before long, and with it came the daily grind. The land was his, paid for by his great, great grandfather, a deal made with one of the Native American tribes, which was never written in a history book. After the family homestead burned down over a decade before, Tommy's grandmother bought the trailer as a temporary living space until the new home was built. She died, God rest her soul, a couple of months into the project.

Since Tommy was the only family member still living because the fire killed his grandfather and father, and his mother had skipped out years earlier and remarried some guy up in California, he inherited everything: the land and the business. Whispering Pines, it was called, was touted as one of the must-see tourist spots in Sedona. Unlike other tourist attractions, Tommy's land didn't rely on colorful vehicles or horses to make it special. Instead, it was a combination of what Sedona was known for, healing and natural beauty. His grandfather had been a businessman in his own right, kept up with the taxes on the land, and put away a nest egg for the family.

The land was covered in pines, towering, ancient, and majestic. Granddaddy Philpot had also grown up at the homestead and had heard stories of the whispering pines. "They hold magic," his father would tell him.

He learned about the native people who lived on the land and how they talked to the trees, and the trees listened. In the heat of the summer, the trees would stand tall and give shade to their people. In the winter, they would offer themselves as sacrifices, as wood to be burned in the tribe's fires. The pines promised to protect those who lived on the land as long as the people saved them. Granddaddy Philpot was not a book-smart man but could sniff out an opportunity.

When Philpot was a teenager, he would walk around town and offer tours of the land, weaving a tapestry of tales about the power of the pines. Locals ate it up; they had heard similar stories before, stories of dying men who were brought to the land to be resurrected, stories of broken arms and legs that were healed when the pines left their whisper on them.

Philpot put a sign at the front of their driveway: "Whispering Pines: Free Healing." The first tour season was slow, with only a few cars that took him up on his magical walk through the pines, but people were affected. They would go back to town and talk about the whispers and how aches and pains were relieved after one touch of a pine. The word spread, and the following year more cars came, and the next year, even more. The family built a small hut near the entrance to sell tickets, and Philpot would take visitors on a trail through the pines. He would tell stories, give firsthand accounts of healing, and answer the tourists' questions. By the time his tour hit its climax, which was in a clearing thickly surrounded by pines where the sun reflected off the red rocks in the distance, making a red spotlight against the pine straw on the ground, creating a pillow, the people were mesmerized and ready to experience healing. He would ask them to lie in the straw, close their eyes, and listen to the pines whispering.

From the oldest grandma to the youngest child, no one seemed to walk away without hearing the pines speak to them. "It's a miracle! I haven't heard out of my right ear in years," one would say. "My nose isn't running anymore," a child would say, wiping at their nose. "That bruise, the one on my elbow, it's gone!" "How 'bout that? I see every cloud in the sky!" Philpot believed every utterance, every single one of them, and took note. He had whispered to those pines before, asking for a fortune, and here he was, surrounded by gold.

The business boomed in the tourist season and lay dormant during winter. They saved their money and continued to make new trails and experiences for tourists. Philpot had his own family that grew up working the land, and he took pride in the legacy he created and was even prouder when he saw his first grandchild, a bouncing baby boy. His name was Tommy, a namesake that would carry on Whispering Pines to the next generation.

Tommy's father learned the ways of Whispering Pines from his daddy but did not respect the land as much as *his* father had. He resented his father's love for the pines and felt that the trees had not blessed his life but instead cursed it. He didn't understand why, with all of their money, they still lived in an old homestead with old cars and old clothes. When he graduated from high school, he left Sedona and took a job in California, apprenticing to become an electrician and working odd jobs as a dishwasher or janitor. He met Martha, a beautiful, tanned, blond girl, his "angel," who looked nothing like the dark-headed women he grew up with. He impressed her with stories of the Whispering Pines, and his life in Sedona enchanted her. When they were married, they moved back to the homestead and helped with the business, which had tapered off a bit. His father was getting older, and the property wasn't as pristine as he had remembered.

Martha helped with the tours and brought charm to the place. "She looks like a fairy that winged her way down from the sunshine," Granddaddy Philpot used to say. And she did. It was as if the pines had called her from the shores of the West. The tourists loved her too, not because she was filled with the wisdom of the pines but because she was beautiful, witty, and worldly. They lived happily there and soon welcomed a baby boy named Tommy.

Tommy grew up learning the ways of Whispering Pines from his daddy and Granddaddy Philpot and his mother. While the men would work the land to "make the trees happy"—that's what Granddaddy Philpot would say—Tommy learned how to talk to the tourists from his mother. "When you speak to them, you have to sell them on the power of this place. Tell them about the weeping mother who lost her child and prayed to the trees for a baby and how she returned to us a year later with a baby in her arms, praising the trees. Let them touch the trees, feel the bark, and then blow in their ears. I hung up special chimes in the pines that make it sound like tinkling and wind sails to amplify the sound. That's

23

how you get them, Tommy. That's why they believe in all of this. Remember," she would say, walking him through the pines, "in the end, the magic of Oz was just in Dorothy's head."

"Don't you believe, Momma?" he asked her once when he was seven. He hoped she would say yes because he wanted to believe. He wanted to love the land like his granddaddy loved the land. He wanted to take care of it and tend to the trees. His momma stopped, crouched down to meet his eyes, and took his hands in hers.

"This is all bullshit, Tommy. It is a tourist trap to make money, and it makes a lot of money. One of these days, when your granddaddy dies, we'll hire a bunch of people to work here, and we can move back to California where there are real people with lives. They eat at restaurants, surf on top of the water, shop for fancy clothes, and watch movies on big screens. Tommy, that's real; that's where the real magic is. It's out there! This," she said, dropping his hands and pointing around her, "this is bullshit."

That descriptive word his mother uttered stuck in Tommy's head and created a palpable tension around the dinner table each night as he watched his mom spin stories about the tourists to his granddaddy. Tommy listened as his grandfather indulged in her stories as he gobbled his chicken, vegetables, and dessert. His love for the pines grew more robust with each word she let drip from her mouth, and Tommy could see that she enjoyed it. Tommy didn't know what to think. He had dreams, too, hopes and dreams that included his family and this place. But the longer he watched his mother sprinkle her sugary words over his father and grandfather, he began to wonder which was easier, to play make believe or to actually believe.

When he turned nine, Tommy started going on tours with his mother. Sometimes he would walk alongside her, make mental notes of her words, and practice them later when everyone was gone and he stood alone under the trees. His words would echo and return to him in small phrases as he pointed to places where healing occurred or led his imaginary tour group into the clearing. Other times, he would pretend to be a tourist in her group and ask her questions or talk to the people. This was his favorite. He aimed to make her laugh by giving himself random names like Gilbert Gruffsickle or James Jollygreen. He would introduce himself loudly to the group and wait for her to snicker. There was nothing more beautiful than his mother's laugh, how her smile would stretch across her face, sending her tanned cheeks up to her eyes as if to greet them. He craved her positivity, her ability to send all those around her into an orbit with one giggle.

One day he noticed her talking to one tourist more than the others. He had come with a group of unusually loud guys who carried open beer containers with koozies that said "Free Dan." The man made his mom giggle, light giggles like she shared with his dad when he kissed her neck on the front porch at night. The man stood with her during the clearing part of the tour instead of lying down, and when they returned to the hut, she walked him to his car along with the others. He returned several times over the next week to take the tour, and Tommy found it odd that he would brush his hand against hers as they walked.

Later that summer, Tommy heard the loud fight between his mom and dad. He heard words

ERO

like *cheat* and *lie*. He heard her say, "I can't do this anymore," and "I don't love you." He heard doors slam and feet loudly stomp across the wooden floors. He heard a car door slam and saw lights disappear down the driveway that night. He crept out of his room and slinked to his parent's room, reaching out to knock, but the door swung open. His father was sitting on the bed facing the window, the pine needles glistening in the moonlight. Tommy saw his shadow fall across the bed, making his father look more like a statue than a person, still and dark.

"Dad?" Tommy spoke softly.

"She's gone, Tommy," he answered.

Tommy knew what that meant. He was nine, not five, and he had watched enough TV and listened to enough music to know that his mother had been "gone" for over an hour. He turned, walked back to his room, and sat on his bed. "It can't all be bull." His lips moved, but no sound came out. "It can't be." The stories his granddaddy had told him flooded his mind, stories of healing, broken bones made whole, babies being born, and people coming back from the dead. "It can't all be bull," he said louder. Before he could think, he was out of his bedroom, down the stairs, and through the front door, the screen door slamming behind him. He ran as fast as he could down the trail, his bare feet slipping and sliding on the straw, the needles poking his feet. He ran, his fingertips brushing the bark, scratching and pushing into the fleshy pads. He ran, seeing his mother before him, her golden hair rushing like a waterfall behind her, her voice whispering in the night, "Tommy, Tommy."

He heard her snicker; he felt her hands grasp his. He ran, seeing beside him glances of his grandfather and father working in the pines, picking up the spikey cones, and raking the straw. He saw his father kiss his mother's neck on the porch and heard the giggle. He ran and fell into the clearing, the moon a sliver among the sea of stars, the shadows of the trees and red-rock skyscrapers above him. He turned, buried his face into the pine straw, and prayed to the trees: "If you can hear me, please bring her back. Please. They're broken; like everyone here, they're broken and need healing. Heal them; please heal them. Please!"

Tears rolled from his eyes and disappeared into the straw below him, a rush of water and pain, violent and tumultuous, years of hopes and dreams planted into the ground. "I know you can hear me. It's not bullshit. It's not…" And there he slept, just as a sapling, alone in the clearing.

She didn't come back, and many years came and went, taking his grandparents, father, and the homestead and leaving behind…bullshit. The land was his, the bones of a new homestead that was starting to rot were his, the temporary home of a trailer was his, the hut with the maps to lead one down the trail to the clearing was his, and the pines, those were his too. He didn't need much, just a cooler of beer and tourists. He made sure the wind chimes and sails were free of debris and whispering and tinkling loudly. He had to keep it alive because he had to stay alive, but he knew the truth. It wasn't that he didn't care; the healing that took place that night was not what he'd asked for. His heart scabbed over and scarred. He couldn't stop scratching it for a few years, couldn't stop letting it bleed with the memories of his family. The tissue hardened when it finally scarred over, leaving behind ugliness, harsh reality, brokenness, and grief.

Alcohol dulled the pain, a joint muted it for a while, and the occasional woman he picked up gave him some satisfaction. Tommy accepted what he had left and on days when he sat on his pathetic excuse of a front porch and watched the cars zoom by at the end of his dusty driveway, past the dilapidated sign with Whispering Pines: Healing for Free barely visible through the chipped paint, he even felt a twinge of thankfulness for his Granddaddy Philpot. *At least I have this*, he thought, taking another swig of beer. "Damn fly." He grunted, swatting with his beer hand at the insect. Just then, the chair's back legs gave way, and he let go of the beer to catch his fall, the can tumbling to his lap. He fell into a drunken heap of sweat and alcohol on the porch, yelling, "This is bullshit."

The words echoed through the trees as if they were mocking him.

Chapter Five

As Cal ascended higher onto the butte, she could see
Sedona below, blending into the surrounding desert. It
was a cool town; she wished she had met it under
different circumstances. It was like going on a date with
someone you felt you could have had fun with if you
were different. Her jeep made it to the ridgeline with
only a few strange knocking sounds; she counted herself
lucky not to have broken down on interview day.

Most of the touring companies in Sedona started in
Uptown at the foot of the trails that led to multiple buttes.
Cal wondered if this new company would be able to
compete. This was a hike, much farther out than the other
popular sites that dotted the landscape. It was true that
the average tourist could walk out of their hotel room and
land on a trail or art gallery or vortex.

Cal almost missed the sign in the distance that said
Belle Butte Touring Company in yellow letters against a
red stacked-stone sign. The building beyond it was even
more camouflaged into the rocks. It would have been
hard to see down the drive if not for the cars that lined
the dirt lot. Cacti of varying sizes and large, dark wood
doors flanked the midcentury-modern frame. Windows
covered the rest of the façade, reflecting the desert
landscape like murals. She parked and walked in. The
inside was incredible with gray stone flooring and the
sound of water trickling somewhere in the room that

instantly made it feel ten degrees cooler than the stifling outdoors.

A voice came from a large, circular desk in the middle of the room. "May I help you?"

"Yes, I have an interview with Mark Courier. I think I'm a little early."

"Oh, he'll like that. Early is on time in his book. Have a seat, and I'll let him know you're here."

Cal hated clichés, but the girl was precious, tiny with red hair and even redder lips. She rocked her look. "He'll see you now. And you're Ms. Novak, correct?"

"Yes, that's me."

"It's kind of like Kim Novak, isn't it? The famous actress?"

"Yes, exactly. Except I'm not a blond bombshell or a lot of things."

The girl giggled as she stood to point Cal toward a door. "I wish you the best of luck. You're funny."

"Come on in, Ms. Novak."

Mark Courier stood up from behind his desk and shook Cal's hand. He wasn't what she expected. Men like Drunk Tommy ran most tourist traps, but Mr. Courier was the opposite. He was tall, well dressed in a gray suit and dark tie, young, with blond hair combed over the side. There was no part of him that looked like a tour guide.

"Have a seat," he said, pointing to one of the chairs facing his desk. A window made up a side of the room that looked directly at one of the red-rock faces, revealing greenery growing up the ledges. She could see water dripping down and puddling outside of the window.

"It's a real modern miracle, this building. This part

of the red rocks is porous, allowing the water to pass through. We're housed on top of an underground river. A lot of history here in these hills. Are you a history buff, Cal?"

"I'm not sure if you can call me a buff, but I do appreciate history."

"I see that you're a writer."

"Editor. I mean, I can write and enjoy doing so, but my expertise is in editing. Unfortunately, it doesn't look like you have a job that matches my passions right now."

"No, we don't, but who knows? Maybe one day, if we grow. Websites are important. We're looking for tour advisors, just a fancy way of saying tour guides. We aren't like most of the other run-of-the-mill places here. They sell kitsch and I want to sell reality. How long have you lived here, Cal?"

"Close to a year."

"You're a glorified tourist then. What brought you to the area?"

"My grandmother. She has health problems, so we moved here for the dry air."

"The dry air or the crystals?"

When he laughed, his smile revealed a row of white teeth. Cal couldn't help but stare. He was the most well-put-together human she had seen outside the movies in over a year. He was big money L.A.; her curiosity peaked, and she couldn't help but speak.

"Why are you here, Mr. Courier? This doesn't seem like the spot a guy like you would open a business. I don't mean to pry…"

"Yes, you do, Ms. Novak. And that's fine. I've always been drawn to Sedona. My dad brought me up here when I was a kid. We hiked, camped under the pines, and bought some magic crystals. It was a good memory, one I held on to and continue to hold on to."

Mr. Courier clasped his hands together as if the memory were tangible and trying to escape. Cal had a memory of her father, just one. Her parents were typical twenty-first-century parents who had a kid because that's what they did and used her as an excuse to work. "We're doing this for you, so you have a better life than we had. It's a legacy, Cal."

Now, their "legacy" was being flushed down the drain of medical expenses. The memory of her father was fuzzy and vague, more of a snapshot. It probably was a snapshot, a Polaroid she saw once, where she was sitting on her father's shoulders, reaching out to touch a horse pressed against a wooden fence. Her father's hair smelled of shampoo and cinnamon.

That's it. That was all. There were no sounds, no words—just a moment in time.

"That seems like a great reason," she blurted, unsure how long her mind had wandered.

"He is a great man. This place is kind of a monument to him. He respected the land and the people who lived on it. I'm just trying to do my part. Now, if you want this job, you'll be required to learn quite a bit about this area and have a script memorized. We also have uniforms and a tight schedule. Can you handle that, especially considering your grandmother's health?"

"She's fine. A nurse comes and stays with her a few days a week."

Cal wasn't sure why she divulged that information, she wasn't much of a sharer, but at this moment, she was surprised by her honesty. It was desperation. She could feel herself on the verge of a breakthrough that would mean less stress, and she didn't want to blow it. "Mr. Courier, I can do this job," she said plainly, confidently.

Mr. Courier nodded and smiled again. "I do not doubt that. Here's the deal: I'm going to send you out on a tour with Clark Haus—he's our general manager—and if you still want to be part of the team, we'll consider you."

Consider me? Why wouldn't they consider me? Who else do they have around here? She tried to shake the negativity. "Sounds good," she mustered.

The door behind her opened. Courier said, "Clark, this is Cal Novak. She's applying to be one of our tour advisors. Will you take her on the tour and show her around?"

Clark was tall, maybe even over six feet, with dark hair peppered with white, which threw Cal off a bit as his dark skin showed no sign of wrinkles. "Yes, sir," he answered with a nod and a turn.

"Thank you, Clark. And it was genuinely nice to meet you, Ms. Novak."

Mr. Courier emerged from behind his desk and shook Cal's hand, smiling again. Cal noticed something on the back of his neck, a tattoo hiding under the collar of his gray suit. She couldn't make it out, but seeing something so carefree on a man who seemed more square than laid back was odd.

"Nice to meet you too," she said.

Clark Haus wasn't much of a talker. He walked through the lobby without saying anything or turning to check if she was still trailing behind. "Where are you from, Mr. Haus?" Cal broke the silence. She wasn't the strong, silent type.

"Down the road," he answered, exiting through

another door into the sunshine, pointing past Sedona.

Cal donned her sunglasses and squinted. "Oh yeah, down the road. I know where that is." She tried to hide the sarcasm, but there wasn't much of a filter.

"As a tour advisor, you'll need to keep that in check," Clark replied without skipping a beat. She couldn't tell whether he was being sarcastic. Cal hoped she could tell soon; there was nothing worse than a weird working relationship with a boss—*if* she got the job.

"That is if you get the job," he added. Cal almost gasped audibly. This guy was astute. "Here's where you'll meet each day." Clark pointed at a log cabin in the shadow of the same large rock face the main building pressed against. Ahead of them the mouth of the mountain gaped.

"Did they build the cabin, or was it on the property?" Cal asked as they walked closer. It looked old yet in good shape. It could easily have been new but made to look old.

"Log cabins wouldn't do well up here in real life." Clark laughed through his nose while he talked. "No, these city guys come up with all sorts of ideas to lure in the tourists. They call this pioneer cabin. If it were up to me, I would do a mud hut or just use the mouth of the cave there."

He motioned toward the spot that had caught Cal's eye earlier. They stepped into the cabin, which was fantastic and beautifully decorated with animal skins on the floor, dark wood furniture, and leather couches. There was a desk in the corner with a TV mounted above it with scenes of Sedona moving across the screen. There was a hallway in the back with a sign for the restrooms.

"Wow, they spared no expense with this place," she

commented, primarily to herself.

"City folks," Clark answered, taking a tablet from the desk. "We'll also use these technological wonders on our tours. We conduct private virtual tours where they can sign up and ask for specific tour advisors. For those, you get extra pay. We'll set up a bio for you and put a picture up on the site. Just one of the many ways we personalize tours here at Belle Butte Touring Company."

"Sounds like a great commercial," Cal said, still looking around the room. The photographs on the walls were reminiscent of the '60s, with a faded but vivid cool coloring in wood frames. She appreciated the style.

"We are all a living commercial right now until this place opens. Here is the basic uniform: khakis, navy blue polo, hiking boots, walkie-talkie, and oh"—he paused and reached down to pick up a wide-brimmed straw hat from the chair behind the desk—"this will be worn at all times."

Cal squinted, noticing the lack of a hat on Clark's head, then thinking of her pile of curly dark hair on her own. She hadn't worn a hat in years and preferred her wild curls to create a 'fro around her head. She tucked her lips in and gave a half smile. "Well, I guess this is why Mr. Courier mentioned the uniform."

"He's big on everyone looking professional. So many touring companies around here are half-assed, but he wants this place to be different. He wants this place to be the resort of touring companies, not the Motel 6 like the rest. Uniforms create unity, a team. Are you someone who can work on a team, Ms. Novak?"

His voice trailed at the end. It was a question she had wondered about herself. She wasn't much of a team player. As an editor, she could always lock herself in her office or room, put in her earbuds, and get lost in her work. A team player?

"Sure, you don't know until you try, right?" she asked with a smile.

Clark didn't seem amused or convinced, but he accepted it as he motioned for her to follow him down the hallway. "Here's the kitchen, restrooms, and locker rooms. Out back here," he said, opening the door leading to a covered porch, "is where the tours begin. I recommend you hold on to this map and follow along as we go. This will be the route you'll take if—"

Cal finished his sentence, "I get the job?"

Haus took in a gulp of air and released it loudly. He did not dignify her with a response. "We start in the caves. Follow me."

The mouth of the cave was tall, over ten feet, but narrower than Cal expected. If a person were overweight, they might not want to enter. It was illuminated inside with high, artistic lighting made from different antlers all shaped together. "Someone dumped a lot of money into the mouth of this cave," she muttered, mostly to herself.

"The tour makes its first stop here, and we talk about the legend of the Narrow Gap cave entrance. You'll memorize a script and answer any questions based on the research that we give you. The legend states that this entrance opened after a boy from a local Native American tribe crawled through and got lost. People heard him inside crying and prayed to the gods to open a passage just large enough for someone to pass through and find the boy. The gods answered their prayers with Narrow Gap. Little did they know that this cave winds through the red rocks."

Clark paused and looked at Cal, who was taking in

the sights around her. The inside of the cave was darker than the bright-red rock on the outside, almost brown. It was also dry, much drier than the caves she explored as a child in the mountains of North Carolina. "Do you have any questions?" he finally asked.

"Oh, no." Cal shook her head and gave him a thumbs-up. "Just taking it all in. Lost boy, gods, prayers, entrance: check!"

He shook his head and pointed. "We make our way into this corridor here."

"What's through there?" Cal walked over to another identical passage next to it.

"Just a storage area," he answered, directing her forward.

Cal wanted to snoop around but decided against it as she followed Haus. *If* she got the job, there would be plenty of time for that. The pathway was like an ordinary hall shrouded in brown rocks with many divots. Edison light bulbs lined the top, and she noticed the sound of Native American flutes all around her.

"Nice touch," she noted.

"What?" Clark yelled back without stopping.

"The flutes, nice touch. The tourists will love it."

"What flutes?" he asked.

She could only assume that he was making fun of her, even though now she was starting to feel more comfortable. Maybe this guy wasn't so bad after all.

Eventually, the passage opened into another large room. The white sand covered the ground, almost fluffy beneath her feet. The walls had large paintings flanked by bright lanterns. Each image attempted to depict different scenes of Native American village life.

"This is the Cavern of Living Remembrance." Clark

bowed his head reverently. "Here we have Native American paintings done by those who lived in this area through the years. Here we pay homage to those who lost their lives in these rocks."

"So, wait, these people died here?" Cal asked, walking around to get a closer look at each painting. "None of these paintings have the mountains or red rocks behind them. Odd choices."

"Do you question everything people say?" Clark sounded annoyed.

"No, but this all seems so dramatic. Why include this at all? Why not do cave drawings in here or turn this into laser tag or something? These paintings are huge, like ten feet tall or something. They can't be originals. If they are, why are they all the same height and done in the same style?" Cal asked, walking back toward him. "Maybe you should ask more questions, Mr. Haus."

"I don't question the man who pays my salary," he answered. "If you want this job, you'll do the same."

Message received. If Cal was going to be a success working for Mark Courier, she would have to play by his rules, even if it meant giving the tourists a little show.

"It gets darker down this pathway, and you'll start to hear the water," Clark said.

"This must be the water Courier was referencing. He said that it runs through the rock and goes underground. Is there a river somewhere?" Cal asked, more seriously this time and watching her tone.

"There are rumors of an underground river. It wouldn't be unheard of. All of this was once underwater, an ocean. You can find seashells out here. Even if there were water under here, it would be impossible to find the source. This butte, like many of the others, is pure sandstone. Any drilling on a large scale would cause irreparable damage."

Cal recalled when her grandparents took her to Linville Caverns in North Carolina as a kid. There was water, and lots of it, all around them. The sound was subtle, like a trickling that echoed and overlapped. There, a cold humidity hung around them. It was different here. Though the cave was considerably cooler, it was not damp. There was no evidence of water in their surroundings.

"How do they know there *is* a river if they've never seen it?" Cal asked as they continued walking.

"Legend, lore, and science. Even if there isn't a river, the water that flows through the butte has to go somewhere. You'll see what I mean in a minute."

Almost immediately, they stepped into a cavern with water rushing down one of the walls and disappearing into the sand as if by magic. It was lit from above with perfectly placed twinkling white lights and spotlights to the side, giving the water a blue tint.

"How did they do that?" Cal asked. Nothing was genuine on this tour. Everything was so fake, almost theatrical at times. Where was the water coming from? How was there so much of it? This wasn't a trickle but a roar of water splashing through the wall and crashing to the ground. The ground seemed to accept it, in all its violence and absorbed it.

"This should be one of the world's natural wonders," Clark said, "but it wasn't discovered until Mr. Courier bought the land. It's a phenomenon. If you were to hike above this spot on the rocks, which you'll do if you work with us, there's no water running up there. The water's coming from the rocks, from inside of them. But how can water flow up and through rocks? Phenomenon!" His hands spread out, waving across his face like a magician.

This, Cal thought, *is a bit more canned.* "So, it's just accepted as a natural exception to the rule, and that's it? Have scientists done any studies?"

"Of course they have, but they say what people have said forever about this place. This type of rock is porous, almost fragile, and has filtered water for years. If anything, it might be the cleanest water in the world, considering the amount of filtration it undergoes."

"I'm assuming this is the shining jewel of Belle Butte. It needs to be on the front page of your website, on every commercial, and highlighted in newspapers. Why haven't you all advertised the water?"

"All of that's coming," he assured her, returning to the entrance from where they emerged. "From here, we'll make our way back out and hike up the rocks. One more thing: don't let anyone touch the water or get too close. We're trying to figure out the best way to rope off this area without puncturing the ground. No one is quite sure what would happen if a person stepped near the water. Quicksand, maybe?"

By the time Cal and Clark exited through the Narrow Gap, the sun was starting to turn downward. Cal looked at her phone and saw it was already three o'clock. She'd been there since noon. "Will we be doing the whole tour today?" she asked as they made their way back to the cabin.

"No, you aren't wearing the proper shoes to do the hiking part. If you get the job, you'll attend an orientation with the other new tour advisors and complete the rest. Do you live in Sedona?"

Cal laughed, remembering how Clark had ignored that question only an hour ago. "Pretty much. I don't live in the downtown area if you can call it that, but around about," she answered. They were inside the cabin now.

"Sedona. The wackos live there," Clark said with a laugh. "Are you a wacko?"

"I'm a transplant, so I don't think I can be considered a wacko yet, though maybe choosing to live there would make me more of one."

"Do you have family there? Is that why you moved?"

"Observant. No job. No family. I moved for my grandma. She has," Cal paused. It was hard to say cancer out loud. Even though the big C had been a part of their lives for a couple of years now, the potential of losing Grandma Ruth brought tears to her eyes. "She has some health problems."

"You moved to Sedona for the magic crystals?"

Hearing the mocking tone of Clark's voice, she said, "No, not the magic crystals." She didn't want to admit that her grandmother had mentioned them more than once. "The dry air. She heard that it would help her."

"Always wondered why there weren't more retirement homes around here because of that. I've lived in the area all my life, and something about it keeps you young." Cal believed him. Even his eyes looked young. "It was nice to meet you, Ms. Novak. I'm sure we'll be getting back to you soon. We want to have the positions filled before the season starts."

"Thank you for your time, Mr. Haus. By the way, is Haus a German name?" She was curious how a man, obviously of Native American descent, ended up with a German last name.

"Observant." He winked, turned, and waved.

On the way back to the car, Cal stopped and looked over the butte to the land below. Sanchez Ranch spanned outward, dotted with cattle, and next to it was Whispering Pines. Beyond that, the ground undulated with hills, flats, and canyons like a sea of sand. It was a beautiful place.

Chapter Six

"Well, did you get the job or not?" Des hit the tap and poured two quick beers into pint glasses.

"Probably not? I may have come on too strong with the guy who would be my boss. I guess you can say that I'm a better tourist than a tour guide," Cal answered, letting the rest of the bourbon she had ordered pour down her throat.

The heat made her drowsy on the stool. She hated that Lucio hadn't gotten a solid door for the hole. Instead, it was more of a jail cell door with bars that were impossible to break into or out of when locked. Cal thought it was a nod to Officer Sanchez.

"I'm sure it wasn't that bad," He hesitated and laughed. "Just kidding, if you thought it was bad, it was probably worse. Why can't you keep your mouth shut?"

"Whatever, Des. One day, people will appreciate that I ask questions." Cal rolled her eyes. "There were some weird parts."

She returned to the waterfall in her mind and Clark Haus, the German Native American, and Mark Courier, the handsome city guy. While driving back to Sedona, her inner skeptic analyzed the interview. Belle Butte suddenly felt like an alien planet or a cast of characters in a play. She understood the connection of Mr. Courier to the land, or least she thought she did.

Memories can be strong and lingering, much like the

heat during the Arizona summers. Cal had her own set of revolving door memories that crept into her mind at night. There was the smell of her mother's hair, like honey, when she leaned in for a hug. Or the blue of her father's eyes when the sun hit them just right. There was the rough touch of her grandfather's hand, calloused from years of working outside, yet gentle and dry.

However, Cal was still trying to figure out how Mark Courier knew about the waterfall. He'd only mentioned camping in the pines. Maybe he didn't tell the whole story. It was a job interview, and it wasn't like she was interviewing him, though, at times, that's exactly what she felt like she was doing. People also didn't just pick up their lives and build a business somewhere because of a memory. There were reasons, especially if you were a businessman. Cal realized how little she knew about Belle Butte Touring Company.

"I think I'm going to head out," she said.

Des was down at the other end of the bar, talking to a couple of men dressed in uniforms belonging to some resort in town.

Des laughed with them, then jogged back. "You can't leave me with that," he said, filling her glass with a quick shot. Cal hoped it was on the house.

"With what?" she asked, digging in her purse for some cash, knowing that's what he wanted.

"What was weird? Come on. It must be legit if you say something is weird here in Sedona in a bar with a hole in the wall."

"It's nothing." She shrugged, knowing the longer she kept him in the shadow of the word, the more he grinned; she loved his smile. "Do you ever work, by the way? I feel like you stand around and talk to hot girls."

"Where?" he said. "You see hot girls? I could strike up a conversation if I saw one."

Cal punched across the bar and landed her fist hard on his chest.

"Ouch! For real? That's harassment, and Lucio takes that seriously. See, you wouldn't make it as a stripper. Hot-headed."

"It's amazing how you don't learn from your mistakes," Cal said, punching him again.

"Hey, hey!" a voice came from behind Cal. She turned to see a short, balding Hispanic man in a bright green T-shirt and shorts, walking toward her, his belly leading the way. "Don't do that! You can't punch people in my bar. I'll throw you out! I'll do it!"

When he wagged a finger in Cal's face, she backed up. "Okay, okay," she said, swirling back around to face Des, who was overly smiling, teeth shining like the Cheshire cat.

"You all come in here acting like you own this town. We own this town—*we do!*" Lucio screeched.

Cal understood what he meant. She had heard it from every local she bumped into. They still considered her a transplant. Even Cal's friends, not that she had many, reminded her daily of her status by saying things like, "You wouldn't understand; you aren't from here" or "It's a Sedona thing."

At first, she ignored it, answering back with a shrug or a snappy comment, but now it was getting old. A year wasn't a lifetime, but it was long enough to know the town gossip. What makes a "local" anyway?

"Coming in here, punching my people...this is my people!" Lucio stood next to Des and looked up at him with a smile. They were exact opposites. Des was tall

45

with light brown skin and a 'fro that he usually made into a bun or ponytail on the back of his head, while Lucio was small in stature, a bit dumpy, with a red tint to his dark skin.

Des laughed, saying, "Take it easy, Lucio. She's just kidding."

"I pay you to make drinks! Not to stand around talking to her!" Lucio muttered as he vacated swiftly through the back door.

"Your boss is creepy, for real. He's what nightmares are made of, all angry and tiny and menacing." Cal let a shiver go through her body and exaggerated its effect. "Dude, I don't know how you work here."

"Wasn't someone asking for a job here the other day? Who was that? It was some desperate chick with black curly hair and questionable taste in shoes," Des said and pointed at Cal.

"Yeah, desperation makes us do crazy things, but stupidity keeps us doing them." She pointed back with one hand while quickly chugging the rest of her drink. "I gotta go," she said, getting up from the stool and finding her feet.

"You gotta pay for that drink," Des shot back.

"I didn't ask for this," she retorted, throwing down a five-dollar bill and making for the door.

The sun began crawling down the horizon, shining a golden light against the storefronts. The heat was unbearable as she made her way to the car. However, someone had already beaten her to it and was leaning against the passenger side. As she moved closer, she made out the figure, looking down and shaking her head. She noticed that her shoes were dirty from the day.

"Officer Sanchez, are you stalking me? Whenever I

46

come out of The Vortex, I swear you're waiting for me. You could get fired for that, you know, abuse of power." Cal was beside him now and saw his smile.

"You flatter yourself, Cal. I was doing some patrolling when I saw your jeep parked out front and noticed the meter had run out on you."

Cal frowned. "You didn't." She shook her head.

"I did! You have to follow the rules like everyone else around here. You can't use 'oh I'm new and didn't know' anymore. We have to make money, too."

"That's crap, and you know it," Cal said, walking around the driver's side. "This is below you. A cop like you? Someone who's been on the force and has fought real crime? Parking-ticket duty? Wow." She opened the door, her eyes wide.

He avoided the pestering with ease. "I heard you had a job interview today."

"How did you know about that? Man, did the town crier tell you that as he rode into town on his horse? Is there nothing else happening here that my interview made the news? Maybe I'm more important than I thought."

His smile widened. "And?"

"And, who knows. At this point, it was a shot in the dark anyway. Just hoping I find something before I'm out of money and ideas."

There was a long silence that told her Sanchez wasn't trying to target her for a parking ticket. She looked out of the corner of her eye and noticed no parking ticket on her windshield. Who knows how long he had been leaning against her jeep?

He was quiet, exhaling slowly. It looked like he wanted to say something, but the words were trapped somewhere inside.

Officer Marcial Sanchez was one of the first people she and her grandmother had met after they moved to Sedona a year ago. Their Rent-A-Truck, a dilapidated trailer filled to the brim with furniture and boxes, broke down just outside the city limits. Cal was hot and totally bummed out, sitting on the hood of the jeep searching for videos online about how to fix a Rent-A-Truck tire when Sanchez pulled up.

Unlike his brother Lucio, owner of The Vortex, Marcial Sanchez was taller and clean-shaven, with less weight in his midsection. He wore a wide-brimmed police hat and dark glasses. Paired with the khaki police uniform, Cal thought she had stepped into a movie scene. In Atlanta, police officers were in their blues with shaved heads and guns camouflaged to their sides. Officer Sanchez's gun seemed to shimmer in the sunlight like a sheriff from a Wild West flick.

"Looks like you could use some assistance," he said, slamming the door of the police cruiser behind him, his Spanish drawl thick and charming.

Cal kicked one of the tires hard enough to make the road dust jump at least six inches. "Seems that your highway here has nails for concrete. These inflatable tire tubes are flat."

"We throw those in for the tourists. They like that whole stranded in the desert, creepy movie vibe."

Cal laughed and nodded, mouthing *yes*. "I think there are spares underneath this thing. Not quite sure how to get to them?" It was a question for which she hoped he had an answer.

He crouched down, his shiny black shoes squeaking like the tin man needing oil lubrication. "Yep, there they are." He pulled a wire, releasing four tires in tandem to the ground.

"Wow, that doesn't seem safe." Cal laughed, pulling one out. "You wouldn't also know how to change one of these too, would you?"

"Cally? Cally?" Grandma Ruth called out.

Cal had forgotten where she was for a moment and jumped up, galloping to the jeep's passenger-side window. "Are you okay? Do you need some water?"

"Aw, Cally, you take such good care of me. Yes, a drink of water would be nice. It's much hotter here than I thought," Grandma Ruth answered. Before she could grab something from the back, a hand reached out with a bottle of water, condensation dripping. Cal turned to see Officer Sanchez standing there.

"Here you go, ma'am," he said, walking to the window and smiling.

"Well, thank you, sir," Grandma Ruth said with a smile and nod. "What a nice young man."

"Welcome to Sedona, the friendliest little town in Arizona. Let's see if we can't get you fixed up and on the way to your home. I can even give you a police escort!" he said, walking toward the back. Cal understood Southern hospitality, but this was a little more Western than Southern and beat out anything she had seen in Atlanta.

She tried to help him, but Officer Sanchez was more interested in asking questions and small talk. It took over an hour to complete the process, and Cal felt like she had made a friend. They did receive a police escort to their new home, and he even came back later that evening to help unload and bring over some food. She learned about his family, which included a wife and three very rambunctious children ranging in age from eight to thirteen, all boys. She met them once when Officer Sanchez invited her and her grandma to their little ranch above Whispering Pines.

It was the first time Cal had ever been to a ranch. Just off the main road was a long driveway with a two-post sign that read Sanchez Ranch with steer horns above the Z. The drive was lined with an electric fence bordering pastures on both sides; the left side featured a line of tall pine trees that shot straight up and, on the right side, red rocks that punctured the sky. She almost felt like both sides were closing in on her as she drove. About a mile or so down, a small one-story house sprouted from the dirt, with barns flanking both sides and cars and trucks parked all over. Some had tires, some were missing doors, and some were skeletons. Dust rose behind the jeep in puffs.

"Could see you comin' from a mile away," a yell came from the front porch. Officer Sanchez wore blue jeans and a white V-neck shirt, sunglasses still covering his eyes. Cal helped Grandma Ruth out of the jeep and met Sanchez's hand with a shake. "So glad you two could join us this evening. We have steaks on the grill out back and tons of sides. Most of my family is here, too, so you'll be able to meet the whole lot of 'em, well, the ones we want you to meet, that is. Come on."

He led them around the back of the house, where there was a large patio with people and the smells of mesquite and meat, corn roasting, and fire. It reminded Cal of when her parents took her to the beach, and they would make a bonfire to roast marshmallows.

"These are my kin, everyone from my aunts and uncles to my cousins and their cousins and my second cousins. They all live around here and work here at the ranch. We've been raising cattle for generations, the best meat on this side of the Mississippi," he said proudly and loudly, and everyone cheered as if they had practiced it as a performance.

"Quite a family. You should be proud!" Grandma Ruth noted. "A legacy, that's what you have here. A living, breathing legacy."

Cal heard a note of sadness in Grandma Ruth's voice, a longing for the family she no longer had. Cal thought of her mom and dad and their obsession with work. Maybe that obsession wouldn't be so bad if it built something like this ranch. The Sanchez family also worked, but they worked together on something that would last forever and could be molded and shaped to fit the times. Cal's legacy from her parents consisted of money, bills, and grief.

"Yes, it is something, Ms. Ruth. I don't know what to do without these people, but family isn't just kinfolk. Here in Sedona, we adopt people into our family. If you ever need anything, we're here." It wasn't lip service; he had proved that already. Cal knew that he was genuine.

That night they enjoyed the company of the Sanchez family, listening to stories about their lives, laughing at mishaps on the ranch, and sharing family secrets. One secret in particular was hushed as soon as it was mentioned.

"Tell them about your brother, Sanchez," a cousin yelled, laughing from one of the picnic tables. He had gotten into the tequila. Quiet went over the crowd, a quiet that made even the fire simmer down low and stop its crackle. In the dark, with only the strung lights above them and the moon and stars beyond, Cal watched as

Sanchez pulled his sunglasses down his nose and growled, "We don't talk about that here."

Cal had never been around an angry bear before, but she imagined that it would sound like that, and its spirit would dominate the air around it as the presence of Sanchez did that night. The party sprung back to life not long after the awkward pause, but Grandma Ruth was ready for bed, and Cal was still getting used to the new time zone.

"It was a pleasure, Officer Sanchez," Grandma Ruth said as he opened the door for her and helped her in.

"Now, Ms. Ruth, you can call me Marcial. No one else does, but you can." He laughed, which made her laugh.

"You have a special woman here, Cal. You're doing a good thing." He nodded in her direction across the hood of the car.

"Thank you for having us. It was enlightening," Cal said, closing the door behind her.

He cared; he always had.

It was hard to believe that it had been under a year since the get-together at the ranch. *And he doesn't hate me yet.*

Cal smiled and said, "I'll be fine. *We* will be fine. You don't have to worry about us." It felt as if she'd lived this exact moment many times. He found her there a year ago, and now, he was once again leaning against her jeep next to The Vortex.

"I don't worry, just checking on my people. You're one of the good ones, Cal, don't forget that. Here if you need me," Officer Sanchez said, backing away. He stopped and turned to look at her again. "Did you see my brother in there?"

"Always do," Cal said, a smirk crawling across her face. "How is it you got the height and the personality, and all he got was a temper?"

He shrugged and laughed, then answered, "I guess some of us get all the luck." Cal watched as he practically skipped down the sidewalk, a shimmer of gold highlighting his footfall as the sun began setting on Sedona's streets.

Chapter Seven

"Seriously? I got the job?" Cal was both surprised and intrigued. After not hearing anything for a few days, the prospect of getting the job had fled as quickly as it had come.

"Congratulations." The chipper female voice was reminiscent of a 1950s phone operator. Cal wondered if it was the same receptionist she'd met the first day at Belle Butte. She pictured the tiny redheaded woman sitting there with a headset, red lipstick, and legs crossed—perfection.

"You're scheduled to start on Monday," the woman chimed. "I'll need a few things from you before you begin, basic information for HR and, of course, your shirt, pants, and shoe size for your uniform. We're so happy you'll join us at Belle Butte Touring Company. Do you have any questions for me?"

Cal thought for a minute. *Yes, lots of questions.* Instead, she replied, "No, ma'am. All set here."

"Awesome! I'll send that email to you right now. See you on Monday!" There was a click, and the voice disappeared.

Wow. I just got a job. With mixed emotions, she texted Des to let him know. *—Can you believe it? I got the job. It was my sparkling personality. I mean, who could say no to that?—*

She put her phone down, left the darkness of the

room, and made her way into the living room where her grandma was sitting in her chair, watching an old Lauren Bacall movie—no cable or satellite, just an old VCR, and a stack of tapes she'd brought with her from North Carolina. The box TV took up much of the corner. Cal felt so secure in that room as if it were lifted from her past and plopped into her present. The rug, chair, bookcase, stack of tapes, hanging plant, and photographs were all from her grandma's living room. There was even a smell that came with it and sounds of the old movies, little crackles that married with the talking characters and background music.

Cal remembered sitting on that rug, going through the tapes, reading the cardboard covers, and studying the pictures, always in black and white or vivid Technicolor with a man and woman smiling or hiding on them. Her grandfather would give his suggestion, her grandmother would give her a synopsis of the plot, and Cal would sit there the whole time, running her palms along the rug until it tickled. They would decide on one, and she would back up to the couch, sit sprawled out on the floor, and absorb everything until her mind wandered.

Funny, I always thought about my parents. What they were doing, what they chose to do instead of being with me. She shuddered to think of the time she wasted missing them. *How can you miss someone you don't know? Is it possible that I loved them, that they meant something more to me than a placeholder?*

Cal had tried to make sense of her emotions many times, but like her attention span during movies, eventually, she lost interest and moved on. Her grandparents were her parents in many ways. She spent more time with them than anyone and felt the closeness she imagined a child would have with their parents. Her grandmother was the disciplinarian, and more than once popped Cal's hand or made her go to her room for one thing or another. Once, Cal strayed too far from home, walking through the woods. When her grandmother called her for lunch, Cal didn't hear and, without a watch, overlooked the time. She was gone for over three hours, wandering around, pretending to be a fairy, knight, or bear. Sticks became swords and tepees; leaves became snow and food. Her imagination ran wild.

When her stomach growled, she returned to her grandparents' house, home. The doors were locked. She knocked and waited, knocked and waited. Cal checked to see if the cars were in the carport. She knocked on the screen door in the back and then the windows; the shades were drawn. Cal remembered the confusion and fear of being alone and feeling forgotten. That feeling was never far from her mind anyway, with her parents out all the time and leaving her with a neighbor, friend, or teenager. But this, this was different. Her grandparents had never done this. She sat on the porch, folded her arms on her knees, and cried large tears that soaked her pants. Cal never knew how long she sat there balled up; it could have been minutes or hours, but mentally it was the stretch of a marathon until finally, a voice rang out in front of her. It was two voices, frantic and high-pitched, shaky. She saw her grandparents jogging through the freshly plowed field across the driveway.

Cal stood up and walked toward them at first and then sped up. She ran, screaming, "You left me! How could you leave me? You weren't here!" Her grandfather scooped her into his arms and hugged her, squeezing her until she could barely breathe.

"Don't ever do that again, ever," he whispered into Cal's ear. Grandma Ruth came huffing and puffing from behind them and, with a warm hand, encompassed Cal's head like a hat and turned it toward her.

"Now you listen to me, Cally. I don't mind if you wander all around those woods. I've never told you that you couldn't." She stopped to take a breath, then moved closer. "But you listen here, don't go so far that you can't hear me calling. If my voice doesn't carry there, come back. This world is strange, getting stranger every day, and we don't always know what's out there. It's better to be close enough that someone can hear you if you need them and if they need you. You're eight years old and ought to know better."

Cal's grandfather put her back down, and she stood small between them, looking up at giants, nervous to hear their next words yet hating the silence.

"I love you. *We* love you," Grandma Ruth said, bringing Cal in for a hug. It was warm, sweaty, and just enough. "You're going to be in your room for a few days for that. I love you, and you must learn to heed my words when you're here."

Cal remembered the stark contrast between punishment and love at that moment. It was almost like it pained Grandma Ruth to say it out loud. The punishment fit the crime too. Being stuck in the tiny room with white walls and nothing but a twin bed, a dresser full of towels and linens, and a chest with old toys wasn't the great outdoors; it was the opposite. But she did feel safe.

Now Cal looked into the living room and saw her grandmother, much older, faded like the furniture, rug, and photographs around her, like the crackle of the black-and-white movie, still playing. She yearned for the days when her grandfather was there, too, when it was easier to plop down on the floor. Her worries were heavy then, but nothing compared to now. *She* was the one who had to be strong and be an adult. Cal felt a surge of inadequacy and uncertainty about her choice to move out here. Maybe she should have said no to Grandma Ruth and made her stay in North Carolina. Perhaps the familiarity would have helped.

Is she getting worse? Would this have been inevitable if I had kept her there, if we had lived in that tiny house instead of this one?

Cal felt a tear, a big one, surging into the corner of her eye. What was she doing here? How could she care for Grandma Ruth as they had cared for her? What if she did get worse? Could she handle the truth that she failed? The tear fell hot down her cheek, and the image of the waterfall in the cave came to her mind, a gush of water so strong yet disappearing into an unseen void. She wondered where her tears came from, how all that confusion and pain fit into one droplet, and how releasing it could feel so free, yet it was all an illusion. It was helplessness—and guilt for feeling helpless.

Grandma Ruth stirred in her chair, her face turning toward Cal, who was still standing in the hallway, watching like a window shopper, trying to figure out if it was all worth it. But this wasn't an expensive dress; this was a costly love and very much worth it. Cal decided not to wake her and instead made dinner while she slept. It was just past four and the sun was starting its westerly drop, making the rooms red again.

She took out a large pot, filled it with water, and brought it to a boil. The noodles came next, then, after pouring the water and noodles into the colander, she used the pot to warm the sauce, just like that, instant dinner. She felt bad for the lack of vegetables and bread. There was enough time to run to the market. Now that she had the job, money wouldn't be as tight. Cal set the food aside and snuck out the front door, heading to the store.

Jenny's Market was the lifeblood of the local crowd. Sure, it was cheaper to buy food at Save-Mart, but supporting local businesses was the key to Sedona's success. The market was half open air and half tin-covered roof. The vegetables were fresh, and the meats were straight off the ranches of people everyone knew. Jenny didn't carry many canned foods or processed items. Everything was organic and crisp, the original fresh market. Sometimes she sold little arts-and-craft items made by local artists, mostly made of crystals from ubiquitous red rocks. There was money in crystals, and people in Sedona were looking to own a trinket from their stay. Cal liked Jenny. She was a transplant, too, who opened a thriving business respected by the locals. Cal filled her arms with lettuce and carrots from cardboard boxes out front before heading inside. For once, she ignored the price. Her credit was good, and by this time next week, a paycheck would be deposited into her account.

"Why, Cal, I haven't seen you in forever! How you been, girl?" a lady in her late forties with a floral dress and off-white apron came from behind a shelf of produce. She was slightly plump, with brown hair in a ponytail, and wore multiple beaded and leather bracelets up her arm and dangling turquoise earrings. Jenny Stanton had earned her tan the old-fashioned way, working outside.

"You know me. I'm always up to something," Cal answered, realizing she had just smooshed her produce in the hug. "Time seems to slip by here, doesn't it?"

"Not from you. You're still just as pretty as can be. Did you hear about my son? My oldest? He was accepted to Arizona State! Can you believe it? I thought I'd be stuck with a houseful of kids until I died." Her laugh was loud and apprehensive as if she were genuinely thankful and terrified simultaneously.

"You truly breed genius kids, Jenny."

Cal knew that was a stretch. The truth was that Jenny's son, Sam, was about as helpful as a stripped screw. She heard he got into college by cheating on everything from term papers to the SATs, though she wasn't quite sure how he pulled that off. Even millionaires couldn't get away with that. "I'm serious, Jenny. One day you'll be telling me how to raise kids."

"Buy yourself a store and make them work in it. That's the best thing for kids: hard work. They learned math and percentages, writing, reading, and work ethic. It's no joke owning a place and knowing that if it fails, it all falls on you." Jenny nodded emphatically.

"How's your husband? Doesn't he get back pretty soon?" Cal inquired.

Jenny's spouse, an officer in the army, had been away for over a year. Jenny had taken the boys to California when he was last on leave. She posted pictures all over Facebook showing the family smiling and laughing throughout the state, from Legoland to the Golden Gate Bridge.

"It'll be another month or so. When he returns, he'll have to work at the base before heading home. It'll be nice to have him back, if not for any other reason than to help with the heavy lifting. Speaking of, I heard you may be looking for a job!"

Cal smiled and nodded. "Yeah, I was, but I recently, as in like an hour ago, accepted one. There's a new touring company up in the rocks called—"

"Belle Butte," Jenny cut in, squinting her eyes and nodding for a minute. "Yeah, I've heard of it. We drive by it when we're going between home and here. It's quite a production up there. I've never seen so many trucks. It must be quite an excavation,"

"Excavation? Well, they did build a pretty large building against one of the rocks. It blends in with the space well. Maybe they had to cut into it a bit."

"Huh." Jenny was quiet, eyes still squinting.

"What?" Cal asked, wondering why Jenny was so quiet. She wasn't one to leave silence in the room for too long.

"Oh, nothing, I'm sure. Only I always heard you couldn't build up there, or at least you couldn't disturb the earth. Something about the rocks?"

Cal knew what Jenny was referencing. She had just heard the same thing. It was odd. Everyone seemed to know about the fragile nature of the rocks on that side of the mountain, yet no one seemed bothered by the construction. How would any environmental agency allow construction there? Cal thought that maybe it was more local lore and didn't put much stock in it.

"When I went up there for the interview, I saw no construction. That must have been before."

There was another pause with lots of nodding from Jenny, who was starting to look slightly uncomfortable, even edgy. "No, it wasn't too long ago...like a week ago. I saw some eighteen-wheelers headed up there. It was quite a parade. Maybe just a delivery of some sort? Who knows?" She threw her hands in the air as if to surrender. "Listen to me going on like I know anything that happens here. Well, congratulations are in order! Are you making a special dinner?"

"Yes, well, I don't know how special it is, but I made some spaghetti and thought I'd make a big salad to go with it. Grandma Ruth loves fresh vegetables."

"Aww, how's Grandma Ruth?"

"She's good. I mean, she's okay. She doesn't get out much and sometimes talks when no one's in the room." Cal wasn't sure why she shared that with Jenny.

"She has the whisper!" Jenny said quickly, pointing at Cal as if she just saw her.

"What's the whisper?"

"I guess you can call it local tribal lore. My husband's family was all into that, being from around here. They said the same magic that makes the trees talk can be transferred into people who are open to them and receptive," she clarified. "It sounds like your grandma is a receiver?"

"Like a TV antenna?" Cal laughed again. It was too unbelievable to take seriously; of course, she had never ventured into Whispering Pines, mainly because Drunk Tommy owned a large part of that land, and he was, well, gross.

"Kind of?" Jenny nodded, her head slightly tilted. "It's the same basic principle. Greg's Aunt Donna told me that when Native Americans from the local tribes died, their spirits got trapped by the pine trees when they were trying to rise into the spirit world. The pines absorbed their spirits and wisdom and would talk to people willing to listen. Sometimes, if you had someone whose mind wasn't as strong in this world, they could channel the spirits of people from the other world, those trapped in the trees. Most people with this ability are older or have weak minds due to mental illness. Aunt Donna's sister was one of them. I never met her, of course, but she would whisper the most miraculous truths about people, things that no one knew. Pretty strange stuff, huh?"

"Sure." Cal kept her answer short. "I'll keep an ear out for the clairvoyant whispers. I hope she whispers some Powerball numbers. Then I won't have to work." Cal forced out a laugh while Jenny chuckled.

"I know, right? Well, I've just talked your ear off, so let me know when you're ready to check out. We have some amazing oil-based dressings in the back fridge. Gladys from down the road makes them with lemon zest and garlic, yum. Healthy and worth checking out," Jenny added, patting Cal on the shoulder. "It does me good seeing you."

"You too," Cal answered. She couldn't count how many times someone from Sedona had told her a story that ended with Native American tribes and magic powers. Grandma Ruth would have loved that story. Cal picked up the rest of the produce, grabbed a jar of Gladys's dressing, and checked out.

On the way home, she could almost taste the fresh vegetables. She was happy about the job and couldn't help but feel excited about trying something new. She was giddy with the prospect of possibilities, of the chance to do something more than edit for Jack and stress about money. This was something to celebrate and who better to eat a victory dinner with than the woman who believed in her the most?

Chapter Eight

After ingesting what a rabbit would eat in a lifetime, Cal got Grandma Ruth ready for bed before heading back to town. She had promised to meet Des there for the second half of his shift. Nothing was worse than late night at The Vortex. It got dicey as the glasses added up, and the stories turned from truth to fiction. Cal didn't mind it much. She found humor in the ridiculous and tried to sit back and listen to the stories.

Tonight, a truck driver named Gary appeared in the bar. He played two racks of pool before settling on one of the barstools to knock back a few pints of beer. Gary was not unlike most of the truck drivers that made the side trip to Sedona to pick up a supply of crystals, as they called it, but most people in town knew that it was fake.

It was also well-known that weed was a cash crop in the area, though it was tough to find if you didn't know the right people. Gary looked like the kind of guy who knew the right people because his pockets were always filled with cash, and he wore a pair of boots that looked to be made from some sort of reptile, possibly a snake. He said he was from Texas but drove his truck from coast to coast. He called the vehicle "Fancy" and talked about it like some would talk about a lover. He went on and on about her shiny wheels, ample backside, and perfect headlights. It made every man at the bar sway side to side in their jeans. After the third beer, he descended into a story about a woman he met down in Louisiana.

"You wouldn't believe the cans she had on her, and I mean tits that flopped off her chest. She was a real beauty, from her neck down." He paused to allow the laughter to feed his ego and for Des to fill his glass. "Y'all, she was special. I saw her across the bar at a watering hole with dim lights and a cigarette machine. It seemed I had stepped back in time. There she was, in a low-cut shirt, showing a canyon about as big as the one you got up there with those red rocks. It was one of those sparkly shirts, green and pink, really eye-catching. Her skirt was tight and black, every curve in just the right place. As I said, I didn't notice her face because that body was enough to make any man sweat. I went right over there and offered to buy her a drink. She wanted one of those prissy martini things, so I sprung for the best." He cupped his hand to the side as if she were there and could hear. "Though I told them to use the stuff on the lower shelf. No woman is worth that much money."

He laughed again, slapping his knee while the others joined in. Even some women had come over to gawk at the tale Gary the truck driver was spinning, some with mouths flopped open with disgust, others laughing at the description. Cal thought more than once about the #metoo campaign and how those women would have cleared him from the bar like a broom sweeping away trash.

"We drank, talked, laughed, then drank, talked, and laughed some more. By the time the bar closed, it was just us. I touched her leg under the table, ran my hand up her thigh...woooo, boys, it was a strong thigh." Chuckles and smiles filled the room, and men turned into schoolboys, looking around to see if their moms had walked into the bar. "I whispered in her ear, 'How about a nightcap? My place?' She said, 'No, let's go to my place.' Not sure how I made it out of the bar or to her house but when I got there, it was heaven, sheer heaven. Her perfume was thick in the air, and before I could focus my eyes, she was there, clothes off with nothing but nothing on. What's a man to do? I pounced and she pounced. We made it onto a bed when she placed a pill onto my tongue. There was kissing, touching, and breathing, and then everything got all swimmy. I was naked and she was naked...then I saw it, slithering out of the bed toward me. I jumped back in horror. Now don't get me wrong, I'm a pretty progressive guy, but when she pulled out that snake, I nearly fell off the bed."

He started to laugh again, but no one else in the bar followed. They sat, staring at him with wide eyes full of questions. Cal smiled, waiting for the gasp of air after the choke.

"It was a python, a real python! It wrapped right around her arm!" There it was—the quick gasp and a laugh made of misconception and relief. "Wait, what did you think I meant? Why are you all laughing at that? It was horrible!" Gary laughed while he said it, and conversations spun into episodes and snippets, the bar buzzing again after the collective breath.

It had been a while since someone rambled in and shook up the place. Tourists wouldn't do that. If they made it into The Vortex, they sat quietly to avoid disturbing the natural habitat, like someone visiting a zoo or museum. Look—don't touch. Outsiders were always welcome though; Lucio made sure of that. Des was good at conversation and community.

Gary the truck driver moved on to another story of

less interest, so Cal turned her attention to bourbon and a couple who had materialized at the end of the bar. They were young, cute, maybe twenty-one. The guy was much tipsier than the girl. His head was closer to the bar, and she watched it slip off his hand where it was propped more than once. The girl was sitting back on her stool, able to hold her head up. Cal thought that drunk people were a lot like toddlers. Sometimes you could decipher what they were saying, they could kind of sit up and eat by themselves, and they were always unpredictable.

"Another drink?" Des said, thumping Cal's arm.

"Why can you harass me, but when I do it, I get kicked out by your leprechaun boss? Double standards, man," she said, shaking her head.

"You're the dude in our relationship," he joked. "People can see that."

"I'll take that. You're more sensitive than I am and probably look much hotter in a bikini. We do have the same hair."

"No, no, my hair is much better. Look at this curl; it's tight!" He gave her 'fro a playful bat. "You got white-girl hair!"

"White-girl hair? At least my 'fro doesn't glisten in the sun! Let your 'fro *glow*!" Cal sang back to him.

"You're funny, hilarious! Racist, man. You're messed up, Cal. You say something like that to the wrong person…"

"And what?" she retorted, leaning across the bar.

"And…" He nodded then punched his hand into his palm. "You know."

"You can't even say it."

"You're just jealous of my locks." Des fluffed his loose ponytail and asked someone behind her what he could get him.

"A shot of vodka. Make it a double."

The voice sounded familiar. Turning, Cal said, "Mr. Courier?" and reached out to shake his hand. He seemed reluctant but stuck out his hand. Cal remembered that when she met him, she was wearing a dress and sandals and had a bit more make-up on, a bit different from tonight's black floral spaghetti-strap shirt, skinny jeans and wedges. "It's Cal, Cal Novak. I interviewed with you last week."

"Oh, Cal Novak, yes." He nodded and shook her hand again. "I didn't recognize you."

"No worries! I'm sure you meet a lot of people," she said, taking a sip. She patted the stool next to her. "Have a seat."

"Oh, no, I can't stay. Just grabbing a quick drink. Never been here before. There's a hole in that wall over there." He pointed. "They should get that fixed."

"It's part of the charm." Cal laughed. This place was opposite Mr. Courier's little haven on Belle Butte.

"Here you go," Des said, handing off the shot.

"This is Mr. Courier. He owns Belle Butte Touring Company," Cal said.

"Nice to meet you. You're a brave man hiring this one. She's fiery," Des said, thumb pointing toward Cal.

"Call me Mark." Mr. Courier coughed. "It's Mark Courier."

"Where are you from, Mark?" Des inquired.

"All over, really. I was born and raised in California. I worked in real estate for a while, mostly commercial, then moved to Mexico to do some resort development, then to Vegas. I got tired of the rush, so I decided to follow a vision. I remembered this place from my childhood and decided this was where I wanted to be."

It was more than he had divulged during the interview, but Cal was glad he filled in some gaps. She had done a little research about him. His father's commercial real estate company was a very successful business in California. He expanded his father's company into resort development, keeping the Courier name and increasing its worth. Cal found pictures of him everywhere, arms around famous politicians and actresses, posing on beaches and yachts, and looking pensive with European landscapes behind him. Sometimes there were repeated women in the photos but mostly just him. She was disappointed with how bland his life seemed despite his conspicuous wealth.

"Cool," Des said. "My parents work at the Red Rock Resort. My dad is the manager of dining services. Not exactly resort development but a cog in the wheel." Cal was always impressed with how easily Des could connect with people, even someone like Mark Courier.

"Red Rock Resort, yeah. I had a meeting over there the other day. It's a beautiful place. I was hoping to get some advertising space for the company there. They all seem like nice people."

"Surprised you didn't open a resort in town." Des nodded back. Cal thought it was a bold assertion.

"The market is a bit saturated here. Most of these places have been around for a while, established and on good land close enough to the tourist spots where people go. Plus, I wanted to do something different." Cal noted his sincerity. He seemed in a hurry when he came in but was pausing to answer questions from a bartender.

"Makes sense. Well, we're glad to have you in town. Looks like a big operation up there. Did you hire a lot of locals?"

"Not really. Cal here is one of the few. I think people are still a little wary of us. Being new and different can be intimidating. Glad we were able to get at least one out of the bunch," he said, nodding to Cal, who smiled and sucked down the rest of her bourbon. "Let's drink to that."

Des filled their glasses and grabbed his water to cheer for Cal's new job.

"I better get going. Your cops here really watch this place. I saw one standing outside when I came in. It looks like he's trying to catch people drinking and driving. Don't want to get off on the wrong foot. I'll see you Monday?"

"Yes, sir, bright and early," Cal said, giving a quick wave.

Mark Courier was a far cry from Gary the Truck Driver and other one-time visitors to The Vortex. She imagined Officer Sanchez approaching him with questions like, "Good evening, sir. What brings you here?" and then, "This isn't exactly the seemliest of places. May I recommend one of the resort bars?"

"That guy. He's posh! How much is he worth?" Des blurted once Mark cleared the door.

"I don't know, like a couple of bucks?" Cal smiled. "Who cares! His money is about to be my money. And who drinks shots of vodka? Chicks who are terrified to gain weight. I was waiting for him to ask for a slice of lemon and lime in that glass."

Des murmured, "Uh oh, trouble's coming. Watch your back." The words barely escaped his mouth before the hand slapped her back.

"Tell me something, Cal—do you ever look ugly?

I've seen you in shorts and a T-shirt, and man, you're still the hottest thing in the room. Do you just stare at yourself in the mirror?"

Drunk Tommy's words were smothered in stale beer. Cal rolled her eyes and didn't turn away from the TV above the bar. "Tell me something," she started. "Do you ever get tired of being the dumbest thing in the room? Notice that I said thing because, let's face it, my barstool has more brains than you."

"Aren't you the smart ass tonight? I guess it's every night. If your personality was just a little better—"

"Then what? You'd give me the time of day? You really do think highly of yourself. Just being next to you is bringing my IQ down." She brushed her hand in the air between them. "Clear off, Tommy. I've hit my quota of idiots today."

"I do love our little talks, but I also like to drink. Bartender? Whiskey, no water."

Des poured the whiskey over ice and slid it to him.

"I thought I told you no water?" Drunk Tommy cocked his head. He pulled an ice cube out of the glass. "What do you call this?"

"Ice," Des answered.

"And what is ice?" Drunk Tommy pushed.

"Water?"

"Good boy. Water. I asked for whiskey, no water."

Des grabbed a pair of tongs and took out each piece, his gaze never leaving Cal, crossing his eyes and making a face. Cal tried to hide her laugh with her glass.

"There, sir," Des thundered. "I hope this meets your expectations."

"I see having a smart mouth is a disease around here. Better leave before I catch it," Drunk Tommy said, moving away.

"Too late," Cal yelled after him. "Pretty sure you're patient zero."

"That guy. How can you be that ridiculous in real life? I mean, he's for real, Cal."

"Oh, I know." She had turned on the stool to watch Drunk Tommy walk through the crowd, giving high fives to his cronies and messing up the hair of some unknown.

Des got busy filling drinks and telling the occasional joke to the patrons. Two drinks in and Cal was feeling friendlier than usual. She made her way to the dartboard. She threw a few, some hitting the board—one slammed off the plastic and onto the floor. As she was picking it up, a whistle pulled her eyes away. Cal knew who it was and didn't want to dignify him with a response; this time he didn't feed it. Drunk Tommy was having a loud conversation with his table.

"They're up to something," he said. "I sat on my porch the other night and watched the lights of eighteen-wheelers drive up toward the butte. What do you make of that, huh? I'll tell you what I think of it." He waved them in like a coach would do to their team.

Cal didn't know why she cared so much. She stepped forward and positioned herself away from the dartboard to throw. Drunk Tommy began again: "I don't think they're taking something up there…I think they're taking something *out* of there."

"Like what?" someone from the group asked. "Magic crystals?" The group laughed out loud, bobbing up and down collectively. Tommy waited until they were quiet again before he spoke. "Who knows? I'll say this, though. Whatever he's doing up there, that transplant, he's being shady as shit. He didn't hire one local from the whole town. He brought in a bunch of out-of-town twits."

The group was quiet again, and Cal looked up slowly. They were all gawking at her, eyes narrowed and searching. She wanted to curtsey or bow, acknowledging that she got a job there and was the one exception, only she knew better. So, she wasn't local; who *cares*?

At first, Cal smirked. "Could he be more ridiculous?" She flicked a dart onto the board, missing altogether. But it wasn't that dumb. Drunk Tommy was the second person she heard talking about the trucks. What would it be if Mark Courier took something out of Belle Butte? Was it the water? What else could it be? Drunk Tommy was an idiot, though, no doubt about that. She felt stupid even giving credit to his conspiracy. The only thing Cal could do was find out the truth. It was good that she was about to have access to all of Belle Butte Touring Company.

Chapter Nine

Cal hadn't experienced an alarming wake-up in a long time, so when the clock screeched loudly in her ear, she rocketed up and screamed, "What the heck?" before crashing back down.

She was surprised to smell bacon crackling in the kitchen. She assumed Alice came early and wanted to do something nice for Grandma Ruth. Cal rolled over and with a yawn asked aloud, "Do I really have to get up?"

Knowing the answer, she peeled herself out of bed. Since she was going to get a uniform and a terrible hat anyway, she wasn't concerned with how she looked. She was ready with a brush of mascara, some eyeliner, and a gargle of mouthwash. By the time she got to the kitchen, the bacon was sitting on a plate beckoning her forward with tempting tendrils of steam.

"I was about to come in there and wake you up myself," Grandma Ruth said, rustling into the kitchen, taking the dirty skillet and rinsing if off in the sink.

Cal was astonished. "Did you make breakfast this morning?" she asked, expecting to see Alice pop through the doorway.

"I woke up early and wanted some bacon," Grandma Ruth responded as if it was a daily occurrence to be active in the kitchen.

Cal wasn't taking the bait. "Where's Alice?"

Over the scrubbing of the skillet, Grandma Ruth

responded, "She isn't here yet. I'm sure she'll be along soon. Now you better hurry if you're going to make it to work on time."

Cal edged over to the sink and stared at her grandmother, the muscles in her arms twitching with each movement of the brush. Was she dreaming?

"You feeling okay this morning, Grandma?"

"Just fine, Cally." Cal loved how Grandma Ruth repeated little phrases. It was like a tic she had developed over time. It was cute and charming, especially for a Southern woman.

"Okay," Cal said, edging back away from the sink, grabbing a handful of bacon for the road. "I'll be gone all day but Alice will stay with you. I have to give the full tour today; wish me luck, but I'll try to take some pictures so you can see how beautiful it is."

Cal followed Grandma Ruth to the living room where she plopped down into her chair and picked up a book. "What is that you're reading?" Cal asked, still processing the change in behavior.

"This is that Daphne du Maurier, *Rebecca.* I've seen the movie more times than I can count and always wanted to read the book. Alice picked it up from the library for me. It's better than the movie," she whispered and smiled.

"I'll read it after you then." Cal kissed Grandma Ruth on the head. "I should be back around six. Alice can make you dinner before she heads home, okay? I love you."

"I love you too, Cally. Now don't wander too far off. If I call you, you better be able to call back."

Cal nodded and backed out of the living room, keeping an eye on her grandmother. From the hallway, it looked as if nothing had changed. Grandma Ruth was still hunched over and pale but, in the kitchen, it was completely different.

Cal looked down at her watch and sped out the door and to her jeep. The heat of the morning was beginning to rise with the sun. Cal opened the windows as she drove to create a breeze since her air conditioner was on the fritz. Downtown Sedona was sleepy, with only a few people out and about looking for coffee and conversation. Cal was a city girl by birth. She lived in Atlanta for most of her life. Even now, she missed the sound of cars and the hustle and bustle of people that created a constant buzz. Mornings in the city were always busy with the rush and the traffic. There was a Starbucks on every corner and the smell of bacon and donuts streamed through the streets. It was hard not to wake up ready to start the day. In Sedona, however, there was no rush to wake, no people to join, or smells of breakfast to crave. Here you were met with heat, the glowing red rocks rising from the ground and the sun, but it had its sense of majesty, quieter and more mysterious.

She drove in the silence, winding through the pines and up into the crest of the canyons. She moved past Whispering Pines and wondered if Drunk Tommy had made it home. The Sanchez Ranch dipped past the trees before she began curving upward toward Belle Butte. Below, Cal could see the cattle at the ranch and, beyond it, the pines. She had never noticed how close Drunk Tommy's place was to the Sanchez family ranch. Beyond that was the town, only the lights visible from the road now, the shadows of the rocks creating the illusion of nighttime. It was a pleasant drive, allowing

Cal to wake up before talking to people.

People.

It wasn't that Cal minded people. City life was about being around others whether you wanted to or not. Tourist season was in full swing when Cal moved to Sedona, making it an easy transition from Atlanta, but when the population dwindled back to the locals, Cal found herself alone. Sure, she had friends now. Des had become one of her closest confidants, but it was different. The city wasn't about having hundreds of friends; it was about hiding in the masses, being part of the wheel. Cal couldn't get lost in the crowds of Sedona any more than one could get lost in their house. People said her name and asked her questions no matter where she went. Atlanta was in the South but held little Southern charm regarding the daily greetings and gossip. She had gotten used to the friendliness she could keep at arm's length. Now Cal would have to get used to a new normal: coworkers.

She pulled into the parking lot just before nine and walked to the cabin. Cal was greeted by a group of people talking and laughing inside. They turned and looked at her and then returned to their conversations without a word. Cal spotted Clark coming through the back carrying cardboard boxes. "You need some help?" she asked, grabbing one off the top.

"Yeah, thanks. Used to doing things on my own up here." He nodded, putting the boxes down on the desk.

"Any more back there? Came ready to work." She smiled, putting her box down.

"I think that's it. Uniforms, shoes, hats." Clark touched each box as he spoke and then looked up. "All here. All right, everyone, gather around."

The others stopped talking and surrounded Clark at the desk.

"I have uniforms here and everything else you'll need. The locker rooms are in the back. Lockers are labeled. Everyone's code is 1234, and you can change it by holding the 4 for twenty seconds, then putting in your new number. Make sure you don't forget it because once it's set, not even I will know it. Get dressed, put your stuff up, and meet back here in fifteen minutes." Clark pointed towards a table with stacks of uniforms labeled with names.

Cal snagged her pile and shuffled through the crowd.

The locker rooms had wood floors, gray-blue walls, industrial lighting, and copper lockers that went from the floor almost to the ceiling.

"It's like that book," a voice interrupted Cal's observation. She turned to see a girl with long blond hair standing beside her. The girl was snapping her fingers and looking up. "You know? With the wardrobe?"

"Oh, yeah. *The Lion, the Witch, and the Wardrobe*," Cal said.

"Yes! Oh my gosh, that would've killed me all day. I'm Nia, Nia Hathaway." She stuck her hand out for a shake.

Cal reached her hand out and said, "Cal Novak. Where are you from? Obviously not Sedona."

"I wish! I'm from Las Vegas."

Cal wondered if her expression had made Nia laugh. She clarified, saying, "Sorry, I didn't mean to look at you like that. I didn't realize anyone came from Las Vegas."

Nia smiled and walked toward the lockers. "Not many people do. I bet it's like Sedona, lots of tourists and transients but very few locals."

"That's pretty much spot-on. I'm not from Sedona. We moved here a year ago," Cal said, finding her name on a locker and punching in the code. She decided to keep 1234. Who had the time to memorize something like that? "How did a girl from Las Vegas find this place? Seems like an odd job to move for."

Nia laughed again, opening her locker and removing her shoes. "I worked for Mark Courier at one of the resorts in Vegas. I managed the adventure facilities, or at least that's what he called them. It was a glorified gym with a climbing wall, indoor and outdoor pools, exercise equipment and classes, and a spa. I loved it there, but I needed a change. When I heard about this place, I applied and he hired me. I got a rental house not too far from here, unfortunately not near Sedona. The prices there are outrageous!"

"Um, yeah. Our house is tiny, and the rent is crazy. I like being near the town," Cal agreed and changed quickly.

"Nice to live close to a town! I feel like I'm out in the middle of nowhere even though I have neighbors. After growing up in Las Vegas, this place feels desolate, you know?" Nia pulled on her shorts and slipped on her boots.

"I grew up in Atlanta, so I know what you mean. I'd say you get used to it, but…"

"At least we'll get a steady stream of new faces here." Nia stood before the mirror, smoothing her hair under the hat. "This is just not going to work." She laughed.

Cal slid off her high-tops, rolling her eyes at the chunky boots before joining Nia at the mirror. She wished she hadn't kept her hair so short. Under the hat it would disappear and make her look like a boy. Even with her curves, she was hidden under the navy-blue collared shirt and baggy khaki shorts that came down to midthigh. There was nothing attractive about the uniform.

"We won't have any trouble keeping the boys away—that's for sure," Nia agreed and made her way to the door. "You coming?"

"Yeah, need to figure out what to do with my 'fro. I'll meet you out there," Cal answered and returned to the mirror.

It didn't matter what she did. The hat sat on top of her head instead of fitting around it. Her curls would have to go on workdays, putting an extra step in Cal's day. When she returned to the cabin's main room, everyone sat on the couches, and Clark talked about schedules.

"Join us," he said, irritation clear in his tone.

She found a seat near Nia and plopped down.

"There are two types of tours: virtual and in-person. You'll log onto your Belle Butte tablet and see your daily schedule. Remember, you'll need to create your profile. We'll take pictures and add them to the profile in a few minutes this afternoon. Tourists will choose their experience and can even choose their tour advisor. They're encouraged to tip you, so the more tours you give, whether virtual or in person, the more money you'll make—it's that simple. The virtual tours are live, so you'll use your tablet to take them on the tour as if they were there. You'll give them the same speech, answer their questions, and take them where they want to go. This is a unique perk to our touring company. Any questions so far?"

Cal looked around the room and noted the faces. They were all in their twenties, athletically built and diverse. She couldn't help but wonder if most of them were handpicked. She didn't recognize them from around Sedona; she had not ventured out much over the last year. Other than a weekend getaway to Phoenix to see a friend, she had stayed in town.

"Okay, moving on," Clark said. "Your tour starts here in the cabin, so we must keep this place nice. I don't mind if you take a break, but know that when tourists come in, you need to put down your phones and treat them like royalty. Meet at the desk, ask them if they want water or a snack, and direct them to the bathrooms. Give them the history at the desk as the pictures appear on the screen." He pointed over to the desk as he referred. "I can't stress this enough: lock your lockers. We're not responsible for stolen items while you're on tours. Do you understand?" Clark paused again and looked at everyone. There was a collective nod.

"Your uniform should be kept clean, wrinkle-free, and together. You'll have an extra one to keep in your locker to switch back and forth. There's a washer and dryer here if you need to use them. No excuses, people. When you wear this uniform, you represent Belle Butte. Consider this when you leave here. Everyone up!" Clark moved his hands like an orchestra conductor. Everyone stood.

"We'll do a walkthrough together. Grab a tablet from the desk and turn the power on. Your name is on the cover. When you log in, you'll see the script. Please memorize it and any extra tidbits that may help you answer questions. 'I don't know' is not an answer. You *will* know."

Cal made her way to the desk again and grabbed a device. The covers were leather with names engraved. "Wow, these are nice," she said to no one in particular. Clark had been right. As soon as the tablet booted up, the screen turned white with a script.

"Twenty pages?" a voice sounded in front of her. "That's not a script; that's a novel!"

"It's lengthy but thorough. Most of you have already been on tour with me. There's nothing short about it," Clark answered. "Today we'll focus on the canyon and rocks."

The group moved toward the back door, and Cal found herself walking next to Nia. "Did you take the full tour since you live here?" Nia asked her.

"No, I didn't do this part. We just focused on the cave through Narrow Gap. How about you?"

"Just a virtual tour. Mr. Courier interviewed me virtually, and Clark walked me through the cave. It was cool. It gave me a good idea of what to expect with those tablet-tour thingies."

"What did you think of that waterfall?" Cal was curious if it looked as mysterious on camera as in person. It was a sight she would have wanted to see in person.

"That was awesome. I can't wait to see it in person." Nia's voice dipped to a whisper. "Do you think we'll get a glance at the source today? I heard you can hear the water flowing through the rocks."

Cal had researched the phenomenon before hearing back about the job at Belle Butte. Apparently, no one had inspected the area before Mr. Courier bought it. She read that the whispering pines and the living rocks were both believed to be spirit-bound, channels where beings who had passed could interact with those still living on Earth.

Unlike the pines, the rocks were dangerous. There were only two deaths in connection with Belle Butte in recent years, and both were climbing accidents by tourists who didn't heed the warnings about free climbing danger due to the fragility of the rocks. Without knowledge and the right equipment, inserting climbing gear into the rock face was hazardous.

Cal couldn't wait to see if it were all true, to peel the rock back with her fingers and put her ear to the ground. Much like the crystals Jack wrote about in his magazine, Cal didn't believe in much of the mysticism and spirituality of Sedona. It was all too much for her taste, not subtle enough. It was like showing up in rural North Carolina, where her grandparents had lived, and seeing a church every mile or so. Was there a connection somewhere, a conduit that it was all plugged into that fed it? She doubted it, but Cal wanted to know for herself.

Cal and Nia were in the back of the group as they started up the path near Narrow Gap on the outside of the rock wall. It was a wide enough path for two, and she could hear Clark saying something about the horses being able to make it up the trail without trouble. The ground was a mixture of crushed rock and sand with wooden slats every few feet to help with footing and drainage. Cal let her hand run against the rock to her left, feeling pieces brush off a little here and there. She couldn't tell whether it was already loose or if she could make it break with the lightest touch. That seemed less likely as she remembered the large paintings and photographs, even the chandelier and lighting hung inside the cave. It had been a long time since she had a geology class; at this point, she was throwing things in the air, hoping that something stuck.

Nia was starting to breathe heavily. Cal turned and asked, "You okay?"

Nia let out an airy laugh and answered, "Yeah. And here I thought I was in shape. Boy, was I wrong. I'm having trouble getting a breath!"

Cal realized that she was laboring a bit too but less severely. She laughed, wondering how she wasn't dying between the heat and the uphill battle.

"I wonder how long this hike is. Did Clark say?"

"If he did, I wasn't listening. I bet our trusty tablet will tell us," Cal answered, lifting the device, her hands sweaty.

Nia shook her head. "I can't imagine many people making it up here. Think about the people who take tours like this. Families? Older folks? No way."

The hike took forty-five minutes before the group crested the top of Belle Butte. It was not the highest rock outcropping in the area but unique. It had a smooth long top with higher, skyscraper-like rocks shooting up into the blue. The group huddled around Clark with *oohs* and *aahs*. Cal couldn't help but agree.

The sun was much higher now, and she guessed it was around ten a.m. Below, she could make out the road coming up from Sedona, winding past Whispering Pines and Sanchez Ranch. Down to the left were other routes and rock outcroppings, green brush, and red desert. There were homes and the reservation and fences dotting their way around properties. The blue of the sky reminded Cal of turquoise with striations of white made by the few streams of clouds. It reminded her of the American flag against the red of the desert and rock. Pride crept up from her soul, pride and peace for some reason. Other than the crushing of the rocks as others walked around her, she was surprised by the quiet of the space.

Clark's voice broke the silence. "This is what people want to see, a view extending for miles and miles. We'll offer a few yoga classes up here each day, and of course, during those times, you won't have tours scheduled." Clark bent down as he talked and touched the ground. "This, however, is why we come up here." He stopped and put his ear down on the ground. The others followed, each one imitating his pose.

Cal slowly got down on her knees and put her ear to the ground. She wasn't sure what to expect. Maybe a rush of water or a trickle like a faucet, but this was not it. It sounded like the ocean, roaring waves pushed back and forth beneath the surface. Cal remembered the Coleridge poem "Kubla Khan," with its underground ocean and icy walls. It was a poet's dream to hear the waters below, not knowing how far away it was.

The others were spread over the rock and heard it—yet there was no logical source. Cal had both hoped and feared the source would be on top of the rock. Like the other rock outcroppings, they jutted high into the sky out of nowhere. Questions flooded Cal's mind.

"You have to show them the waterfall first," Clark said, his voice above the rest. "Then when they hear it, they'll understand. They'll look at where Belle Butte starts and stops and be in awe. This is why they'll choose us over the rest. It's magical."

He was right; the longer Cal was present inside the bubble of the butte, the more she was affected by its power. People would see and believe. When she was a kid, Cal's grandparents took her to Mystery Hill in the mountains of North Carolina. She was only a child, so the mystery was real to her, a place where a ball could roll uphill, and you could feel gravity in a new way. Cal returned to Mystery Hill when she was older and learned what an illusion it was. She questioned her senses as she walked through the building and reminded herself that it was all a trick, a simple mind game. But Belle Butte was no illusion. It was as real as the rock she was standing on, and whatever was happening beneath the surface was living. They were veins carrying life through the rock.

"Pretty cool," Nia said in such a matter-of-fact way that it surprised Cal.

"Pretty cool? It's amazing!" Cal said, standing. "Though it doesn't make sense."

"Honestly? It sounds like the wind."

"But there's not even a breeze up here, Nia. It's absolutely still."

"Whatever, I just don't get it. It's water. If it were pink with glitter, Mr. Courier would have a better shot of making his money back from this rock. Can you imagine spending millions of dollars on this place? I don't know how he will make enough money to keep this tourist trap afloat."

"You definitely don't get this place. He has to compete with magical crystals that bring enlightenment, whispering pine trees that can heal you, and resorts that are an oasis in the desert with golf and spas. This place stands out like a gem; trust me. People will come."

"Oh, I get it. I came from Vegas, remember? People will pay, sure." Nia stopped and looked around her. "They'll come at first, and he'll get an initial boon of tourism, but it'll taper off like those other places you mentioned."

"I'm not saying this place has healing powers like

the trees. I'm saying that it's a miracle. Nia, water is flowing up and down and all around us, defying gravity. Something down there is pumping water through the rock. You don't find that even a little intriguing?"

"I didn't mean to offend you. Your sarcasm won't get you far here. Don't you worry. When I take tours, I'll put on my best cheerleader smile and be the most excited person in the room about Belle Butte. When I'm alone, I'll think of this place as any other tourist trap for the weak-minded with nothing better to do than throw good money away on a lie. It's just nature, Cal. Nature does crazy stuff. Sorry, I'm just not blown away. I guess I was expecting the fountain of youth or something."

At that, Nia walked over to Clark and started talking to him. Cal bent back down, put her fingertips on the ground, and swore she felt the Earth moving below her. She couldn't control what Nia thought about this place, but she could outdo her by taking more tours. At that moment, it was on, a competition had been planted, and Cal was ready to water it.

The trip down the rock was faster than the uphill. Cal walked in the back, alone, watching the group pair up, catching bits and pieces of conversation that ranged from "Where did you come from?" to "Do you have a girlfriend?" She felt like she was working at a summer camp.

Clark stopped at the entrance to Narrow Gap to give directions. "If you haven't been inside the cave, I'll take you in now. The rest of you can return to the cabin and set up your profile before lunch."

As much as Cal wanted to see the waterfall again, she didn't want to be near Nia, so she headed to the cabin. The profile took less than thirty minutes, which gave her enough time to call and check in on Grandma Ruth before the other tour returned. Clark wrapped up the afternoon with a lecture about expectations and guidelines. The company had ordered an array of wraps and salads from a local deli for lunch. Cal wondered if Mr. Courier would make an appearance.

She met a few other tour advisors: a guy named Will from California, who had just moved to Sedona, and a girl named Maria, who was born and raised on a nearby reservation. They made small talk during lunch, though Cal was not convinced they would be lifelong friends, especially after the strange interaction with Nia on the rock. She kept reminding herself of the temporary status of the job. At the end of the day, the group signed paperwork for HR before heading out. It was a long day, an actual nine to nearly five. Cal hadn't done a day like that in a long time. She had enjoyed the freedom of editing jobs.

It was strange to feel impacted by a place. Cal had often wondered why people felt drawn to the natural surroundings in the area and why they went on yoga excursions or mindfulness hikes. Maybe it was because she grew up in the city or because she floated between her grandparents' house and Atlanta and never felt the comfort that came with home, but over the last few days, Cal felt a calling, a beckoning to step into a new world. Once upon a time, she was likely on par with Nia's disbelief, but something had changed. She had changed.

****

Cal slept hard that night, the sleep that comes with work. She awoke in the early morning hours. At first Cal thought people were walking outside the house. The walls were relatively thin, and she often felt they were pointless regarding the weather and sound. On more than one occasion, she had heard coyotes howling and fighting in the distance. Cal got out of bed to investigate the sound, tiptoeing in the hall not to awaken Grandma Ruth. She was surprised to hear the voices coming out of the living room.

Cal rushed in, half expecting to see multiple people, but there was just Grandma Ruth. She was having a conversation in the dark. Cal had read that you shouldn't wake someone who was sleepwalking or talking but instead create a safe space for them to process. She sat down in the hallway outside the living room and listened. The conversation came in snippets, almost like tweets.

"I know. She's okay. I promise. Yes. Working. Yes. It's all around. I feel it, too. She can't. Yes. Me too. No. She can't. I know," Grandma Ruth chirped. Her voice stayed nearly monotone with little inflection.

At first Cal thought it odd that the phrases were short and repetitive. Then she wondered why it had sounded like two separate voices before she came into the room. There had been a male voice—she could have sworn it. Maybe it was just how her grandmother spoke, emotionless, almost cold.

Cal realized that her grandmother had stopped talking and decided to wait in the hallway for a bit longer in case she started up again. The light through the window, likely a streetlight, cast a silver gleam on Grandma Ruth's profile. Cal stared at her, studying the little hairs on her face, monitoring her breathing, wishing there was a way to ease her mind. *Something must be going on in there, more than what I understand.*

She wanted to reach out to her, hug her, and snuggle against her as she had done as a child. Everything changed so quickly. One moment Cal was living her dream, interning for a publisher in Atlanta, her grandparents alive. They were gardening, having get-togethers, drinking iced tea on the front porch, and going to church, and now…that all seemed like a dream. Now she was caring for her grandma in Sedona, in a tiny house with paper-thin walls and howling beasts outside her windows. She worked at a tourist trap and drank at a bar with a hole in the wall. This was her life. The day-to-day didn't seem so bad, but to break it down on a dark night against the memories of her past life, it seemed foreign, unreal.

Cal fell asleep against the wall in the hallway.

Chapter Ten

Jack Miller was a born journalist. From the time he was a child, he knew that he wanted to write. He didn't care what he wrote about. He started a middle school newspaper and found a passion for news. He enjoyed tracking down a story and learning every angle, asking the tough questions, and getting answers that both shocked and inspired his readers. He once investigated and reported on the mystery of a cracked parking lot. It was such a hit that the local paper picked it up and printed it in their weekly circular. It was a special weed with chemical properties that corroded the cement and pushed upward, creating a large crack.

By high school, he had made a name for himself and became the paper's editor, though he didn't like that as much. Jack enjoyed the grit it took to be an investigative journalist. He received a full scholarship to Arizona State where he studied journalism. In his junior year, he took a trip with friends to Sedona. For as long as he had lived in Arizona, he had never been there, writing it off as a place where hippies went to get high and worship rocks. On further investigation, he found what he considered "truth and revelation."

Jack's girlfriend of two years broke up with him right before the trip, leaving a hole in his heart. He had moped around for weeks before the Sedona trip without any relief from his pain. His friends told him that Sedona would hold the answers, that there he would find the peace he needed. Assuming his friends meant other women and alcohol, he agreed to suck it up and go. It did not disappoint. On day one, they found themselves in a shop filled with little glass-like rocks ranging from transparent to green to purple. His friends laughed at the hokey nature of the store, but Jack was intrigued. How could something so beautiful exist, and how could people like diamonds more than these crystals?

It wasn't just the beauty of the rocks. As he walked around, picking up each stone and studying its flat sides and variations, a lady came out from the back and approached him. "Can I help you, young man? I see you understand them."

Jack looked at the lady who dressed like a Gypsy with a pink bandana covering her hair, a long, flowery skirt, and dark shirt. "Understand who?"

"Why, the crystals, of course." She picked up a large blue crystal, holding it to the light. "They can speak, you know. They talk to people, and the chosen ones listen. They hear wisdom in their whispers."

He decided to humor her. "What do they say?"

"That depends on the person. If you believe in their magic, they can make things happen. What is it you desire? Healing?"

Jack wasn't sure how to answer, but it didn't matter because his mouth moved before his brain could stop him. "Yes, healing." Surprised, he wished he could have held it back.

"You must find one that speaks to you. Look around; touch them. Hold them to the light and ask them questions. You'll find answers. Just believe."

Jack nodded and browsed with intention. He held a

yellow one up to the light and a green one. He held a purple one and asked for help healing his broken heart. He found himself begging each crystal he touched, hoping for an answer. Jack could hear his friends in the background. They were joking and laughing, wondering why Jack was being so ridiculous. He didn't answer their jests but continued his quest until he came to a tiny pink stone so small that he was almost afraid to put it between his fingers. Jack held it to the light and asked it to remove his pain and heal his broken heart. He was mesmerized that something that once meant nothing to him suddenly meant the world. He would later take the small pink crystal and make it into an engagement ring for his wife. With each crystal, he saw something different that fascinated him, that made him forget the pain little by little. He wanted to know more about the crystals. He wanted to know their names and why they were the way they were. He tried to understand them, cry and laugh with them. He fell in love with the crystals that day.

After college, Jack moved to Sedona and started a magazine specializing in crystals. He learned everything about how they were created, how to mine for them, and the years and years of lore surrounding their magical existence. He got to know the little Gypsy woman named Dandelion who owned the crystal store where he fell in love. One of his first interviews was with her, the perfect way to start his journey into a new world.

Since then, he'd heard of success from celebrities who wrote to the magazine about their experiences with crystals and geologists who specialized in their formation. There was money and a small amount of fame.

But by the time Cal came to his door begging for

work, Jack's magazine was an afterthought to most. Instead of fascinating articles about crystals, there were advertisements for various tourist spots. He'd never transitioned the magazine online; print was expensive, but Jack didn't want to be digital. He was a journalist and wanted to give people something they could hold, touch, and keep. Jack thought this was his chance. He couldn't afford Cal, but he saw something he once had in her. It was a hunger and a need for words, the first powerful "crystals" with which he had fallen in love.

"So, do I have the job?" she asked, a short, curly-headed girl with jeans and a t-shirt who looked more suited for a ranch than a desk job.

"I don't know how I would use you?" Jack's response was truth and disappointment.

"Well, I'm an editor, so I guess I could edit things?" Her voice went up as she spoke.

"True." Jack sat back in his chair and continued, "But there isn't much to edit. This magazine used to be a must-read in Sedona and throughout the country, but now my readership has dwindled."

"Have you thought of going online? Lots of magazines do well digitally."

The words made Jack cringe. If he had a nickel for every time someone suggested going digital; he wouldn't need to worry about advertisers. Heck, he wouldn't have to worry about anything.

"I've considered it, but I'm not interested in putting the magazine online. People who believe in the power of crystals are tactile. They need to touch them, breathe them in, if you will. These people wouldn't read my magazine online. They look forward to receiving a physical copy, feeling the pages, and studying the photographs."

Cal's expression didn't change, and Jack was surprised she didn't fight him. She was a confident young lady.

"I like you, kid. I can't afford you, but I like you. We have a few articles that come out along with many advertisements during tourist season, but there's nothing new during the off-season. We circulate the same advertisements. It wouldn't be full-time work—"

"That's okay!" Cal cut in. "I just need something," she said quickly and added, "maybe this can at least give me a start."

"That's a good way to look at it." Jack stood up, and Cal followed. "I'll hire you as a contract editor. You can work remotely or come into the office if you want. As a journalist, I always hated sitting at a desk to write."

"Where did you work?"

"The *Phoenix Times*. It was a real rush. Mostly did investigative journalism, so there weren't a lot of stories, but the ones that came together, well, I guess you could say I was pretty good."

"I didn't realize I was standing amid greatness." Cal chuckled, but Jack noticed it was the laughter of excitement and not mockery.

"Wouldn't say great. I enjoyed the life while I led it," he said.

"Then you moved here. Fell in love with a local?"

"You could say that, if you call crystals locals. Eventually there was a girl, is a girl. My wife's name is Eve. We have a house up near Courthouse Butte. We'll have you out sometime." Jack held out his hand for a shake. Cal reciprocated.

"Thank you, Mr....?" she trailed off, looking

perplexed.

"You can call me Jack. No need for formalities when you write about crystals," he laughed.

Jack often thought back to his first meeting with Cal and how she seemed so ready for a change. He felt the same pull. It wasn't that he was giving up on his crystals; in fact he was holding on to them more than ever before. He did however understand that he needed to make a change and that meant making a phone call to a friend:

"Oliver, hey, it's Jack. Yes, Jack Wendall. How are you, buddy? I'm great. Eve's great too. The magazine business is slow, so I wondered if you had any jobs for an old journalist like me. Any assignments in this area? Yeah, I'd be up for that. Sure! Okay, I'll put it on my calendar and do that for you. Absolutely. Look, Oliver, I really appreciate it. No, I still believe in crystals. Ha! Yeah, okay. Talk to you soon."

The conversation was quick, which was not a surprise. Jack and Oliver had been friends since college, and Oliver had suggested the trip to Sedona many years ago. Taking on a job for the *Times* was a step in the right direction. If he could establish himself now with an article here and there, Jack could get back in the business and put the magazine to the side. He had to start thinking of Eve, retirement, and the prospect that even crystals changed. He needed to find a big story and show Oliver and the *Times* what he could do. It was either that or plan B, and he didn't want to make that call, not yet.

Chapter Eleven

Cal made it to work two days in a row, which was quite a victory in her book. After a rough night of falling asleep in the hallway and a long hike the day before, she felt fatigue in her muscles and bones. The drive up to Belle Butte wasn't as enchanting, and the prospect of seeing a roomful of faces was not as exciting. Cal was no quitter. She parked and reached the cabin without collapsing into a heap of sleep. Inside, the air was cool and quieter than the day before. She thought she was the only one affected by the long day.

"All right, team," Clark shouted. Cal grimaced and wished there was a way to turn down his volume. "Today we're setting up for the grand-opening event we're hosting tomorrow night. You're expected to be here. Don't worry; we won't require uniforms that night. Instead, wear cocktail attire and be ready to do a lot of smiling. You're the bright, shiny faces of this operation. The event will host local businesses and investors from the area. Be on your best behavior and remember who you represent. I've split you up into two teams for today. Half of you will clean up the grounds and get pamphlets set out. The other half will be setting up the rooms in the main building. Let's finish this before lunchtime so you can spend half the day memorizing those scripts. Any questions?"

There were questions; there were always questions.

Cal was impatient to find out what her job was going to be. She hoped for the setup crew, mainly because the heat would make her sleepy. Clark showed the two columns of names on the TV screen behind the desk. Cal saw her name with the setup crew and gave a sigh of relief.

"I guess we're stuck together today," Nia said, moving next to Cal.

Cal fought off the urge to roll her eyes. She had overreacted yesterday and felt somewhat foolish. Whatever, she had moved on, and now she just wanted to get things set up so she could go home and take a nap.

"Yep, the old setup crew," Cal joked back. "At least we aren't outside today. Yesterday got to me a bit."

"I admit that I was praying for a miracle there. Not sure how I'm going to deal with the heat daily. By the time I got home last night, I was ready for bed. I passed out on the couch while I was eating dinner. Pathetic." Nia laughed.

Cal changed the subject. "Do you know any of the others on our team?"

"Yeah, I met them yesterday. They seem nice. Honestly, small talk doesn't tell me much about people. None of them are local; I know that."

"Don't you think that's weird?" Cal asked.

"What's weird?"

"Why would Mr. Courier ship people in to work here? Some people in town, or at least around here, need jobs. Why hire a bunch of outsiders? No offense," she added quickly, remembering that Nia was from Vegas.

"Not sure if he shipped them in, but the company did send out sort of an all-call to the other resorts, I think. I'm sure it's easier to train people who already know the ins and outs of the company," Nia added.

"Makes sense, I guess. I mean, how hard is it to be a tour guide?" Cal wanted to add "no offense" again but thought it would be redundant. Nia didn't look upset by the question. She nodded her head and smiled with what seemed like agreement.

Clark called the setup team to the right and introduced them to the event planner. Her name was Jenna, and with the fewest words possible, she explained where the tables and chairs needed to be, how the clothes and centerpieces needed to look, and other little tidbits. Cal took mental notes and hoped she didn't have to make things look fancy. While she took pride in her attention to detail regarding editing, decorating was not her forte.

Between the five tour advisors, they had everything done in two hours. "Remember, everyone," Clark stressed to the team, which was scattered all over the main room of the building, "tomorrow night, cocktail attire. Be here by six-thirty. Guests will arrive at seven. Oh, I almost forgot. You can bring a date or a person if you'd like. Just remember that your job is to mingle."

Cal was one of the first through the door to the parking lot.

"Hey, Cal, are you bringing a date tomorrow night?" Nia yelled across the lot.

"Uh, not sure. Maybe?" she answered.

In her desire to leave, Cal had only half heard Clark. If she had the choice, she would bring Des, but that was probably out; Des always worked on Friday nights. She heard Nia laugh as she climbed into her jeep. Her insecurity wove a web of assumptions as to the meaning of the laugh. It could have been innocent, or it could have been catty. Either way, Cal stared at Nia through the rearview mirror and watched the leggy blonde step into her BMW convertible, wondering why someone like that would move here.

She stopped at The Vortex on the way home. There was time, and she hoped to convince Des to take the night off so he could be her date. Cal plopped down on a barstool and knocked her knuckles on the bar.

"Bartender?" she said, accentuating the *en*.

Des ended his conversation with several guys perched near the bar's end. "Yes, ma'am, what can I serve you?" he said as he swaggered up. "Don't you look like"—he looked her up and down and eventually came up with—"like a tour guide."

"That was the best you could come up with? Not a ranger or a zoo-animal tamer? Even a pool cleaner would have been better than the truth. And you made it sound so degrading. I want to remind you that the work I do is life changing. Soon people will pay a lot of money to hear my words and see what I've seen. You're basically talking to a celebrity." Cal laughed. "I'll switch it up. Give me a margarita."

"Whoa, are we celebrating tonight?" Des laughed, taking a glass out from behind the bar.

Cal didn't understand why her nerves were firing, sending butterflies through her stomach. "Not exactly, but I have a favor to ask you."

"I'm intrigued." He moved the shaker up and down, mixing her margarita. "Do ask."

"We're having a grand-opening party up at Belle Butte tomorrow night, and I was wondering if you might perhaps want to—"

Before she could finish, Des jumped in. "Oh wow, are you about to ask me as your date? Where's my phone? Seriously, I need to get this on camera. Cal Novak is about to ask a boy on a date! And not just any boy, Des Adams. That's me, people," he yelled to the bar. There were some chuckles, mercy ones, that trickled out.

"Shut up." Cal rolled her eyes. "F it then. No, I was not and will not ask you, my *friend*, to go with me. And just so you know? It's a bunch of bigwigs, investors, and people like that who you could have rubbed elbows with so that one day you could be more than the local bartender. Just saying." She smiled. "Not that you would have gotten the chance...because I wasn't going to ask you."

Des smiled back and added, "Yeah, too bad. I missed my chance." He walked away, turned around quickly, and pointed his finger toward Cal. "Oh yeah, I forgot to mention that I *will* be at that little soiree tomorrow night. Mr. Courier asked Lucio to provide the bar for the night, so of course he asked the star bartender to work the event. So, I guess that means I'll see you there?"

As much as it annoyed Cal that Des had made fun of her asking him, she felt comforted knowing he would be there. She assumed she wouldn't make it far from the bar anyway, so having him on the other side was a plus. There was no way she was going to admit that to Des. He looked like he was having way too much fun.

"I probably won't even see you there since I have to rub elbows, but if I happen to, I'll say hello." She knocked a few chunks of salt from the rim of her glass onto the bar.

Suddenly, Des was across the bar, his face close to hers. "You better come to the bar. I can't wait to see you in a dress!" he said, blowing the salt back at her.

Cal pushed him away and realized, *Oh crap, I need a dress!* She couldn't spare the cash for a new one and she didn't have a good witch with a magic wand begging to help her.

"I need a dress," she finally said out loud. "This is when it doesn't pay only to have guy friends. Where am I going to find a free cocktail dress?"

"Ha! Can't help you with that."

Cal visualized her closet, which was more like a pile of clothing than an actual place where clothes hung. She did have a couple of black dresses that might work. Black never went out of style. She could even add some of her grandmother's jewelry or local pieces she had picked up over the last year. "I'll figure it out," she managed to say through a gulp of margarita.

Des was almost too quiet as he dried a glass with a towel. Cal had been curious as to what he would have worn. She assumed he would be in black tomorrow night as it was a catered event. Lucio wasn't the classiest guy, but he knew the rules. She was surprised that Mr. Courier hired a local bar owner to schmooze his big dogs.

He must want to show the local faire tomorrow night. But why? How would that impress them? They're used to eating at the club at the Red Rock Resort. He would have an easier time getting more money from them with fancy cocktails.

"I would've said yes," Des said quietly.

"Huh?" Cal wasn't sure what he was talking about. *Did I say something out loud?*

"If you'd asked, which I'm pretty sure you were going to, I would've said yes." It was the sheepish grin he flashed that brought down Cal's guard. It was true. He would have said yes, and Cal knew that.

Over the last year, she considered Des her best friend, someone she could count on. Thinking of him as her date was strange, but she couldn't deny that the thought had crossed her mind. Des was handsome with his caramel-colored skin, lean build, black 'fro, though not as cool as her own, and his laid-back style. He could sing, dance, and make a mean Old Fashioned, and he never failed to make her laugh. It wasn't that she didn't want to date him, but the hesitation was natural, and she couldn't shake the fear that a date would mean awkward conversations and late-night sessions with less McDonald's and more snuggling. No, it was not the time, and she smiled back, acknowledging his "semi-apology" for mocking her. Maybe he felt the same way she did. Again, it was not the time.

"Oh yeah? Well, I wasn't going to ask. I was going to see if you knew Drunk Tommy's number because I heard he makes a mean date, and I do have a thing for men in their forties. I think he would change his shirt and everything and, you know, be the talk of the party. I might score some points with the boss." She laughed.

"Yeah, yeah." He put the glass down and pushed his hand away at the air between them. Tension was broken, and for now, Cal was glad that they were friends.

When she got home, Cal spotted a note from Alice on the refrigerator. *"Took your grandmother for a walk today. I could barely keep up! They did her blood work at the doctor today. You should get those results back in twenty-four hours. Keep an eye on her. She's a quick one."*

Cal smirked at first then thought back to the other morning. It seemed that Grandma Ruth was turning the corner, was it possible that she was getting better? The clock on the wall reminded her of the time and Cal ran to take a shower.

After toweling off, Cal went through her closet and tried on both dresses, one long and black and the other short and black, a bit tighter. She had a multistrand turquoise necklace that paired well with the long, flowy strapless dress, so she made her final decision. She remembered the last time she wore the dress.

It was a date with a guy named Tanner. He was a banker she had met at a publishing party, a night she wasn't super proud of. He was another lady's date that she stole. They stood on the balcony of the high-rise office building talking about everything from books they were reading to current events. He asked her on a date for the next night, and she donned the long black dress and paired it with a simple silver necklace that hung loosely at her collarbone. Over dinner, he told her how he wanted to kiss every inch of that bone and how jealous he was of her necklace. They drank champagne and eventually returned to his apartment where he spent the night doing just that. She was drunk and happy, lost in the moment of life going her way.

The following day, her phone rang, and she rolled over to answer it. The voice, drenched in tears, at the other end was Grandma Ruth, who said, "Cally? Oh, Cally, he's dead. Your granddad is dead." Cal pulled her dress back on, walked out of Tanner's apartment, and never looked back. After the funeral in North Carolina, her grandmother's health worsened, and Cal decided to take care of her.

Cal placed the dress on the edge of her bed and looked in the mirror again. She didn't look that much older. Sure, years had passed and with it perhaps an extra pound in her midsection, or two, but she was still young.

Des has never asked me out. I wonder why? Let's see what he thinks of this.

She looked back at the dress and smiled.

Chapter Twelve

On the night of the party, Cal pulled up to Belle Butte Touring Company, confident with her final look. Other than the jeep that served as her coach, she felt posh and put together, more like her years working in Atlanta. The air was still hot so sweat rolled down her back and front, dampening her dress. It was a smart call to wear black, and she gave herself another mental pat on the back. Others emerged from their cars, wearing suits, sports coats, and colorful dresses that complemented the desert's colors with blues, greens, and reds.

She entered the building and was immediately impressed with the setup. The tables looked great with succulents and candles, and the lighting created a soft glow throughout. Through the windows, the sky's blue made a nice contrast against the white tablecloths. The bar was in the back with a tiered champagne fountain to one side. Des was moving bottles around and taking out glasses. Music played throughout the building, a moody, atmospheric playlist that Cal assumed was chosen by Mark Courier. She'd imagined his taste would be more folk.

"You clean up nicely." Nia, sporting a two-piece outfit with a long black-and-blue skirt and a black crop top halter, walked toward her.

Cal had never seen someone pull off an outfit like that in real life. It seemed like something a model would wear on the runway. "Wow, you do too. Just something you had lying around?"

Nia laughed. "My closet is full of pieces like this from Vegas. I guess I won't have many opportunities to wear them out here."

"Oh, I don't know. You'd be amazed how many people throw parties in the resorts around here, or at their million-dollar mansions in the mountains. I've never been to them but heard about 'em." Cal tried to comfort Nia. She caught Des' eye; he waved Cal over. "Hey, I'll be right back."

Cal made her way to the bar and twirled. Des' mouth gaped open. "Okay, okay." He laughed. "And I suppose this was the dress you *didn't* have?"

"This old thing?" Cal said with her thickest Atlanta-born accent. "I'm a Southern lady, and we always have the right clothes. In the words of Otis Redding, girls get weary wearing that same old dress."

"I've never seen you wear a dress like that in the year you've been here in Sedona, though those shoes—" Des shook his head. "You didn't have any high heels to match the outfit?"

Cal followed his eyes to her red high-tops and laughed. "Well, I can't leave the house without them."

Des smiled and changed the subject. "This place is amazing. I can't believe you get to work here. Do you have an office?"

Cal burst into laughter. "Are you kidding me? We have a cabin in the back, the nicest cabin you can imagine. Maybe I can take you on a tour at the end of your shift?"

"A private tour with a beautiful woman? Yes. What can I get you to drink?"

Cal glanced around to take in the scene. "An Old Fashioned, of course."

"I should've known you'd be the first at the bar." Mark Courier was next to her in a casual suit, his hair styled to the side, wearing a toothy grin. "Hope you approve of my choice of bartenders."

Cal wasn't sure what to say. She hadn't seen Mark Courier since she started her job and had forgotten about him. This was a pleasant surprise. She finally came up with, "It was a good choice. Honestly, the whole place is beautiful. Did you come up with this idea?"

He laughed then sighed. "No, I believe this was all my personal assistant Jenna's vision. She has a knack for party planning, though I will say the fountain was my idea. I never throw a party without one. What do you think? Too much?"

"Nah, I don't think you can go over the top at a cocktail party." Des put Cal's drink next to her hand. "And this location, how did you find this? I remember you saying something about being a kid and coming up here, but I can't believe you found this spot. People from all over Arizona would come for this view," Des said, his voice in awe with his eyes on the floor-to-ceiling window. "You can see Cathedral, Courthouse, and Tempe Rock in the distance. Quite a view, Courier, quite a view."

"Glad you approve, Des. It took some finagling, but I don't take no for an answer. It was this butte or nothing. But you know, I'm always thankful for the support of the locals. Tourists will come and go, but locals will be our neighbors," Mark rattled off. "I hope you see this place as part of Sedona's landscape, something you all can be proud of. I plan to be here for a long time."

Cal had read something similar in an interview Mr. Courier had given. She tried to remember where it was.

"I better get back to the crowd. I'm going to talk with the staff before we get started. Coming, Cal?" he asked. She nodded and followed him away from the bar.

"Can I get your attention, please?" he said loudly. "I want to thank all of you for your hard work this week and for some of you, beyond. I am proud to have such a lovely staff ready to kick off Belle Butte Touring Company next week. We have tours and events planned already, and we hope you're as excited as we are to begin the season. It's important that those coming here tonight also feel appreciated. Please take time to talk with them and get to know them. Enjoy yourselves!" The staff clapped and smiled.

Mr. Courier walked away, shaking hands as he went. She watched him, confident and calm in his element, as he had mini conversations with each person he passed. Cal heard Nia's voice, "He's amazing, isn't he? Can you imagine that much charisma in one person? I've seen him make these speeches so many times, and it never gets old. He glimmers!"

Cal never took her eyes off the man. "He does seem to enjoy it, doesn't he?"

"Are you ready to get to know a bunch of bureaucrats?" Nia laughed and walked away.

Cal looked around and saw Nia stroll over to a group of men who had just walked in, immediately making them laugh. That wasn't Cal's style, and insecurity began to creep in as she noticed all the staff intermingled with people entering the room. She saw a familiar face coming through the door in her peripheral vision.

"Jack?" she asked and walked in his direction.

"Hey, you!" he exclaimed and went in for a hug.

"What are you doing here? Is Eve with you?"

"I'm covering the event for the *Phoenix Times*. Just a little side job while the magazine waits for the hordes of tourists." He laughed. "Did I miss anything? I thought this thing started at seven?"

Cal was excited to see his journalism in action. She had heard the stories about his investigative talents. "It does. Mr. Courier gave a little speech to the staff to start it off, though I don't think that would make good news. So, are you going to be walking around asking people questions?"

"You seem too eager. How about I let you ask the questions, and I'll walk around taking notes?"

"I wouldn't know what to ask. Remember, I'm the editor type, not the writer," Cal said,

"Oh please. Anyone who pays as much attention as you do to detail can write. Have you ever tried?"

"Sure, I've written things, but nothing of worth. I'm waiting for the big story," Cal joked. "Can I get you anything?"

"Nah, I don't drink on the job. I need to be coherent. Where should I start? Maybe with that lady right there?" he asked. "Isn't she a congresswoman?"

"No idea. I'm not into politics."

It made Cal wonder. Suppose that was a congresswoman, and she did spot the mayor and many other politicians and businesspeople. Why would they come to an opening of a random touring company in Sedona, Arizona? She couldn't imagine them descending on Drunk Tommy's Whispering Pines and sitting with him on his front porch, celebrating the opening of his season.

"When do they start the tour?" Jack asked.

"A tour? At night?" Cal hadn't heard anything about that.

"Yeah, it was in my press packet, a nighttime tour of the caves. I was excited about that part."

"I'm guessing Clark will be giving that tour. He's the expert. Strange, though, I haven't seen him tonight. He's probably hiding—not much of a big crowd kind of guy." Cal couldn't even imagine him dressed up.

"I'm off to ask a lot of annoying questions. See you in a bit?" Jack touched her shoulder and walked off.

She was alone again, standing in the middle of the room, surrounded by strangers. She wasn't sure if she should run back to the bar or attempt a conversation. It felt foreign to be there, though her previous life wasn't far removed from this world. Cal had buzzed around publishing parties and book signings. She had even spoken in front of people, but this was different. Everyone here had an agenda, some unknown reason to be here. Her mind wandered back to Drunk Tommy in the bar, and she was immediately disappointed that she was thinking of him at a party. Is a new tourist spot worth all this hype?

Without thinking, she returned to the comfort of the bar and greeted Des with a smile and the empty glass. "Another one of these, bartender."

"Thirsty tonight? It's a bit warm in here," Des rebutted, busy pouring a row of shots.

"Looks like I'm not the only one," Cal answered. "Look around and tell me what you see." She glanced from side to side as she posed the statement.

Des took the bait and looked around. "A bunch of white people drinking in a glass house?" He laughed. Cal rolled her eyes. "Okay, okay. Umm, I see wealthy people. This is like the who's who of Sedona. These are the people who make decisions around here for us lowly folk. Mr. Courier has some rich and powerful friends already."

"He does, doesn't he?"

"Notice that none of the other tourist traps are here. No Tommy from Whispering Pines, Dandelion from the Crystal Shop, Johnson's Mining Company, or even Garcia's Canyon Tours. Courier has his priorities right— I'll give him that," Des answered.

Nia approached the bar and placed an empty glass beside Cal's. "And who do we have here?"

"This is Des Adams, friend and local bartender extraordinaire," Cal said.

"Where do you hide?" Nia's eyes were glued to Des. "There's no way you're local."

"Sadly, yes," he said, "and I hide behind a bar most days. I work at The Vortex downtown."

"It looks like I have a reason to drive into Sedona. I'll take a vodka and soda, lemon and lime please. What do you think so far?" Nia asked, turning toward Cal.

"It's nice. Not really into the whole schmooze thing, but I like the overall vibe. Do you know who's giving the tour later?" Cal asked, knowing the answer, but the small talk was enough to make her look busy.

Nia grinned. "Probably Clark, though I don't see him anywhere. I'm sure he's in the cabin sucking whiskey before the spotlight hits him. He doesn't seem like the kind of guy who would volunteer willingly, but Mark can be rather convincing."

Cal heard the name *Mark* like a resounding gong. So, it was Mark now? What happened to Mark Courier or Mr. Courier? Cal had had her suspicions before this moment. Nia was a beautiful girl, straight off the pages of a fashion magazine but she didn't fit the job—and looked more like a politician's wife than a tour guide.

Nia and Mark were more involved than they let on, and Cal figured another vodka soda might reveal the truth. She began formulating the questions in her mind, channeling her inner Jack with his investigative journalism, which felt good.

"I know you said you worked at the Vegas resort that Mr. Courier developed, but you didn't mention whether you knew him," Cal pressed.

Nia ignored her, eyes still on Des. "What's The Vortex like? Is it one of those rustic places where people drink out of jars?"

Des laughed. "No, the owner would never do anything so tacky. We're much classier than that with our original dark wood flooring, shiplap wood walls, and the obligatory neon beer signs. It's a sight, almost like you're stepping into a boat."

"Charming," Nia said, taking a sip from her glass, then swirling the remaining contents. "I'll have to stop by soon. I need a place to blow off steam."

Des leaned in close. "The Vortex has some local flare. Stick close to me, and I'll introduce you around."

Cal blurted out, "So how long have you known Mark?" Both Des and Nia turned their heads, facing her. She felt blood rush into her head and flush her cheeks.

"Oh, uh, a few years, I guess?" Nia said. "Not really sure. I started working at the Platinum Resort right after it opened. He was there a lot, trying to work out the kinks. Mark said that he wanted people to feel like they were a part of nature so the whole place looked, well, a lot like this. It's his signature, I think. Clean lines, minimalist, no fuss—that's the kind of guy he is."

Nia took another drink. "I was introduced to him after a staff meeting. He stayed behind to shake hands, and I couldn't help myself. I've never been one to shy away from an opportunity to meet the boss. There I was, with my yoga outfit on among the other uniformed workers, probably looking like a bum, shaking his hand. He asked for my name and…" Her voice trailed off in an invitation to have the blanks filled.

Cal wanted to fill in the gap with "my number" but didn't feel the need. The silence was enough to make the inference.

"Let's just say we worked together and played together." Nia smiled coyly. "I wasn't the only one. Other women found him handsome and kind, and I'm sure he obliged. I've never been a one-person type of girl, so it didn't bother me. Then he left for weeks at a time, and we saw each other less and less. We texted back and forth, nothing too nefarious, and then nothing. The last time we saw each other in Vegas he told me about this place. At first, I didn't understand the vision. A touring company in the middle of nowhere? It didn't sound like his style. But then the more he talked, the more he revealed his dream. I was enchanted."

"What was so special about his dream? I can't imagine Sedona being more attractive to a city girl than Los Angeles or Las Vegas," Des said, mixing a cocktail.

"The red rocks, the cactus, yoga on top of the world, it sounded heavenly. So, I applied for the job, and he hired me as a tour advisor and yoga instructor. I took it as a positive sign that maybe we were moving in a relationship direction. Why would he hire someone so far away to work in Sedona when surely there were locals he could hire? I didn't need the job; honestly, I was fishing. But when I arrived, and everyone was from somewhere else, I realized I was probably no one. There was no intention behind hiring me other than to fill a need here. We haven't even texted or spoken since I moved in, and I'm not the kind of girl to fall into a puddle over a man." Nia lifted her glass and let the rest of the contents disappear down her throat.

Cal felt guilty for opening a wound. Nia may deny her true feelings, but Cal could tell she had it bad for Mark Courier, bad enough to leave her life behind and move to Sedona. If this was Nia's backstory, how about the rest of the staff that moved from other areas? He couldn't have slept with all of them.

"He sounds like a jerk," Des said, taking her glass and putting down a fresh one. "He's not worthy of a chick like you."

"You're too kind," Nia said. "Trust me, I'm not losing sleep over Mark, just treading lightly until I figure out the game. There's always a game with people like him. It's like chess, but you don't know who's a pawn or the king."

Cal could see her point. Tonight felt like a chess match.

And the game just got interesting.

Chapter Thirteen

Halfway through the party, Clark Haus took the microphone to invite the guests to join him on a private moonlight tour of Narrow Gap. He instructed the press to be upfront so they could hear and add information to their articles.

"Are you gonna go?" Des asked Cal.

Cal didn't want to sit around and wait for the crowd to return. "I don't think we're allowed to crowd up the space. It looks like everyone is leaving. Are you supposed to clean up the bar?"

"Lucio said I could take a break. I was hoping you could take me on that private tour?" Des threw down his bar towel and winked.

Cal could feel the butterflies again and wasn't sure whether it was the potential of being alone with him in the dark or getting to sneak around a bit. Either way, she was in. "Sure," she responded, gulping down the rest of her drink and feeling the warm, numbing effects. "I'll show you the cabin."

"Why don't we start with this building?" he asked.

"What you see is what you get here. This room takes up most of the space. Mr. Courier's office and a boardroom are over there to the right, and—"

"And how about the elevator?" Des cut in, pointing behind him.

"Oh," she said with surprise. She hadn't noticed the

door before. Unlike others, this one blended into the wall, the same red-stained oak that lined the other walls. "I've never been in that elevator before. We don't come into this building."

"Then this is the place to start," he said, grabbing her hand and pulling her toward the door. There was only one button, and Des pressed it quickly, but nothing happened, no sound at all. "Strange. Maybe it doesn't work?"

"Maybe? Or it could be one of those fingerprint ones that you have to have access to," Cal suggested. Strange indeed. Why would you need a special access elevator in a touring company? What would you possibly need to keep that secret from tourists and staff?

"Show me the cabin then," Des said with disappointment.

Cal still had the elevator in her mind as they left the main building and headed to the cabin. A nice breeze dulled the night's heat, and the moon lit the path against the dark sky.

"Not a shabby place to work," Des said, looking around. "Compared to my hole in the wall, this place is divine. Now I know why you took the job."

"That and the intrigue." Cal laughed. "There's a story here; I feel it."

Des chuckled. "Yeah, apparently every place has a story in Sedona. If I didn't know better, I'd say you're getting swept up. Whoa, this is the cabin?"

"This is it," she said, opening the door. "I better not turn on the lights, or they'll notice."

"It's okay. We got that natural light going on through the windows. This is posh. These chairs are genuine leather, and are these lamps made from antlers?"

He brushed his hand against one of the lights.

Cal laughed, saying, "Yeah, they spare no expense for the staff. This is all for the guests. They start their tour here."

She moved past him to one of the windows that faced the cave entrance. She could see the back of the main building too. Cal couldn't stop thinking about the elevator. The shaft didn't go up, as a window started about ten feet from the ground above where the elevator would have been. "That means it would have to go down," she said quietly.

"What would have to go down?" Des asked, appearing next to her. "Is that the cave?" he pointed toward Narrow Gap. The light was streaming out of the mouth.

"That's the entrance. Des, the elevator must go down, but how? I thought Mr. Courier said in my interview that they couldn't dig into the rock, which was too fragile. How can he have an elevator that goes down? Do you think he found the source?"

"The source of what?" he asked, his tone one of confusion.

"The water, the source of the water. What if he built that elevator down into the rock to see how the water could pump up and through Belle Butte, through the rock? I mean, think about it. All the people here tonight would be interested in investing in something filling their pockets with cash. Water has little overhead and a lot of return. This is one of the few spots in Arizona that isn't a national park or trust area, and it can be capitalized on if it all starts here," Cal said, feeling like a detective who had just solved a mystery.

"Not to burst your bubble here, Cal, but who cares

about water? We have water. Why is that such a big deal?" Des sounded almost annoyed at this point.

Cal tried to ignore his ignorance and looked him in the eye. "Water is a resource, like oil, and it won't be abundant forever. I've seen it rushing through these rocks, clear and violent. There's a lot of it somewhere. An underground river, possibly free from environmental toxins."

"You do know toxins seep into the earth, Cal," Des said, nodding his head. Cal put her hands out and held him still. His skin felt warm, and there was a buzz between them.

"Enough water to flood the valley leading to Sedona to make a river to bring more tourism and hydroelectricity. Rafting underground? Possibilities are endless," she said, moving closer to Des. "Don't you see it? This isn't just a touring company of a local butte—this is potential. And that's what he'll show them tonight in that cave…potential." Her lips were close to Des now, eyes on his.

Cal wanted Des to meet her halfway, hoping he would lean down at that moment and acknowledge that her crush was reciprocated on his end, but he didn't move. He stood still and statuesque in the window's light before eventually saying, "That would change everything."

Amid a victory, Cal had missed something, but she wasn't sure what. *Why did he turn cold?*

Des pulled his hands away and stepped back. "What would it change other than expanding yet another tourist trap or even better, industry?" she asked. "You must see that the money it would bring would boost the economy. I mean, Des, you've never lived away from here. Towns must have some industry to keep them alive, or eventually they die. You couldn't imagine the number of meat-processing plants there are in North Carolina alone. Do you not see how awesome it would be to discover an underground river?" Cal was baffled, flushed, and a bit dizzy.

"We have an industry—tourism, and we make it work. Look." He walked to the windows on the opposite side of the room and pointed down. "There, do you see those flickering lights? That's Officer Sanchez's place and Whispering Pines. And over there? In the distance? That's Sedona. You act like living here all my life has been a detriment, like I haven't seen things, but you're wrong. I've seen a community embrace the people who float in and out of it each summer and see them band together in the other months and support one another. We're a family."

Des drew in a breath and turned to face Cal. "You flippantly mention flooding the valley, which I know would never happen because the impacts would be far-reaching, but you say it like it's nothing. But that would be a big deal, Cal. This is home. Everything we do affects someone else, something else. So, if your boy up here is selling a story about water, it better be that little natural phenomenon you mentioned, not something large-scale. I better get back. Lucio will wonder where I am."

Unsure of what to say, she stood there. What just happened? She thought this was a moment, a shared moment. Was she that off? Oh, she was off; the ground seemed to quake beneath her feet, and her head was swimmy. Why did she spout off about the water? What was she thinking?

"You coming?" he asked, the door now open.

"Yeah," she said, brushing past him. Cal wanted to ask him what had happened. She wanted to understand where she had gone wrong. *Was it me? We were just standing there, talking about the water in the moonlight. It all seemed right.*

Whatever it was, it had affected Des. He didn't say a word as they returned to the main building. When they got inside, he went back behind the bar and put away some of the dirty glasses. Cal took the hint and walked to the front of the main building. She plopped down into a chair and stared out the front window.

"I was hoping I'd see you here." It was the voice of the little secretary from the day of her interview. "Cal, right?"

"Yes," she answered, trying to smile. She was never a good actress.

"Novak." The little lady pointed to her. "Kim Novak was my mother's favorite actress. My father liked her too, but most fathers did." She laughed with a snort. "I'm so glad you got the job. Are you settling in okay?"

"Yes, I am. Looking forward to starting the tours next week," Cal replied.

"I saw you had a few lined up right off the bat. It's a beautiful place, isn't it?"

"It is." Cal turned and looked behind her to check if Des was there, but he had disappeared. In his place was the elevator door. If anyone knew about that door, wouldn't the secretary?

"I didn't catch your name," Cal said, putting her hand out.

"Oh, it's Christy Hammond at your service."

"Have you worked here since the beginning?" Cal asked.

"Pretty much, yes. I've known Mr. Courier for a long time. I've known Mr. Courier senior. He gave me my first job when I was living in California. I was a lowly secretary then, now I'm an executive assistant," she said proudly. Cal felt silly not knowing the difference between the two concepts. "This has been a dream job, really, starting from the ground up. Mr. Courier has created something special for people to experience."

"Well said. Christy, do you know where that elevator leads?" Cal wanted to hold her breath and wait until the big reveal. She was desperate for an answer to turn her night around from the awkward moment with Des. It had been a whirlwind.

"Oh, that?" Christy asked, pointing toward the hidden door. "Funny you should ask. I've never actually been down the elevator before. When they first built it, it didn't lead anywhere. I thought it was going to be another door leading outside. It isn't what it appears though. Have you ever been down a coal shaft or explored a mine?"

Cal nodded, though she had not done either; however the conversation was leading to answers, and she didn't want it to lose steam.

"It's like that, or at least it seems to be. Again, I haven't been inside. I've just seen Mr. Courier and others go in there. It doesn't look safe and sounds rickety. Why do you ask?"

"Curious. Seems an odd place for an elevator when there doesn't appear to be other floors to this place," Cal quickly answered.

"Definitely no other floors. To tell you the truth, this building isn't the most structurally sound. I've noticed movement, even with items on my desk. The original renderings of this place were more like a lodge than a mid-century-modern concept, but then the engineers said they had to be changed due to the rock. Apparently, it isn't the best to build on up here. I hope I was able to answer your questions. I can't offer much." Christy laughed off the comment innocently.

"You've been a great help, thank you," Cal assured her. "I find it all so fascinating."

"It was nice to sit and talk with you," Christy said. "It looks like the tour is finishing up. I better go see if Mr. Courier needs anything."

They said their goodbyes to one another, and Cal watched Christy walk over to a grinning Mr. Courier. After the awkward moment with Des, Cal was even more curious about Belle Butte and its owner. Tonight had lit the fire of intrigue, and Cal realized that she was indeed dealing with a puzzle. There was staff from all over, even places where the Couriers had their resorts. There was Nia, who followed Mr. Courier to Arizona because she clearly loved him. There was the elevator that led to nowhere. There were the bureaucrats, politicians, wealthy locals, and the press who came to the grand opening of a somewhat over-the-top tourist attraction.

She thought of the cliché "Where there's smoke, there's fire," and wondered if there was truth right here. She didn't have enough now, but she knew it was worth looking into.

Mr. Courier wrapped up the night with another speech that thanked everyone for coming and investing in his dream. He took them all through a montage of memories he had after visiting the area with his father on vacation and was mesmerized by the views and the people. It was a heartfelt and seemingly honest speech, but Cal didn't trust it. Nothing was as it appeared at Belle Butte as if someone had placed strange lenses into her eyes that distorted the view. As much as she wanted to focus on the task at hand, a job that offered security for Grandma Ruth and herself, which would allow her to enjoy the magnificence of the rocks and water, there was a strange itch irritating her mind.

Combined with the weird moment in the cabin with Des, Cal felt a bit dizzy and drunk. She counted the number of drinks she had that night and landed on five, a bit above her normal average. As the speech wrapped up, Cal headed to the bathroom near the boardroom to cool off and get her bearings before heading home. A hand landed on her shoulder, turning her around.

"Jack, you scared me to death," Cal nearly yelled.

"You don't look so hot, kid. Maybe you should sit down," Jack responded. A flash of worry went across his face in the form of furrowing brows and wrinkles.

"I'm fine. I need to get some cool water for my face. I was overserved." She laughed with a hiccup. Cal was immediately embarrassed. How could she have allowed this to happen?

"No, have a seat in here." Jack opened the door to the boardroom and led her inside. It was mostly dark with light streaming in from the large floor-to-ceiling windows. She plopped into a rolling chair and put her head down on the wooden table. The room smelled like it had never been used, as if it were still wrapped in plastic. "I'll go get you some water. Sit tight."

Cal tried to think straight, but the room was spinning. Whether she opened or closed her eyes, it didn't matter; everything was moving. Jack was back quickly. "Here," he said, handing her a glass of water. "I told your friend, Des, that he should be ashamed of himself for fixing you so many drinks."

"You said what?" Now Cal was embarrassed. As if Des wasn't annoyed with her enough for some reason. "What did he say?"

"He seemed worried. He asked if you were okay and if you needed anything. I told him you needed to chug water and sober up. You're going to feel awful tomorrow." Jack laughed and pulled out a pack of cigarettes. He glanced around the room as if looking to see if he would get caught, lit one and sat a few chairs down from her at the head of the table. "Check this room out. Can you imagine leading a meeting from here? This is classy!"

Cal tried to laugh, but it came out like a burst of air. She took a swig of the water and let it drain down her throat.

"Tonight was educational. I learned a lot, more than I had bargained for." Jack laughed again, smoke trailing out of his mouth.

"What did you learn?" Cal wanted to know more; if this conversation had happened thirty minutes earlier, she would have asked questions until she was blue in the face, but now she was green and a little less enthusiastic.

"I knew this guy was rich and well connected, but I didn't know how rich or well connected. He had to jump through a lot of hoops to get that piece of land. He could have built this little dream company in other places, but he was only interested in this spot. He was often told it wasn't suitable to build on or ridiculous to try. Now look!" He waved his hand around the room and added, "Why do you think he wanted this place so badly, huh?"

"I think he said something about his childhood a

couple of times," Cal answered, perking up.

"Oh yeah." Jack laughed. "Some trip with his dear old dad. Do you know anything about Courier Sr.? He wasn't exactly the fatherly type. I wouldn't doubt if that was a lie."

"The waterfall?" Cal offered.

"The waterfall. He had to have known about it as it is the only redeeming factor of this butte, but how?" Jack puffed his cigarette in thought.

"Had a friend here?" Cal slurred and took another drink of water. "What do we know about Clark?"

"Wait, Clark? Who's Clark?"

"The guy that took you on the tour: Clark Haus."

"The German Native American. Oh yeah..." Jack was quiet. "Maybe he's our connection here. We need to find out more about Clark."

"We?" Cal asked, sitting up slowly. "I need to get home and sleep off this situation."

"I need you, Cal. You're the only one who can get some answers. I can probably dig something up on Clark, but I need to know more about this place. Maybe the bigwigs are here as a thank-you for helping him gain the land, but what's in it for them? Why help at all? What's his connection to Sedona?"

Cal had questions too, a nice list that had accumulated over the last couple of days. She was beginning to think she was being dramatic, but Jack seemed to feel the same way. "I may be able to help you with this. I've recently learned a few things myself," she said, barely audible.

Jack leaned forward, eyes wild, sparkling. "Do I sense a partnership?"

"What does that include?" Cal asked, wondering

what her part would entail.

"We investigate and we write. We do this together. Let's find out what's really going on here, and let's expose it." He was getting louder with excitement.

"But what if nothing is going on here? What if we waste time digging for something that isn't there? Don't get me wrong, I love a good mystery and getting answers from people, but I just got this job. By next week, I'll be swamped with tours."

"You have something I don't: a position. People know me as the crazy guy who created a magazine about crystals. Now that I'm writing an article for the *Times* here and there, I'm a nosy reporter, and they'll tell me what they want me to know. Unless we have more nights like this where the alcohol is flowing, I'll be out of luck. You're the insider. You can do this, Cal." He almost sounded as if he were begging.

This could be the opportunity she had hoped for. Belle Butte may not be the ladder she could climb, but it could give her access to one. She wasn't a terrible writer, and even though her people skills were a little rusty, she was about to get a lot of practice. She was already investigating Belle Butte on her own accord, and this could help her smooth things over with Des to show him she was on Sedona's side. Belle Butte was working its magic again.

"I'm in," she said.

He smiled at her. "That's my girl."

Chapter Fourteen

The next morning Cal woke up, feeling like death. The light escaped through the sides of her blackout curtains.

It's probably afternoon.

A half-empty glass of water was next to her bed, along with an open bottle of ibuprofen. Cal took out three and swallowed hard, hoping her stomach would accept them. Her phone lit up. She didn't have the sea legs to get up, but curiosity made her stand, cross the room and reach to obtain the device before crashing down into her bed.

She found a string of texts from Des:

—9:08 I'm sure you feel like crap this morning but please call me when you get this message.—

—10:22 Okay, look. If you are up, call me, okay? I need to talk to you.

Then there were the four missed calls before his final text message.

—12:05 So are you mad at me? Because if you are, that's not fair. It was awkward as hell last night and I hated that. I hated it more that you went home without saying goodbye. Friends, we are friends.—

Cal didn't want to remember the weird moment in the cabin. Things were a bit fuzzy anyway, but that moment was clear. It was the alcohol because otherwise Cal would never have made that move. What was she thinking? He had every right to be upset. She practically said it would be beneficial to flood part of Sedona. She clicked Des's name and let the phone ring away from her ear.

"Hello?"

"Des, hey, it's Cal," she said back, unsure how to approach the situation.

"How are you feelin'? Can't remember how many of those drinks I made you, but it was more than two."

Cal laughed. "Yeah, try five or so. Lost count. Apparently, my insecurity leads to bad decisions. Usually I'm not that bad." She cut to the chase. "What happened with us last night?"

It was a brave move that possibly caught Des off guard, but Cal didn't want to sit on the phone rehashing everything that happened. There was a long pause with an audible sigh.

"Okay, well, I wanted to kiss you. I've wanted to for a while, so trust me, it was hard not to kiss you back. But you'd been drinking, and your mouth got ahead of your brain. You looked out that window and very coldly—"

"I know, Des, and I'm so sorry," Cal interrupted.

"You talked about it like it was nothing; if it happened, it wouldn't be the end of the world. But, Cal, it *would* be the end of my world. I know that sounds stupid, and I know you were rambling and that nothing will *ever* happen like that, but it was how you said it. You've been here a year, and you know this place and the people. I mean, can you imagine what something like that would do?"

She wasn't sure how to respond. He called her cold, and basically unfeeling where it concerned Sedona. *Was she?* "I get what you're saying, but it seems dramatic. I

129

care about Sedona, and I care about the people who live here. Dude, I live here! Yes, I had been drinking, and yes, I probably got caught up in my train of thought, and I guess I shouldn't have said anything out loud."

"It wasn't what you said; it was how you said it. I know you were drunk, and I'm not being dramatic. You could have said all of that with a bit more care. You sounded almost excited about the prospect!"

He sounded much more irritated now, and Cal didn't like that the conversation was happening on the phone. "Look—I'm sorry. This place is home to me, and I wouldn't want anything to happen to it. I wish you knew me better than that."

She let the last sentence linger in the air. The effect would be enough to help Des see her perspective. She was hungover, and last night brought a list of revelations that she had trouble remembering. She wanted to survive this conversation and walk away with a small wound and a giant headache.

"Okay, so I'm being dramatic. Maybe I was disappointed in what you said, and then I was disappointed by not kissing you…" His voice trailed. Cal imagined that he ran his fingers through his hair at that moment. He often did that when he was nervous.

"It wasn't meant to happen last night. Can you imagine us being part of a cliché like that? The girl gets dressed up, the guy falls in love with her, and there's a magical kiss in the moonlight. Gross…plus I don't think kissing your bartender is ethical. Think of all of those free drinks!" she joked.

"Yeah, if there is anything we aren't, it's cliché." Des laughed. "Look, I need to get ready for work. You coming to The Vortex tonight?"

Cal laughed; the last place she wanted to go was a bar. "No, I'll stay home tonight and crawl under my pillow. There's no need to address the public in this state."

"Take care of yourself. Oh, and look, I don't care how cliché it sounds. My best friend is a chick I think about kissing; call me a 1980s movie." Des laughed. "Talk to you later."

"Bye," Cal was able to say before the click at the other end. That was that.

She lay back on her bed, hearing Alice talking to Grandma Ruth in the living room. She wanted to go to the kitchen and get something to eat but didn't want to bump into anyone. The conversation with Des was the only social interaction Cal wanted for the day. Slowly her mind drifted back to the first time she met him.

****

Within the first few weeks of moving to Sedona, Cal had wandered the streets, exploring the nooks and crannies of shops and restaurants. It was strange being surrounded by people who dressed like they had stepped out of Woodstock and onto the streets of Sedona. Cal felt like an outsider in skinny jeans with a white oversized V-neck t-shirt half tucked in, a layered silver chain necklace with various charms, and her trusty red high tops. She dipped into a pharmacy, dropped off Grandma Ruth's prescriptions, and bought a Coke in a glass bottle.

The heat was insane and unlike anything in Atlanta, which was accompanied by a thick, stagnant cloud of humidity. Arizona was dry and deceiving. Cal peered through the windows of gift shops and stores that specialized in rocks and crystals that she had heard so much about. She saw an office tucked between two larger stores with *Crystal Publications* written on a faded plaque. She took a picture of it with her phone and made a mental note to do some research. If they were going to make things work in Sedona, she needed a job.

Cal crossed the street and heard the familiar beat of reggae echoing from a building ahead. The front of it looked smashed as if there'd been an accident, and the sign above it said *The Vortex*. A familiar clinking of glasses and laughter echoed from inside, beckoning her in. The contrast between the blinding sunshine and the bar's dim light made it hard for her to see at first. She sat down at a barstool and took it all in.

"What can I get you?" a slender guy, Cal guessed was in his mid-twenties, asked, walking over.

"Bourbon on the rocks," she answered. "I like the hair," Cal added, touching her own. She couldn't help but note the similarity. While his was thicker and filled in with a few tight curls, hers was bouncy with large curls, making more of a helmet around her head. His was somewhat tied back.

"Thanks! Tell that to my boss. He gives me a hard time. It adds character, even though a mixed guy like myself is already a bit of a commodity around here." He laughed, sliding the drink down the bar to Cal.

"Noticed that." Cal laughed. "It doesn't look like that where I'm from."

"Where would that be?" He leaned against the back of the bar.

"Atlanta," she replied, taking a sip of the drink.

"Hotlanta!" He laughed. "Yeah, much more colorful there. Never been but I've always wanted to go. I was born and raised right here. I did get away for college but it called me back. What can I say? I'm a sucker for crystals and mysticism," he said, his eyes widening.

Cal laughed, adding, "To live here, I'm guessing you need some special power or a magical niche. I was half expecting to see a wand shop in town."

"Oh, you mean Wanda's Wand Shop! Yeah, it's on the next street over," he said, nodding as if swearing it was real.

"I'll have to make my way over there next. If I'm going to be a local, I need to do what locals do," she answered mockingly.

"A local? Uh oh! You moved here?"

"Yeah, about two weeks ago, me and my grandma."

"Not many people choose to live here full-time. Most people visit for the summer, and that's all they can handle. It gets empty during the off-season. Were you fans of the place?"

"We had never been here before. My grandma read all about it and had some health issues, so we decided it was a good place to settle for a bit."

"Cool. I mean, not cool about your grandma, but yeah. What do you do for work?"

"I was doing some editing, freelance mostly while interning for a publishing house in Atlanta, but now I'm just looking for something to keep us floating. I saw that Crystal Publishing place down the road; do you know anything about that?" She pointed out the door as if he could see the place.

"Not really. But hey, there is always online work. Isn't that a thing?"

"Yeah, it's a thing but you have to find clients. It's more luck of the draw. It might be easier if I was a writer, but I'm an editor."

"I would have liked having you around in college. I

was a horrible writer—I mean horrible. My papers were littered with red marks and symbols. It looked more like some ancient language instead of a college essay."

Cal laughed, remembering the people she helped in college with the same problem.

"So, what's your name? If you're going to be local, we have to be on a first-name basis." He smiled. "I'm Des."

"Cal," she said. "Kind of like California but not…"

"Ha! Well, if not California, what's the full name?"

"Just Cal. My grandma calls me Cally, but she's the only one. It's always been Cal." She smiled. "How about you? Desmond?"

"Yeah, after my great-grandfather. They've also always called me Des so…"

"It's nice to meet you, Des," Cal said, drinking the rest of her bourbon.

"You too, Cal."

A couple came in, and he took their order. Cal watched him laugh and smile easily, much like he had with her. She put a wad of cash on the bar and jumped off the stool. Cal was almost to the door when a finger tapped her shoulder. She whirled around to see Des standing behind her, a huge smile on his face.

"That was a massive overtip there," he said, handing her a stack of bills back. "Drinks aren't that expensive in Sedona."

Cal was embarrassed and amused. "You better be here the next time I come around. You're worth every penny."

She winked and walked through the hole that served as a door. Cal meant to ask him about the hole, but she had an idea this wouldn't be the last she saw of Des.

****

Thinking about that day, and how far they'd come, was strange. They were a million conversations from small talk and trying to think of what to say. There hadn't been a "what's your favorite" fill-in-the-blank or a "what would you do if" moment. Their relationship was not in foundation mode; it was in finishing touches. For it to have been just a year was unfathomable. Cal wasn't about to let something as silly as a drunken conversation, tone of voice, or a kiss that never happened, end what they had built.

She picked up her phone and texted Des immediately:

—*Cal: Hey, do you remember the night Drunk Tommy spit in that biker's drink and that guy drank it?*—

—*Des: LOL. I had forgotten all about that. Yeah! That guy slapped him, like a girl slap...no offense because it was the loudest smack I have ever heard in my life.*—

—*Cal: No joke, like, I felt the wind coming from behind the guy. I am amazed Tommy didn't lose a tooth.*—

—*Des: But he had that print, that big ol' handprint across his face. Oh my gosh, that was freaking hilarious.*—

—*Cal: LOL*—

That was all that needed to be said. It was a subtle reminder that "hey, we have history, and it means something to me."

With that, she passed out.

Chapter Fifteen

Cal survived her first few weeks of work like a champ. She booked a good number of tours and received positive ratings. By week three, she was in the top two for number of tours given, a massive victory for an introvert. There were moments when she wondered what she had gotten herself into.

She laughed when she remembered the couple on their honeymoon who wanted to be left alone in the cave; they even asked about the door in the cave entrance, to which Cal quickly responded, "It's a death trap. No lovemaking in there." Then there was the family with teenagers who kept throwing rocks into the waterfall after being asked not to. They laughed and mocked her until she finally escorted them out.

The family with young children was the scariest. One little kid kept running toward the edge at the top of the butte, and Cal had to chase her. It was not a good day. Even with all that, she enjoyed it and was in good spirits when she made her way to The Vortex after work that Friday night. Officer Sanchez was writing parking tickets out front when she walked up.

"I'm afraid the bar is closed tonight. Too many illegal parkers," he said, putting a ticket on a car.

"You'll have to do better than that. I survived yet another work week, so I believe that merits a drink," Cal replied, leaning against a light post near the bar's entrance. "Why are you always writing tickets right here? There's a whole street!" she said, waving her hand from one end of the street to the other.

"This one is of special interest. If I can get people to stop staying in this establishment and giving my brother money, then maybe, just maybe, he'll come crawling back to me and apologize," Officer Sanchez said with a laugh and a glare at the hole. "Why won't he fix that hole? It makes downtown look so trashy. At least have a little pride in your space."

"I believe it brings some charm. It beckons people to enter."

"I wouldn't say beckons, exactly," he argued politely.

"Well, well, well," Drunk Tommy slurred as he sidled up next to Cal. "If it isn't our fearless officer in arms and our local nonlocal. Tell me something, Cal— do you often spend time on street corners, leaning up against lampposts? Because if you do, I'll throw a couple of bucks your way."

"That's enough," Officer Sanchez snarled. "We don't speak to ladies like that."

"If you can point out a lady, I'll be sure to keep that in mind," Drunk Tommy quickly responded, pulling his pants up and dusting off his shirt. He wore his large-brimmed cowboy hat with a three-day beard matching his dirty-tan skin.

For the first time. Cal noticed his tattoo. "I didn't take you for a religious man, Tommy. A drunk man, a stupid man, maybe even a nonhuman," she said, pointing to the tattoo.

"Now that's where I draw the line there, lady. That right there." Tommy pushed a pointer finger down on his bicep. "That's a tattoo dedicated to my grandfather. I carry on his legacy."

Cal liked the tat and thought it was well conceived with a pine tree cross and a cloud blowing air through the branches; however, she would never admit that to Tommy.

"Whispering Pines is a big deal. You can come by for a private tour if you'd like," he whispered the last part toward her ear.

Cal snatched her head back. "I think I'd rather jump into a hole full of snakes, Tommy, but thanks for the offer." She took a deep breath and noticed a strong odor coming from somewhere outside. "Do you smell that?" she asked Officer Sanchez.

"Smell what?" Drunk Tommy responded quickly, his eyes narrowing.

"I don't have much experience with this, but it kind of smells like...pot?" she questioned, her attention still turned toward Officer Sanchez.

"Huh, yeah, I think I smell that, too," Drunk Tommy said. "Maybe you should go check that out, Officer. Do your job." There was a booming laugh. "I guess I'll see you inside," he said, pointing to Cal.

"Great, that just ruined my night," she said, looking at Tommy.

"Do you think it's pot?" Cal asked, still waiting for Officer Sanchez to respond.

He just stood quietly, looking around. "It's possible. Sedona isn't exactly known for being marijuana free. In fact, I think we're known to be the opposite. It's hard to keep the town clean with the tourists coming in. Did you notice the influx of cars out here?"

"I heard this weekend is going to be even worse. My

boss has most of us working Saturday, but I have it off so I can spend time with Grandma Ruth."

He pulled his hat down a little over his eyes. "Your boss sounds more reasonable than I thought."

"What do you mean?" Cal thought it was a curious statement. Why would Officer Sanchez have any knowledge of her boss?

"It's nothing. Just something I saw that I probably wasn't supposed to see," he said, pushing the words away with his hands.

"You can't leave me hanging. Come on; tell me what you saw," she pleaded, stepping toward him.

"Seriously, Cal, I don't know why I said that. It isn't my place."

She cocked her head to the side and smiled, trying to look as innocent as possible. She found that even at her age, she could put others at ease with a youthful grin.

"Now, this doesn't go beyond us, Cal. I mean it!"

Cal nodded in agreement and stepped closer.

"I was at the courthouse the other day and had to make a phone call, so I stepped inside an office waiting room and saw your boss, Mr. Courier, sitting there. We made small talk, just the basic 'Hey, how are ya?' kind, and then I excused myself to make that call. When I returned, I had forgotten my hat and had to grab it. Well, on the desk was an open file with papers scattered out a bit. I saw one with a rendering of Sedona, only the town had moved, and in its place was like a lake or something. I thought that was strange because there isn't a large body of water like that near here. The other page was a contract with the National Park Service concerning his land. I thought that was strange too. He just developed that land with his little touring company, so why would he sell or give it or whatever to the National Park Service?"

Sanchez took a handkerchief from his pocket and dabbed his face. "It was probably nothing, Cal. I shouldn't have looked and shouldn't have told you, so you just put that right out of your mind, you hear?"

She wasn't sure what to say. A week ago, she had spent a night listening to stories about Mr. Courier and Belle Butte and had put it out of her mind. Now she couldn't wait to tell Jack what she heard. Part of her wanted to deny the claim, to say to Officer Sanchez that it was ridiculous, but another part knew that, again, where there was smoke, there was fire. Was Mr. Courier an innocent man who just loved the area, or was there something sinister about his plans?

"That was a lot of information," she finally said, scratching her forehead. "Not sure how to take that."

Sanchez laughed. "I don't think you should take it as anything but gossip. You have a good thing going up there, and the last thing I want is for you to ruin that by listening to a townie like me."

"Only you aren't just any townie, and you wouldn't lie to me. Thank you for telling me, whatever your reasons. I like to know who I'm dealing with. I better dip inside. Des is expecting me. Don't put a ticket on my car," she yelled over her shoulder.

Sanchez's voice faded as Cal walked through the hole to the bar. "If you parked on this side, I will."

It was crowded tonight, with more than enough locals to even out the tourists. Cal saw Drunk Tommy in the back of the room around the pool tables, one of many cowboy hats bobbing up and down with conversation. Jenny was also there with a group of girls, and a few others she recognized spread throughout. Lucio and Des were behind the bar, each on a different half.

Cal made her way to his end and stood. "This place is bumpin' tonight. Is Lucio finally doing a BOGO deal?" she yelled back.

"You wish! This is the beginning of tourist season. You hate it and love it. The energy is addicting, a natural high, you know?"

Cal nodded. She didn't mind the people, but the volume was intense. It was hard to enjoy sipping a beverage when you couldn't talk to anyone. "You guys should figure out some outdoor seating to help with overflow and noise," she suggested.

"Funny you should mention that," Des said over his shoulder as he fixed a few drinks. "Lucio's been working on that. There's a zoning issue, thanks to his brother. He's been jumping through hoops to open a rooftop bar. How cool would that be? He said if we build it, we might get to add some live music."

"That'd be awesome. Then maybe I'd get to see some of those musical skills I've heard about."

"I don't know about that, but it would help. I'm always open to change. You're friends with his brother, right? Maybe you could talk with him about it?"

"First, I don't think an officer can halt a project like that. Secondly, he's trying to shut you guys down, so Lucio should avoid any conversation with him. It's so weird how much they hate each other. Get over it already."

"It's not that easy." Lucio appeared behind Cal, making her jump. He went through a side door and returned with several barstools, one for Cal and another for himself. "I don't expect a transplant to understand the value of land and legacy."

"I didn't mean to—" Cal started.

"You never do. Tell me, Cal, do you spy on me when you come here? Do you spy and then run and tell my brother what you heard? What do you hear and see?"

"What would I tell him? That you run a successful bar that people love?" She laughed. Lucio was not amused.

"The Vortex is the most successful business in downtown Sedona. Not many establishments make the money I do, bring in the cash I do. Marcial never saw my vision." Lucio coiled up on the stool like a snake, his frustration creating tension before the strike. "But he will, senorita, he will. This place will tower over him one day, and he'll feel the chill of living in my shadow."

"A little intense there, Lucio. Maybe you need a drink," Des said sarcastically, pouring a shot of tequila and sliding it toward him.

"Gracias." Lucio downed the shot and slammed the glass down on the bar. "Look around you. Locals and tourists together, a friendship. You don't see that in any of those tourist traps or gift shops or resorts. We turn into a bunch of servants there, but here, here, we're equals. I created that; it was my dream. You tell my brother that. I was making things happen while Marcial ran off with Tommy over there. Look at him." Lucio discreetly pointed in Drunk Tommy's direction, and all three looked.

He was still with the group of men, playing pool and drinking, laughing, and telling stories. Drunk Tommy was the center of attention, all eyes on him.

"They were best friends, Marcial and Tommy. You wouldn't know that now. Ended up like cops and robbers and yet, I see them talking. Old habits die hard."

Cal took all of Lucio's words with a grain of salt. She had spent time with Officer Sanchez, and there was a definite difference between him and Drunk Tommy. If anything, Lucio was way shadier. The cops were good guys, even with bad friends, but Lucio was a bar owner. Where was his credibility?

"Let's just say I make money the honorable way. I don't sell…magic." Lucio stood up and walked off.

"That was weird." Des laughed. "Maybe he's been sipping from his barrel over there."

"Barrel?" Cal asked.

"Yeah, down under the counter. He makes his own stuff and calls it his *Espiritu Loco*. Says it keeps him young. It smells like pure rocket fuel and is eerily clear."

"Have you ever tried it?"

"Nah, not my thing."

"Seems like everyone is into something around here."

"Of course they are. Sedona is a hotbed of lore and mysticism. Some believe that the tribes who originated here were the most powerful beings in the world. Their reservation may have been 'given' to them by the government, but they had always lived there as one of the oldest societies in the world. They were Earth worshipers and gained wisdom from listening to the sky, wind, trees, plants, and rocks. My mom hates this stuff." Des stopped and laughed. "She thinks that it's atheistic, that somehow it diminishes God."

"What do you think?" Cal asked.

"I think that there must be some power around Sedona. I've seen things, people who have been healed or look younger or are even just super happy. Sometimes

I wish my parents would jump on board; they would probably be happier."

"I don't know if I believe all of that. We've been here for over a year, and all I've seen from my grandmother is—"

"Cancer that hasn't spread."

The words struck Cal like an arrow. That was true. It hadn't spread and over the last few weeks, she had noticed a change. "I hadn't thought about it until now. Maybe it's the air."

"Or it's everything from the water to the rocks. There must be a reason why people continue to believe in a thing for generations. Just sayin'."

Cal wasn't ready to fully succumb to the fantasy world that Des was peddling, but she could acknowledge there was something. The locals seemed vibrant now that the tourists were there, almost as if their spirits fed on their energy. Even on tours, Cal noticed herself genuinely smiling. They added something to the land, like fertilizer for plants. If locals were colors, they were once sepia-toned, and now they were Technicolor. She couldn't deny the difference. It was like the locals harvested the tourists and stored them to survive. A cold chill ran through her body.

When she returned home, she stopped by the living room and observed Grandma Ruth sleeping peacefully. Cal recalled the insane laugh from a few weeks ago, the one accompanied by the story following her vein. She found the blue line and followed it in the moonlight until it disappeared on the other side of her cheek. It was faint, fainter than she had recalled, but still there. Cal thought back to what Des had discussed at the bar and her conversation with Clark on the day of her interview. She was tired, she knew that, and maybe the alcohol was getting to her, but she couldn't deny a connection between the water and the veins, the living, breathing rocks that were never built on until now and where they could lead. Cal went to the back stoop and looked across the patchy grass and rock to the black-rock skyscrapers that plateaued in the distance.

"It's out there; Belle Butte and the reservation are out there. All of it's out there," she said in the night, under the stars. Cal wasn't superstitious or religious, and for a year, she had brushed off the stories she was told about Sedona like they were nothing, but were they? Was there credence to the lore of this place? Was she missing something because of her cynicism?

She found her way to her bedroom and crashed. Her dreams led her on a journey from Atlanta to North Carolina to Sedona, a meandering trail of faces and events. Images flashed, faces from Sedona, native people dancing around fires and singing to the sky, spirits rising from the rocks into the trees. Cal heard chanting, flutes, water rushing, and trees whispering in the breeze. Everything moved quickly until deep sleep came on her, and the early morning hours arrived.

Chapter Sixteen

Cal spent Saturday morning typing notes on her computer. Since the party, she hadn't spoken to Jack for over a week and didn't want to until she had something to share. With evidence stacking up against Mark Courier and Belle Butte, she decided to do a little research, this time digging into the man behind the man. She'd already done a preliminary search before she got the job; now was the time to dig a little deeper.

She typed his last name and looked up *resort development*. His father's company came up first, Courier's Resort Development, along with a list of projects on the West Coast. Like the others Cal had seen, their resorts catered to the wealthy and elite. Then she typed in *Mark Courier* and *resorts*. She clicked through ten pages of the same information from various news sites until she got to page eleven. It was there that she started seeing news articles connecting Courier to a resort in Mexico.

She opened the articles, then read through them, each one more horrifying than the last. Hundreds of locals and tourists died from exposure to chemical waste linked to Casa Grande Resort. The resort was shut down and eventually sold; the Courier Resort Development team claimed it was due to other investment opportunities. However, the more obscure websites called out the company, saying that the deaths were evidence enough of something sinister.

"It can't be me," she said out loud. "I can't be the only person who noticed this."

But she felt like she was. She quickly copied and pasted the articles into the document and bookmarked the pages. This was the story. It made sense that Courier hadn't hired a bunch of locals. He wanted people he could trust so he could get away with whatever he was doing. But what was it? Was water the connection? Was the cave a connection? There was the passageway used as "storage" that she had yet to check out and the elevator. Could those lead to the answer?

There was only one way to find out.

Cal didn't have tours scheduled that day, but she figured no one would notice if she showed up on campus. She called Jack on the way. When he didn't answer, she left a quick message. "You probably found the same thing I did: there is a story here, and it's a big one. Going up to Belle Butte now to see what I can find out. Call me."

The drive went by quickly; her mind raced the entire way. It felt surreal that she had uncovered something that others hadn't. *This is a real knight in shining armor takes down a villain kind of story.* She imagined the headline. *Local editor and investigative journalist take down resort giant.*

She pulled into the parking lot at Belle Butte and headed to the cave. That was the obvious starting point. When she got there, a tour was starting, so she hung back and waited. It was a perfect day, like most in Sedona, though she had read that a weather system might bring storms through the area in the next week or so.

The group departed, and she crept to the left inside

the entrance and down the passageway. Sure enough, there was a door, a locked door. *Keys, who has the keys?* Cal placed her forehead on the door and jiggled the knob impatiently.

She envisioned Clark's obscene ring of keys that possibly unlocked every door in Sedona and grunted. *Those never leave his pocket.* She ran back down to the cabin and entered through the back. A group tour was sitting in the main room, and one of the guides was behind the desk. "Hey, do you know where Clark is?" Cal asked her.

"Um, not sure. I haven't seen him," the girl said. Cal didn't remember the girl's name, but she was in too much of a hurry to care.

How would she get the keys from Clark even if she did find him? There wasn't a place the tour advisors went that needed keys, and he would probably want to walk with her if there were. No, there had to be another way. *Christy, I bet she has the keys.* It was perfect. Christy was the most unassuming, precious little person and seemed to like Cal. If there were any individual she could get the keys from, it would be her, that is if she had them.

She ran to the back entrance of the main building and slowed down when she hit the door. She mustn't look too desperate. Cal concocted a plan that would hopefully negate the need for Clark to enter the picture.

"Christy, thank God you're here," Cal said.

"Cal! I didn't know you were working today. I didn't see your name on the schedule."

Shoot. She hadn't realized that Christy had kept up with that kind of stuff. "No, I actually left something in my locker and had to come back. Such a bummer on my day off. I went up to say hey to a friend who was giving a tour at Narrow Gap and heard a sound coming from that locked passage door, and it was Clark yelling away. He got locked in or something. Maybe the door got jammed?"

"Oh no," Christy said, like she was in pain for Clark. "I have a set of keys right here. I'll run up there right now."

Double shoot. "Let me do that. Your shoes are way too pretty to get dirtied up with that dust. I'll bring them right back."

"Are you sure? You aren't even supposed to be working."

"Absolutely, don't mind a bit," Cal assured her.

Christy handed a ring of keys to her and pointed out the one with the blue around the edges. "I hope he isn't too mad when he gets out."

Cal quickly walked to the door and disappeared up the hill to the cave. With no one in sight, it was the perfect time to see what was hidden inside the passage. She inserted the blue key and turned it, not knowing what to expect. The wait had filled her with anticipation, sweet anxiety that propelled her forward.

"A closet," she said. It was just a closet with a dirt floor. To the left was a pile of boxes with pictures of light sconces, a toolbox, broom, rake, and on the back wall, shelves with sound equipment. "The flutes." She laughed. It was disappointing. Again, Cal didn't know what was in the room, but there were hopes at least of another tunnel or something.

She closed the door behind her and returned to the main building. The cave was just a cave, but the elevator was something more, it had to be. The keys in her hand were like a magnet, and Cal wondered if one of them might help get into the elevator.

What could she do about Christy? Even Christy wasn't allowed down the elevator, and even with her perky, somewhat ditzy personality, she knew who was working and who wasn't. There was a reason why Mr. Courier had asked her to work on this project. *Perhaps a spy.* Regardless, Christy needed to leave the lobby for Cal to get to the elevator. It couldn't be anything crazy, or she would call for Mr. Courier, who was in his office or somewhere on campus. Cal had seen his silver Porsche parked out front.

"I didn't know you were working today," Nia said from behind her.

Cal whirled, hiding the keys behind her back. "Oh, well, not technically. I left something in my locker, or I thought I did, but I didn't see it so I went up to the cave and, no luck."

"Maybe I can help you look. I just gave my last tour," Nia said with a sigh. "It's been crazy up here. Apparently, some kid fell while up at the top of the butte. Mark went up there along with some others. I could tell they were nervous."

Cal had an idea. It wasn't great, but it might be enough to take Christy off her hands. "That sounds awful," she said, exaggerating her voice with a Southern drawl on the *aw*. "Christy should go bring them some bottles of water or something. It's a hot day."

"That's a great idea. I can cover that; there's nothing else to do." Nia started to walk toward the building.

"No!" Cal yelled and then dialed it back. "No, she can do that. She seems bored in there. Why don't you go in and suggest it?"

"Oh, okay. I hope you find what you are looking for," Nia said, heading inside.

Cal nodded and headed back around to the other side of the building. She didn't want Christy to see her when she came out of the back. She watched out the window as Nia talked to Christy. They both headed outside a moment later. Quickly, Cal opened the main doors and went inside, making a beeline for the elevator. There was no time to waste. She didn't know if Christy or maybe the whole group would return in minutes or hours.

The elevator had a keyhole; she began trying each key, making mental notes of the ones that didn't fit. She was about seven in when a strange key caught her eye. It was shaped differently from the others, so she inserted it in the hole and turned. It worked, and the door opened.

Christy was right; it wasn't like a standard elevator. There were walls in the shaft but not actual *walls*. Once inside, there was a lever instead of a button; she pulled it. A light came on as the elevator began to slowly move downward.

Soon, the walls disappeared, and she found herself in an open space—and it wasn't what she'd expected. The entire building was built on a thin layer of rock, and underneath were giant metal stilts, almost like what Cal had seen at beach houses on the coast of North Carolina. In some places, the stilts were thick, and in others, thin. There was a halt and jolt; the elevator had reached its destination. It was dark, with only a few lights scattered above her. She always wondered what the underbelly of a building looked like exposed. The quiet and cold were startling. Cal walked off the platform onto the ground, taking her phone out to light her way.

There was nothing. It might as well have had boxes

for wall sconces because this was even less interesting than the closet. There were hooks on the wall near the elevator with yellow suits and helmets hung neatly in a row with large storage containers stacked next to them. Cal made her way to the left, figuring the cave to be in that direction, and there, against the wall, going down into the depths, was a sealed maintenance hole with a handle.

She tugged three times before the seal popped. The opening was narrow and pitch black. "What am I doing?" She peered into the hole. She could hear the water even more loudly through the hole. Inside there was a ladder against the left side. With a deep breath, she put her phone in her back pocket and stepped down into the hole. Darkness engulfed her.

Her shirt caught on the narrow sides of the hole as she descended; down and down into the black she went until her foot hit hard on the bottom. She felt around and noticed it had opened behind her but was too dark to see. The sound of water was everywhere now, like waves crashing continuously against a shoreline. Cal took her phone out and turned on the flashlight. At first it wasn't easy to see, even with the light.

She stepped forward and kicked something metallic; it was a lantern. With one click, the darkness faded into light and true illumination. It looked like an underground ocean, rushing and gushing before her with a powerful pull, seeping into the walls around it, stretching as far as the eye could see.

"I can't be that deep, can I?" Her voice echoed slightly in the cavernous space but barely audible over the water.

She walked over to the edge where the ground

dropped into the water. The sand was white, and the water was almost red. There was so much potential around her, truly a place of discovery. *How did Courier know this was here? Had he known when he bought it?*

Cal turned to look at the rest of the space. Behind her, metal canisters were stacked as high as she could see along the wall. She walked toward them, trying to make out the labels. None were in English, and there were no pictures on the labels. She looked back toward the entrance, then it hit her.

"Those suits…those helmets…this place…the hole was sealed!" It all began to connect. Mexico, the hazardous waste at the resort, and now Sedona and Belle Butte.

"He's doing it again! That monster is doing it again!"

Each part of Mark Courier's past and present became dots as she drew mental lines connecting them. There were the deaths in Mexico that his company caused somehow, then covered up. There were the loyal employees who traveled with him wherever he went, leaving their lives behind. There was the party with anyone and everyone who would benefit from such a scheme, possible money under the table or promises made.

There was this place, an underground treasure trove of, what Cal assumed, toxic waste of some sort in the perfect place where no one would go. Mark Courier wouldn't want to release this water; he would want to keep it, hoard it, and protect it because if it got anywhere, his secret would poison everything in its reach. Cal took pictures of the canisters and returned to the ladder, quickly jostling up the rungs and through the maintenance hole.

After she reached the top, she shut the circular door and heard the seal lock in. She snapped pictures of the suits on the wall next to the elevator before getting on and pushing the button to go up. *I've got him. I've got the story.*

The elevator opened to the main room, the light almost blinding Cal as she stepped out. She looked around to see if anyone had noticed her appearance, but the space was empty. She stashed the keys back where she found them, walking quickly toward the entrance and straight to her jeep without looking back. She felt the adrenaline, the giddiness of fear and excitement rising through her veins. It was as if the water had followed her and rushed through her body in torrents.

There was a sense of responsibility now. She had been chosen to save the water, to save Sedona. The article was writing itself in her head as she drove off, speeding toward the computer that awaited her.

When she got to the first stoplight in Sedona, she took out her phone and texted Des:

—*I got him. I got them all!*—

Chapter Seventeen

It was pride that drove Cal to lift her hands in the air and let a silent scream of victory escape her lungs. Stepping away from the computer, she knew she had composed a symphony of truth that would bring the hammer down on Mark Courier and his company. She was breathless, dizzy with exhaustion, and feeling the exhilaration of the moment.

She'd never considered herself a writer, but now she wondered if she had missed her calling. There were Jenny's words, Officer Sanchez, Lucio, and even Tommy's: first-person accounts of Mark Courier's plans for Belle Butte and the future of Sedona. She sat back down at the computer and composed the email to Jack.

Jack,

Here it is. Every word was backed up with interviews like you asked. I edited it myself. It's ready for your connection in Phoenix. Once it hits, you'll be a hero. We will be heroes. Let's take this guy down. Cal.

The words were simple, almost too simple. And it was true, once the story hit the *Phoenix Times*, Mark Courier would have the entire state against him; hell, he'd have the Environmental Protection Agency against him. Cal attached the document and hit send. It was out of her hands now, out in the digital landscape. This was no longer about helping Jack or trying something new. Cal had a responsibility now, like a superhero who had just discovered their powers, only hers were derived from a keyboard. Adrenaline surged through her body, and she wanted to get out and run, jump, drink, or something. She picked up her phone and looked at the time; it was well after eleven and suddenly she heard something coming from the front of the house.

She left her room and crept down the hallway, peeking into the living room. Grandma Ruth was sound asleep, yet light streamed through the window. Looking out, she saw a vehicle parked in the front yard. At first, she thought it might be Des, but he wouldn't be off work yet. The lights were bright and almost met her eye line. The vehicle was tall.

She walked onto the front porch. "Who's there?" she called out, putting her hand up to shade her eyes. Someone moved in the car. "Who's there?" she yelled louder. Cal didn't want the commotion to stir Grandma Ruth. A figure emerged.

"I hope you're smarter than I think you are." It was a man's voice, still more of a shadow than a human. The car lights were off now as well as the engine. Only Cal and the figure stood. "I know who you've been talking to and what they told you. It's all a lie, Cal. Every bit of it is a lie."

Cal knew who it was, and her adrenaline started to wane. "What are you doing here, Mark?" she asked, moving back to the porch, her hand grasping the doorknob.

He was close enough to where she could see his face in the dim streetlights. He didn't look like himself. His face sprouted stubble along the jawline, his eyes were sunken in a bit, and the hair that was usually fixed was everywhere. He looked older and younger at the same time. For the first time, Cal realized that she wasn't sure of Mark's age.

He bent over and put his hands on his knees. "Belle Butte is what Belle Butte is. And what are they telling you about me? About that place? It's all wrong. You know me! You work for me!" he sounded desperate, frantic even.

"You're wrong," Cal answered. "I don't know you. You spun some story about coming here because of a memory you had long ago, yet all you've done is keep secrets. I saw the elevator and the stairs leading under the building. You hired a bunch of outside help, and they're all connected to your business. I heard about Mexico and what you did there. People got sick and died, yet you're willing to do it all again. You're willing to risk so much, and for what? A pipe dream? Your real dream? Are you so intent on your father's legacy that you could destroy the legacy of others?"

The last sting was a big one, and Cal knew it. Mark moved ahead up the stairs, clumsy, like a zombie in the night. Cal tried to open the screen door, but he pushed his hand into it, breaking through the mesh.

"Let go," she said quietly, then louder, "let go of the door."

He grabbed Cal's arm with his other hand, a pleading hold, not one of pain. "You're wrong, about everything. If that story gets published, it will ruin my life. Yes, I found the water, and yes, I may not have followed every rule technically, but all of it is on my property, which makes it my property, so if I want to bottle it and use it, I—"

"Wait, just wait." Cal wasn't sure what to say next. A million questions flooded her head. What did he intend to bottle? What was he saying about the water? Her stomach sank, and she was glad she hadn't thought to eat that day as she feared it would all come up. "You're doing what with the water?" she finally asked, meeting his eyes.

"Bottling it. The limestone here acts like a filter, and with the way the water moves through it and dumps down into the river, it purifies it. I've never seen anything like it," he answered, shaking his head. "Look, if you publish that story"—he paused and took a deep breath— "it's over for me. The EPA will come first, then the politicians, the conservationists, the big-business guys, and your little tourist town will be mixed up in more scandal than you'll ever know. People will come with signs and protest on the streets and agendas in their back pockets. Everything you love about this place will die out. I've seen it before. I saw it in Mexico. That town."

Mark stopped and shook his head again, taking a step back. "That little spot on the coast was a gem of mine—it was. Beautiful beaches, jungle. We built a resort with huts and pools, nothing crazy, but we didn't know about the cave. No one ever told us. We talked to locals; we followed the rules. The price was right, and no one lived near it."

Mark paused, letting the sounds of the desert filter through the quiet, a chorus of *yips* and *howls* that echoed in the distance. Cal kept her focus on him, not wanting to say anything that might stop this moment of revelation. "That radioactive waste was not ours. It had been dumped on that site, and it was too late when we found it and saw that it had seeped into the groundwater. Tourists got sick and died. The locals who worked there got sick and died. It was awful, so very awful. I still have nightmares about it. I hated myself. My dad tried to help by sending me to Vegas, hoping I would come out of it." He backed off the porch. "I left, Cal. I left and tried something different. This was my chance to redeem myself, to show that I was not the monster that people thought me to be. They wanted a face on those deaths, and as hard as my dad tried to make sure that face wasn't mine, I saw the truth every time I looked in the mirror. I should have done more."

Cal didn't know what to say. He could be lying, but it didn't seem likely. Mark poured his heart out on her porch; his blood, sweat, and tears were all that remained. It couldn't be a mistake. How could all those pieces fit so well together? How about everything she saw at Belle Butte? She didn't make it up. Or she didn't imagine it?

Cal took her hand off the door and sat on the porch steps. She wasn't afraid of him now. "Tell me about the stairs and the construction equipment. Tell me about the elevator that leads down below ground."

"Because of the rocks, we had to be creative with how we built that main building. It was truly an engineering feat. We tried using exceptionally light building material and lots of plastic you see as our windows. There's minimal furniture, light composite wooden materials only. We made strides at first, but honestly, it was still too heavy. I had this vision…" he trailed off. "No matter what we did, the building wanted to sink. My engineering firm decided to add these underground stilts placed on the stronger rocks beneath, so they had to dig out. Upon digging, we discovered the river, which I'm guessing you've seen. At first we didn't know what we had; it was untapped potential, and then we tested it. Not sure if you noticed, but it's red! Can you imagine? Pure, clean water the color of blood rushing throughout Belle Butte and under the canyons."

She noticed how his face lit up as he spoke, how the streetlights danced on his cheekbones and flickered in his eyes. For a moment, he seemed to forget that he was begging for his life, and Cal couldn't shake the guilt that crept in. She had made a horrible mistake. Assuming the worst of others wasn't usually in her character yet turning Mark into a villain had been easy. The evidence had stacked against him.

"I saw it," she admitted, letting the tension turn her into a statue.

"You saw what?"

"It...the river. I went down there, saw the containers, and thought they were something else. I took a picture of them. I couldn't read the words; they weren't in English."

"No, they're in German. I had to order a special barrel to ship the water."

"Right." Cal succumbed to her astonishment and plopped her head into her hands. "I saw the suits, the yellow suits."

He made his way over to Cal and sat next to her. "When we started going down, we didn't want to contaminate the water. We couldn't bring equipment down there with just the tiny maintenance hole to work out of, so we had to make it as sanitary as possible. It was quite an operation.

"With my track record, they won't believe me. They'll invent stories like you did. Even when they find out the truth, it'll be too late. As I said before, I didn't follow all the rules at Belle Butte. I wasn't supposed to drill. I wasn't supposed to build that huge structure…I did it because I knew I could get away with it. I can schmooze and smile and, in the end, get what I want." He laughed and lifted his head. "Or I guess I thought I could. Maybe it's for the best. What was I thinking?"

They sat silently, only the distant sound of the wind whipping through the canyons behind them.

"It was going to be magic water." Mark broke in with another laugh.

"Magic water?" Cal was amused but not enough to ease the pain in her stomach.

"Yep, straight from the red rocks of Sedona. Magic water, like the whispering pines and vortexes and crystals. It would fit right in with the spirituality of this place. Come see the magical waterfall and drink of its power!" he yelled into the sky.

"Shhhh." Cal put her finger to her lips and then pointed to the window next to the front door. "My grandmother's asleep."

"Sorry." He looked down again, shaking his head. It was as if it was barely attached to his neck, drooping down like a flower beginning to wilt. "I wish I had gotten to meet her."

"I already sent it, Mark," Cal said, letting the words seep into the air around them before adding, "but it's not too late. I sent it to a friend of mine who has a friend at the *Times*. I'm sure he's sleeping. I can call him and tell him not to submit it."

Cal looked at him, hoping her words would rejuvenate the little flower. The adrenaline she had felt only a few hours ago had faded into nothing. She wasn't sure what she knew anymore and felt betrayed by her own mind. How did she get so caught up?

"Will you call him?" Mark finally said, looking at Cal, blinking in the darkness.

Cal took out her phone, found Jack's name and called. No answer, straight to voicemail. He was sleeping, so she left the message: "Hey, Jack, it's Cal. I sent you an email, but you need to delete it. It was all"— she stopped and stared at Mark— "my imagination. It wasn't real. Call me back when you get this and delete the email, okay. Thanks." She ended the call and put her phone on the steps.

"Thank you," Mark said, a small smile of gratitude breaking the frozen fear that had taken over his face.

"I never thought I could get wrapped up in a witch hunt. I'm so stupid. I believed Drunk Tommy, for goodness sake. What was I thinking?" Cal felt the air leaving her lungs, her mind beginning to wander.

"You didn't know, Cal. You thought it was the right thing to do. I wouldn't have done anything differently except maybe ask questions of the right people," Mark assured her. "Now what?"

"Now I call Jack again in the morning to make sure he got the message…and tell a few people the truth. They may not believe me, and that's my fault."

"Don't worry about it. Luckily, I don't need the locals to like me; I need the tourists to."

"Actually, you do need them. I guess the locals here are like all small towns, except a bit more desperate. They thrive off people, like parasites. They get fat and happy during summer so they don't waste away during the off-season. You're competition. That has to be it."

She was thinking out loud, trying to rearrange the pieces of the puzzle that she was so eager to put together. She couldn't simply let it go. It wasn't in her nature to "drop it." If it were, she never would have ended up in Sedona in the first place. She began flipping through the mental images of conversations with Drunk Tommy, Marcial Sanchez, Des, Jack, and the people at the party. What had she missed? Was their motivation to tear down the competition? Wouldn't Belle Butte bring in its own clientele and buffer the community? What were they so afraid of?

"Maybe you're right, but I'm too tired to think about pleasing them now," Mark answered, standing and walking a few steps. "I've been pleasing people my whole life, and I'm old enough to know that you can't please everyone. This is one blip on the map, Cal, and a small one at that. Look around you. In the end, places like this are a dime a dozen; people like these locals are a dime a dozen."

"Well, this dime a dozen almost took you down." She stood to face him, seeing his face change from near depression to anger. "It might benefit you to make an effort here."

"Like you did?" he asked.

Cal wasn't sure how to respond to those words. She could feel her face contort into confusion, and she blurted out, "What the hell is that supposed to mean?"

"You made an effort here and look what they did. They used you to get to me. You aren't a local; you're an outsider just like me, only you aren't a threat."

"I don't know that they were using me."

"Of course they were, Cal! These ideas didn't come from you. You weren't looking for trouble or looking to take me down. You got a job, the only one in town who got a job at Belle Butte. You were the perfect pawn for them. Are you desperate to be a part of Sedona? Do you

---

want to fit in here?"

"I've never fit anywhere, and honestly, I don't get why any of this matters right now. I know my mind, Mark, and while I obviously grasped for straws, I was the one grasping. No one told me to do that."

"Are you sure about that? What led you to snoop around? What led you to write the article?" Mark stepped nearer to Cal, their faces inches away from each other. "Your curiosity didn't morph into malicious contempt on its own. Something forced your hand, and it wasn't me. Think about it."

Cal couldn't think. She was exhausted, and the tension made her dizzy with confusion. Did she make it all up alone, or was she listening to others? Why would they have chosen her? Why didn't they go to Jack? He couldn't have gotten into the elevator or learned about the water. They needed her. They needed her to see it. Cal was looking at Mark, but she saw beyond him to the town of people that she thought she knew. The only one who hadn't pushed her was Des.

"Look, I could be wrong. I think that someone like you wouldn't automatically go to the extreme of taking someone down. I know you're probably thinking, 'How does he know?' And you're right; I don't know you." Mark looked away and sighed. "I think it's time for me to go."

Cal was relieved. She had experienced a roller coaster of emotions in the last few hours, from victory to failure, and now she was questioning everyone, even herself.

"Not sure when I'll see you again," she said, walking with him to his car.

"Why not?" he asked quickly. "You planning to quit

on me?"

"Well, I wouldn't expect you'd keep me on after this."

"Yes, you still have a job," Mark answered, opening his car door and hopping in. "I'll see you Monday."

That was that. He drove away, leaving Cal with the aftermath of her own hurricane. She was embarrassed and confused, yet something about tonight gave her clarity.

****

Sleep did not come quickly that night. Cal was plagued with dreams of Sedona underwater, spirits swimming through the liquid, screaming and grasping at her as she drowned amid the buildings and people she had come to love. At one point, Des reached out and yelled for help, but she couldn't reach him. Cal woke up, her breathing hard. She went to the bathroom and splashed her face with cold water. It didn't make sense that she would get caught up in this. It was as if everyone planted seeds in her, seeds meant to bloom at just the right time, only when it grew, it became a weedy monster. The clock read seven when she called Jack again, this time getting a faint answer.

"Cal, it's seven in the freaking morning. What do you want?"

"I know. Did you get my message? My email from last night?"

"I haven't even gotten my coffee yet," Jack whined. "Are you serious?"

"Very serious. Look, I was wrong about everything. Mark Courier wasn't being shady."

His voice sounded more awake at this prospect. "Did you talk to him?"

"He came to my house last night. He heard that I'd been snooping around."

There was a pause before Jack asked, "Did you let him in?"

"No. I'm not an idiot. I went outside."

"You are an idiot. If someone comes to your house, especially one who likely has beef with you, you don't meet them outside. You're lucky he didn't hurt you."

"Hurt me? Seriously, Jack? He was more desperate than mad, and what he said made sense."

"Yeah, I'm sure it did, kid. He probably had time to think about the whole thing after he heard about it. He had time to think about what you needed to hear. Damn, Cal, you're going to make a horrible journalist."

"I'm not trying to be a journalist. I never wanted to be part of this anyway. I was just the…"

"You were just what? The listening ear? The therapist? The gossip queen? The nosy neighbor?"

"Oh, come on. That's not fair. You even thought this was a good story, that it would blow the roof off this guy. You encouraged me to go for it. Don't you dare get onto me about this."

"Please, take responsibility. You got too close to the story. You believed people over substance. You didn't fact-check."

"Changing your tune, aren't you? I thought you just implied that Mark Courier was lying?"

"I'm not implying anything. You're messing up my Saturday morning. Who calls someone at the crack of dawn on a Saturday morning anyway?"

"I do. Someone who cares about doing the right thing."

"Fact-check, that would be the right thing. Luckily,

I've not sent it, but I won't lie to you. I wish I could."
The phone went silent, then he said, "I don't know, Cal."

"You don't know what?" She was confused and curious.

"The magazine is not lucrative anymore. I pushed this on you before you were ready, and I'm sorry for that. You were going to be my way out of a failing business, help me make my big break back into real journalism."

Cal didn't know what to say. Mark had been right; Jack had used her to get to him. But she did feel bad for Jack, the man who believed in the power of the magic crystals. He had built his career on those little stones, only to realize they were nothing but rocks. He sold his soul for a story and banked on it being flawless, like his stones. Jack wasn't a mentor; he was a scam. Cal wasn't angry.

"You didn't let me down, Jack. You don't owe me anything. I'm just sorry I got your hopes up. I thought I had it right but didn't know what I had." She sighed audibly. She felt guilty again for being sad that it was all a lie. Why was it so hard to be happy that Mark Courier wasn't some money-grubbing big shot? Was she really that bad of a person?

"I should have listened," he admitted. "Well, it's over now. If you ever do decide to write again, let me know. You have talent, Cal. Take it from me. You shouldn't edit other people's work; you should write your own. Be confident. And, you could make one hell of a journalist if you could distance yourself from the story."

Cal said, "Thanks, but I doubt I'll be doing that again anytime soon. I almost ruined a man's life. I'm just glad you like to sleep in on Saturday mornings."

"Yeah, me too." He laughed. "Talk to you later."

"Bye, Jack," Cal said, hitting *end* on her phone. It was officially done. The story was dead. Now it was time to figure out what people really knew.

There had to be a reason why so many nuggets of information were thrown at her.

Chapter Eighteen

"Relax, Marcial. Sit back, drink a beer and chill out," Tommy advised Officer Sanchez and pushed a beer at him.

Tommy's porch had been cleaned off, and his trailer had been recently pressure washed. He had gone to great lengths to prepare it for the tourists, who had been trickling in little by little.

Irritated at Tommy's laid-back attitude, Sanchez pushed the beer away and sat in the other lawn chair beside Tommy. "I can't relax. What if she gets cold feet? What if they don't run the story? The point was to shut down that place before the tourist season started, and they're already here. What's the backup plan?"

Tommy opened his beer and took a few gulps. "Backup plan? There's no backup plan. We don't need one, Marcial. That story will kill his business and get rid of the whole operation. Belle Butte will stay dormant forever because no one will know what to do with it. Worst-case scenario, some conservation group buys it to make sure no one else messes with it."

"That's a worst-case scenario. We've gotten away with this so far because no one could see what we were doing. Anyone up on that rock can possibly see it." Sanchez took his hat off and wiped his head. The heat was getting to him.

"Well, they couldn't smell it over all of the cow shit,

that's for sure." Tommy laughed. Sanchez rolled his eyes and wanted badly to correct Tommy's reference but knew that was what he wanted. "Look, that marijuana has been growing out there for years; you know that. No one has ever seen it or suspected it. Damn, we have the best setup of anyone. Between your shit and my land, and of course these beautiful magic trees, we're practically famous for our Sedona Crystal Bud. Folks come from all over...and it's right under their noses. And, of course, I have the law on my side, so I feel pretty good about this."

"You don't have as much to lose as I do. My ranch? My job? My reputation? My family? It never felt right, but now, now it's just too much." Sanchez tapped his fingers against the side of his pants. "I need to get out."

Tommy stood and walked behind Marcial. In an instant, he took a knife out of his pocket and brought it to Sanchez's throat, poking the blade into his skin.

"What the hell, Tommy? Put that away!"

He had known Tommy all his life, and while his bark was often worse than his bite, desperation could turn a man into someone else. There was the time when his grandma died, and he went out and set fire to the skeleton of the new house they were building, and Sanchez had to rush over and put it out. "I know you aren't going to kill me, Tommy, but you could hurt me. Is that what you really want?"

Tommy flicked the knife into the air and watched it stick into a pine off the side of the porch. He circled around to face Sanchez. "You're wrong, Marcial. See, you still see me as that kid. You know that kid who used to run off with you to the reservation and play poker, drink, and knock over mailboxes. You still see me as weak. But while you've been messing around, pretending to be a cop, I've been learning some things too. There's no way out for people like us. The only exit is either prison or death. I can survive prison, but you, you're a faker, a self-righteous faker at that. If you go to prison, they will rule you because you aren't a man yet. You haven't been tested. You got your wife over there, your boys, your family, hell, you have a whole town down there. And you know something? You hide behind all of 'em. Me? I live out in the open. I grow our pot and deal our pot—"

"And I make sure you don't get caught. Do you know how often I've had to step in for you? You're messy and undisciplined. You'd be in prison already if it weren't for me and my job. You misunderstand what I do, Tommy. Who do you think people are going to believe when this blows up? Me, the respected family man, an officer of the law, or you, the drunk, sketchy local boy who lost it all."

Sanchez knew what he had built over the years and that he would be safe. He didn't want to take Tommy down, but he didn't want to be part of it anymore. Belle Butte Touring Company was likely the beginning. Before they came, Tommy could stop them with his hole-in-the-wall tourist trap. There was no reason for people to go to the rocks above. At one time, it was a deserted road that led to nowhere. Now it was a noose waiting to hang them both. In the views from the top of the rocks, you could see the field peeking out of one of the back clearings, an area overflowing with marijuana that had fed their pockets and the town's for years.

Most of the locals benefited from the money in one way or the other, either as dealers, customers, or those who needed loans. Jenny's Market was basically owned by the Sanchez family. All he wanted out of the deal was for his family's ranch to be safe. Before he became a cop, it seemed like a good deal. He and Tommy had seen a patch much like theirs on a reservation down the road. It was a worthy investment that paid off, and with the lack of accountability around that area, it wasn't much of a risk.

Tommy chugged the rest of his beer then crushed the can. "You think you're better than me? We both have legacies here, not just you. This land has been our land before we were part of it. I may drink my money away, and you may give yours to keep that cow farm alive, but we're the same, you and me. There ain't nothin' different about us. If I go down, you go down, even if you get out. People will connect the dots, and that weed field is not just on my property; it's on our property."

"Let's dig it up, burn it. Let's get out of it altogether before it blows up," Sanchez offered.

Tommy just laughed. "What if your little wanna-be sleuth peddles that story like we planned? Why would we destroy a good thing? You never think, Marcial. Nah, we won't be diggin' up anything. Patience and cool-headedness are the keys right now, and I've got plenty of both."

Sanchez wanted to laugh. If Tommy was cool-headed, then he was Mother Teresa. He did agree with him, though. Maybe waiting and seeing what happened with the story was a good idea. Even if it were a temporary fix, it would calm the situation, and then he could talk Tommy into shutting down the operation. Sanchez had enough money to buy him off if he had to. At this point, it wasn't worth it to keep up the ruse, not worth the ulcer in his stomach, sleepless nights, staking out The Vortex, and looking out for Tommy. He wanted a fresh start.

"All right. We'll wait," he agreed, looking off into the pines.

A familiar car was parked at his house after Sanchez left Tommy's. It was Cal's jeep, and a trail of dust still lingered in the air. He parked the police cruiser next to her and saw her sitting there. She hadn't been to his house since the night of the dinner when she brought Grandma Ruth, and he thought it odd that she would come now. Recognizing his paranoia, he shook it off and exited the car. "What brings the famous Cal Ripken Jr. to my ranch?"

Cal got out of the jeep, let the door slam shut behind her back. "I'm not sure why I'm here. In most cases, I would have just waited until I saw you on patrol downtown. It's been a weird twenty-four hours."

"Everything okay? Grandma Ruth?" he inquired, taking a step toward her.

"Yeah, she's fine. Everything is fine. It's just…" her voice trailed before she said, "I had a visitor last night."

"A visitor?" he asked, worrying that Cal may have been robbed. "Did they take anything? Hurt anyone?"

"No, no, nothing like that," she assured him. "It was Mark Courier. Not sure how he knew I had been looking into him, but he was upset. He debunked everything, and I mean everything. He didn't make any questionable plans, Officer Sanchez, none. I got wrapped up in it and created a story without one. I was able to make sure it didn't get published, but something still doesn't seem right."

"And what story did you create?" he asked.

"There's this elevator at Belle Butte that goes under the main building and then this manhole that continues down into the rocks and then a river, an underground river."

"Wait...a river?"

"Yes, but he isn't planning to do anything with it, well not anything you'd seen on those plans."

It was everything Marcial had feared. Cal may have taken the bait, but she wasn't hooked, and Mark Courier was much more connected than he had anticipated. Sanchez had lied about seeing the blueprints; he couldn't get out of that, though he had a feeling that the fish was now fishing. He was surprised the river existed; at least his lie had some clout. However, Mark Courier must have told her what he was planning; otherwise, she would still question his motives. Cal said that the story didn't seem right. She had known the locals in town for much longer. It seemed a fact that you'd believe family over a stranger. Maybe it wasn't too late to salvage the lie and float it as truth.

"I thought you were looking too hard for something. What doesn't seem right?" he asked with a laugh. He hoped by making her feel silly that she would feel more comfortable. He could tell this had thrown her for a loop.

"There wasn't a story, but I feel like people wanted me to think there was. Since I started working there, everyone has wanted to tell me something about Belle Butte. Even you. I'm not saying you did anything wrong, but it was odd, you know?"

Sanchez kept his cool, remembering she was a twenty-two-year-old kid who didn't know the rules. She always asked a lot of questions, and he could see that it was taking a toll on her. At the same time, his guilt was starting to grow. He hated that she was a pawn in his plan, that Tommy had talked him into using her. If this were going to work, he would have to continue lying. He would have to convince her that Mark Courier was still the villain in the story. It had to be now. The situation was fragile, a thin pane of glass close to being shattered, but was it worth it?

Yes, it's worth it. Belle Butte could not continue; it was too dangerous for him. He would have to find a way to make the pot field disappear or make Belle Butte fail. Sanchez was aware of the heat and yet felt the bumps on his skin rise and his blood pressure climb.

"Let's say you believed Mark Courier was innocent—would he come to your house at night and tell you his story? Doesn't that seem desperate?" He thought the question would help her talk.

"Funny you asked. Jack said the same thing. I don't think it was that odd. If you thought that someone was about to bring the world down on your own head, wouldn't you try? He must've been somewhere around someone that told him that night." Sanchez could see Cal's wheels turning with the last syllable. She broke the silence. "The Vortex. He had to have been there that night."

Cal opened the door of her jeep and looked ready to jump back in without another word. Sanchez didn't know whether he should stop her or let her go. If Cal found out who Courier talked to that night, she could find out whose side the person was on. He thought the most obvious candidate to be Des Adams, who spoke to everyone about everything. It was both a talent and a curse. Des would be a safe person.

"Thank you!" she said.

"What did I do?" he yelled through the passenger window.

Cal rolled it down and said, "You listened. Not sure if I should listen more carefully or stop listening altogether. See you later!"

With that she was gone, leaving him in the dust. It wasn't entirely out of his control. He took a breath and headed to the house, dreading the phone call he needed to make to Tommy.

Chapter Nineteen

The Vortex, like every bar, was much less entertaining during the daylight hours. Not that you could tell it was daytime when you were in the cave. Light spilled through the hole, leaving shadows of the barred door across the floor. Cal was almost breathless when she arrived.

On the way, she had texted Des to see if he was working that day but hadn't gotten a response. She decided it was easier to go and wait for him, maybe have a drink to calm down. Lucio was behind the bar, and a few early patrons sat at tables or played pool.

"Bourbon on the rocks," Cal said, hitting her knuckle against the bar.

"A little early for you, isn't it?" Lucio said, grabbing a glass.

"Not really. It's five o'clock somewhere," Cal mocked. She had always hated that phrase. "Besides, you'd think a bartender wouldn't make fun of when people drink. Don't you need the business?"

"Actually, things are looking up for me. I have a feeling that everything's going to be okay," Lucio said with a smirk.

Cal wasn't a fan of Lucio, primarily because of her relationship with Officer Sanchez, but she did enjoy his establishment, so she forgave his words. "Good for you," Cal said, nodding. She changed the subject quickly.

"Was Des working last night?"

"He works every night. Why? Keeping tabs on the boyfriend now?"

"Not my boyfriend and, no, not keeping tabs. I was just curious. Were you here last night?"

"I'm always here, too. Friday nights are our busiest, so I help with bartending and occasionally breaking up a fight. That's what you get for owning a bar."

"Ah yes, the master of the house." Lucio handed her the drink, and she took a sip. Cal's phone buzzed with a text message. She saw it was from Des.

—Yes. I got home around 3:00 or 4:00. I have to be back there at 5:00. Why? What's up?—

Cal quickly typed *—Was Courier at the bar last night?—*

Lucio was serving someone a beer at the other end of the bar, and Cal took another drink as she waited for Des to answer.

—He was there. He left a little before I did. He was pretty wasted and looked upset—.

She said back *—Did you talk to him?—*

—Not really. He was talking to Lucio most of the time. Why?—

Cal put her phone down and looked at Lucio, who was now drying some glasses. "Hey, did you talk to Mark Courier last night?"

Lucio walked over. "Yeah, who's asking?"

"I don't believe anyone asked anything. Just curious. Did you talk about sports? Taxes? Tourists?"

"You're nosier than usual," Lucio answered, leaning on the bar and smirking at her again. "What kind of bee is caught up in that bonnet?"

"A bee who could use some information. I need to

know what you two talked about last night," she said, hoping that she could keep the sarcasm suppressed so as not to scare him away.

"Oh, we talked about this and that. You know, basic stuff like sports and taxes and tourists." He laughed and dried another glass. "He's a good man. I told him there was some talk in town about his business on the butte. Des told me about your little theory and your attempt to expose his plan. He didn't much like that; in fact, he had a million reasons as to how you were wrong. He went on and on about how you knew nothing and that the people here in Sedona were full of it. You know what I think?"

Cal didn't want to know what he thought, but she knew he needed to be appeased. "What?"

"I think you're probably going to get fired. Can't imagine you'd keep your job after this. You'll be back to asking me for one."

"Actually, I spoke to Mark Courier last night. After he left here, he dropped by my house, and we had a little chat. He dispelled the rumors—"

"Lies," Lucio interrupted with a scoff.

"And asked me not to publish the article I was writing. And you know what, Lucio?" she asked snidely.

He laughed again and looked down. "What's that, Cal?"

"He said I could keep my job. What do you think of that? I guess he wasn't as mad as you thought. Is that really why you told him? To get me fired? When have I ever done anything to you? Did I make fun of you too much? Was it because I'm friends with your brother? Is that it?"

"You have no reason to mention him in my bar," Lucio said forcefully, stepping up to the bar.

Those were fighting words, and Cal immediately regretted them. They stared at each other. She wasn't sure what to do with the information. At least now she knew that Lucio told Courier, someone who was disconnected from the rest of her story. Now it did all seem like a coincidence. She sat back on the stool and said, "Yeah, sorry about that," sounding almost disinterested.

"You don't know everything, Cal. You think you do, just like everyone your age. You hear what you want to hear. That's what makes you dangerous. I'd thank your lucky stars that you have a job and ignore all the rest of that gossip. You'll end up on the wrong side if you don't. These locals have secrets and agendas that would keep this place stuck in the past. If it were up to my brother, we would never be allowed to go out independently and make something of ourselves. There'd be nothing new here in Sedona. People like Mark Courier have a vision for the future. They can bring this place back to life. I've heard many things in my day, being behind this bar like Des. You take some with a grain of salt and some as wisdom. You take things for what they are."

Lucio spoke eloquently, sounding more like Officer Sanchez at the moment. She found it hard to believe the two men had a father in common. Cal couldn't help but mull over his words as he walked away. There was no conspiracy; no one was at fault. It was time to drop it.

She spent the rest of the weekend at home with Grandma Ruth. She needed a break from everyone, a clean slate. She saw on her tablet that she had multiple tours scheduled on Monday. Cal prepared, going over her notes and practicing her speech. She still needed to remember all the script and memorizing was not one of her strong suits. Between practice rounds, she checked her email, hoping for an editing job to pop up. With the revelations of the weekend, she could use some normalcy. The ground had shaken beneath her feet.

On Sunday, she took Grandma Ruth for a walk and even dug up one of the flower beds in front of the house. Cal wanted Grandma Ruth to see them from her window. She chose annuals that bloomed with large pink blossoms and dark green leaves. It had been a long time since she had planted anything yet stabbing into the earth and disturbing the space felt therapeutic. While she was watering the new beds, Grandma Ruth appeared on the porch. Cal noted that her posture had improved, and she was walking with a more steady gait. She seemed stronger than she was a year ago when they first moved to Sedona.

The blood work came back from the doctor's office a few weeks ago, touting good numbers. Alice claimed that Grandma Ruth was sweeping the kitchen one day and hanging laundry on the line in the back yard on another. Could it be that Sedona was working its magic on Grandma Ruth? And if it was, could Cal establish herself enough to keep them both comfortable for the long haul? Grandma Ruth took a seat on the porch step and took in a deep breath.

There was minimal breeze, and the air was dry as always. Grandma Ruth mentioned missing the thickness of the North Carolina summer. "You could bite into that air; do you remember?" she asked. Cal remembered it well. Even Atlanta had humidity that made everything stick to you. "You don't really sweat the same sweat here," Grandma Ruth said and laughed. "I won't feel it dripping down my cheek until we get inside, and then it'll hit me."

"So true." It was like that when she took people on tours as well. No one complained about the heat until they sat in the cabin. Spending time with Grandma Ruth brought perspective. All the drama was out there somewhere, not in their little house. Cal sat beside her and observed her profile. A year ago, Grandma Ruth was starting to deteriorate, her cancer little by little taking over the once lithe body. Now she seemed restored. Her skin was brighter, her arms held a hint of strength, and her eyes were sharp. Just a few months ago Grandma Ruth had babbled about the red rocks in the living room, giving Cal the chills. Now they were back to having a real conversation.

"I used to love summertime," Grandma Ruth said, breathing in the air, her chest lifting. "I used to love the smells of summer: fresh-cut grass, burgers on the grill, chlorine. You don't smell those smells here, well, other than the grill." She laughed. "There's that one smell, earthy and sweet. I asked Jennings about it once, and she said it was the creosote. That's them over there." She pointed to a large shrub with white poofs around it. "It smells like the rain here, doesn't it?"

Cal hadn't thought about the rain much. City rain had a distinct smell of rubber and pavement, but desert rain smelled of oil almost. Cal watched her grandmother continue to breathe, watched the smile on her face expand, and watched her peace of mind. She wanted that peace. The last couple of weeks had been like a speeding train going nowhere. It was time to come clean and spill it all to Grandma Ruth, if for no other reason than to bury it for good.

"I have to tell you something."

Grandma Ruth sat still, eyes closed, still smiling and nodded.

"I think I let my imagination get the best of me, yet I still feel like I missed something. You know my boss, Mark Courier? Well, you don't know him, but you've maybe heard me mention him?" Cal didn't remember whether she had or hadn't. The timeline was becoming a blur. She had only worked at Belle Butte Touring Company for a few weeks, yet it seemed like more. "It all started with something I heard from Drunk, I mean, Tommy who owns Whispering Pines. One night, I heard him talking at the bar, saying something about trucks coming down from Belle Butte as if something were being taken out."

"Is that odd? When doing construction, don't you have to clear the land and make room?" Grandma Ruth inquired.

"To an extent but you can't really 'clear' a butte, at least not that one. The thing is, I thought I was onto something, found something that needed to be exposed, but now I just…" Cal's voice cut short, unable to verbalize the confusion and anxiety streaming through her mind and body. Maybe it was all a mirage, but it didn't feel like it. She needed advice. She needed to know that she wasn't crazy.

"Cally, it sounds to me like you need to listen to the whisper," Grandma Ruth said calmly. Her demeanor hadn't changed.

"What does that mean?" Cal asked, unsure how to take the advice.

"Information overload. You have so much going on in your little head, and yet you haven't stopped to listen. You are *hearing* it but not listening. Take a deep breath."

Grandma Ruth demonstrated with a deep breath of her own. She released it slowly and said, "Go ahead. You try."

With that, Cal took a breath through her nose and let it seep out slowly. It was true; introversion played a big part in her thought process. Once her mind started working, it was hard to shut it off. In college she called it the "Death Spiral." Round and round it would go until eventually she would crash. "Breathe," she told herself. "Just breathe."

So many voices had leant themselves to her thoughts lately: Drunk Tommy, Nia, Christy, Jenny, Officer Sanchez, Jack, Mark Courier, Des, and even Lucio. It was interesting how they almost paired up when it came to "sides" of the story.

Lucio, a fan of Mark Courier, was quick to tear down Officer Sanchez, though that was a regular occurrence. Drunk Tommy and Officer Sanchez seemed to be on the same page in shutting down Belle Butte Touring Company, which made some sense if Courier was planning to do something with the water that would affect their land, their legacies. But if it weren't true, Mark had squashed the rumor, yet Officer Sanchez didn't seem convinced.

Someone was lying, and it all hinged on the blueprints—either they existed, or they didn't.

"Who would you trust, someone you have known for a good chunk of time or someone that you don't really know at all?" Cal asked, breaking the silence.

"I don't know if the passage of time creates liars or honest people, Cally. People do what they feel they need to do. You have to trust yourself."

"I'm not sure I can trust myself, not with this."

"And why do you feel like you have to be in the middle of it? Were you chosen for some reason?"

"Chosen?" Cal repeated, mulling over the word and its implications.

As an editor, she understood that words held power; they were charged with it. The word *chosen* meant there was intent. Was she chosen? Was there a reason why people had talked to her? Why was she the cog in the wheel and not someone else? What did she have? Lucio had said in the bar the other day that locals had secrets and agendas, and she was not privy to them. So why her? Was it because she was an outsider? Everyone who had talked to her knew her, and the fuel to the fire was Jack, who seemed very interested in the story being significant in blowing the top off of things. Then he apologized for pressing and humbled himself. If the story had gotten out, it would have saved Sedona and bumped Courier off the map, and who would that benefit from her list?

"Officer Sanchez and Tommy," Cal said quietly. "They were the ones who offered the most information, one way or the other. That's the link."

"Whispers," Grandma Ruth said, turning toward Cal. "You listened and they spoke."

"And now it's time for me to find out the truth," Cal responded, looking back over the flowers.

Chapter Twenty

"Des, I need you to help me with something," Cal said as soon as he answered his phone.

"It's way too early. Can we have this conversation some other time?" he said sleepily.

"No, we can't; it's urgent. I need to go out to Whispering Pines, and I need you to go with me."

"Hell no, I'm not going out to Drunk Tommy's little tree farm. In case you hadn't noticed, that place is shady as—"

"Yeah, because of the large trees. I know this sounds crazy, but I think he's hiding something, and I hate to admit it, but I believe Officer Sanchez might be in on it."

"I thought you dropped this. There's no need to dig around anymore. All that stuff you learned was hearsay, coincidence. You're messing around in other people's garbage makes you a rat. That doesn't suit you."

"Thank you, oh moral compass," she mocked loudly, "but I had an epiphany yesterday."

"Oh yeah? Were you smoking some of that weed you keep smelling?"

"No drugs involved, just Grandma Ruth's ancient wisdom, or Alice, actually. But that's beside the point. The point is I think there's a reason why the two of them kept divulging information which I think has something to do with their land. Think about it. Those two plots have been there for years, side by side, with nothing nearby except the reservation. Then, here comes Mark Courier and his touring company that sets up camp right above them, instant neighbors. Before they even open, Drunk Tommy starts spreading rumors about the water there. Wouldn't he have said something before if he were so concerned about the water?"

"You're reaching again," Des reasoned. "Look, he owns a tourist trap, and the guy opens a bigger and better tourist trap basically next to his. It makes sense that he complains about it in the bar when he's drunk and tells everyone he sees. He doesn't have to have some sinister reason other than losing money."

"Yeah, but for all intents and purposes, his business doesn't seem to make a lot anyway, and yet he goes out and drinks every night, and people in town seem to love him, other than those with any sense."

"You're reaching again, inferring things that aren't real. I know many poor people who go out and drink every night…"

"And do they have new cowboy boots and hats? Do they sit around all day and drink, even in the off-season?"

The silence on the other end of the line told Cal he was rolling his eyes. "What do you hope to find out there?" he finally asked.

"I don't know, and it may be nothing, and if it is, then I'll drop it, Des. I promise. But I have to know. I can't just keep thinking about this every second of the day—it's driving me nuts."

"It's driving me nuts, too." After a moment of silence, he sighed. "Okay, I'll pick you up in an hour, and we'll go. You better have a plan."

"Oh, I have a plan. See you soon." Cal hung up.

She didn't have a plan yet and realized that it was time to think of something. They couldn't just go on a tour because Drunk Tommy would just take them where he wanted them to go and hound them along the way. She needed to see more. Cal got dressed quickly and told Grandma Ruth that she was going out. "I'll be back in a few hours," she started, then stopped.

What if I don't come back? What if something goes wrong?

It was the first time that it seemed real, that there was a possibility that Drunk Tommy was actually a villain and not just the town drunk. Someone could get hurt. "If I'm not back in a few hours, please call the police," Cal said. "Excuse me?" Grandma Ruth sounded almost offended as she leaned up in her chair. "You'll tell me what's going on right now or you're not leaving this house."

"I can't tell you what I don't know. Please don't worry about me. I'll be fine; I have to see something," she explained, inching toward the front door.

"No, Cally, I don't like this at all," Grandma Ruth said forcefully, jumping up with the cat-like reflexes of an Olympic gymnast that sent Cal back pedaling into the hallway. "I don't have a good feeling about this."

What just happened? Her grandmother had suddenly become her seventy-year-old self before Cal's very eyes. It was too much to process. Cal didn't want to provoke her, but she didn't want to lie. She was a little nervous and wanted someone to know where she was, just in case.

She went with a simple explanation. "Des and I are just going to check on the competition at Whispering Pines. I need to know what their tours look like." The answer was quick and gave just enough information so that if something were to go down, Grandma Ruth would know where she was headed.

"I still don't like it," Grandma Ruth said, softer now. "Just don't wander off."

It was her go-to, a simple phrase that told Cal "I love you" and "I'm worried" at the same time.

"I won't," Cal promised, edging toward the front door. Part of her wanted to stand there and take in her grandmother, this miraculous woman that was rising from the depths of cancer but she knew she had to leave. Time was running out. Cal smiled at her grandmother and left.

Des was waiting on the street when Cal walked out. She jumped in the car, and they made their way to Whispering Pines.

"All right, what's the plan?" Des asked, keeping his eyes on the road.

"Pretty simple, TV-show-plot stuff. We'll ask for the tour and midway through, I'll need to go to the bathroom. Drunk Tommy will tell me to go into the trees, and I'll refuse because that's gross, and I'll run back to…wherever the bathrooms are and snoop around a bit," she said, almost excitedly.

"In this plan, I'm by myself with Tommy? You've got to be kidding me." Des looked angry. Cal hoped he would suck it up and go along with the plan, but he wasn't convinced. "Even if I stay with him, I doubt the tour lasts that long. Do you have any clue what you're looking for or where you would snoop?"

"I told you. I think there's something on the border of Sanchez Ranch and Whispering Pines. I'll aim in that direction as soon as you two are out of sight and earshot.

You'll have to keep him busy for as long as possible."

"I'll try. I could ask him what his favorite drinks are but, oh yeah, I serve him those, so that's about our only connection."

"I'm sure you can come up with something. You're an intelligent young man…"

"You don't have to butter me up. I'm already coming along," Des said. The jeep was quiet. *The calm before the storm*, Cal thought.

"What if he has tours going already?" Des asked.

It was a good question, and Cal had thought about it. "It would work to our advantage if there were tours. We can join in, and he couldn't say anything gross when I have to go back." Cal was hopeful.

****

They pulled up at Whispering Pines at around three. The sign was weathered, but Tommy had obviously repainted it before the season started. Even the driveway had some new gravel. There were cars parked on both sides as they drove up. Parking along the driveway, Cal looked at Des and asked, "Are you ready for this?"

"Not sure what to say other than yes," Des said hesitantly. "Just be safe, okay?"

"I will. I'm not nervous about this," Cal said, grabbing the door handle. Des's hand grabbed her arm and she turned around into a kiss. It was startling and exciting, unexpected and perfectly timed. It was over as quickly as it started, as they pulled apart from each other and stared. "Wow, I was not—"

"Yes, you were," Des added. "Now let's go get this over with."

Cal sighed and they got out.

Up ahead, a crowd of people surrounded a hut. The

familiar voice of Drunk Tommy rose over the group. "You'll be amazed at the beauty of the pines and their voices. They sound like angels singing if you listen carefully. Stay on the path…" Drunk Tommy broke off, his head peeking above the crowd toward Des and Cal.

"Great, he saw us," Des said.

"Locals, the first wild animals that you'll see on our journey." Drunk Tommy laughed. "It's not free for locals. You'll have to ante up like the rest of them." He walked through the people who were giggling and laughing, jostling about. "It's ten bucks a piece. Tell me something—did you come all the way out here to support little ol' me? I feel honored."

The words slid out of his mouth like oil.

As much as Cal wanted to make a remark of disgust, she knew her role. "I'm not really a local, am I?" she said. It sounded both sarcastic and truthful.

Tommy laughed. "That says it all, doesn't it?"

Des handed him a twenty-dollar bill that slid into a shake. "How's it goin', man?"

"Can't complain. Trees are free, and the tourists are buying," Drunk Tommy said, then turned to the group. "All right, let's get this show started. Here we go!"

He made his way to the front of the group and started walking. The tourists followed, and Des and Cal found their way toward the middle. Cal hoped they could blend in and be forgotten by the pack's leader, but Drunk Tommy turned around multiple times and seemed to be looking for them.

"He's got his eyes on us," Des said to Cal.

"Yeah, he definitely knows where we are," Cal answered.

The trail was broad and covered in pine straw with

trees as far as they could see. Even without a breeze, the trees seemed to blow and swing in tandem. There was a constant sound of tinkling in the distance. If it were any other circumstance, Cal would have enjoyed the walk. It was hard to enjoy the tour with her plan replaying in her mind. They had been walking for about fifteen minutes when the group stopped.

"This is the thickest part of the pine tree forest. If you look left and right, you'll see the wall of gray from the trunks. You can't see much through the trees," Drunk Tommy yelled.

There were close to thirty people in the crowd, of varying ages. Hands began to rise with a list of questions that Cal couldn't hear. Being in the middle had disadvantages as the class pets were in the front. She decided to make her move. She strode to the front and waited until the last person finished.

"Are there any more questions?" Tommy asked.

Cal scuttled to the front, leaving Des behind. "Um, Tommy, I have to go to the bathroom," she said almost in a whisper.

"You serious? Damn, Cal. Tell me something— didn't your mama ever tell you to use the bathroom before going out?" he asked, obviously peeved.

She watched his lips mouth *damn*. "I actually did, but you know, call of nature."

"All right, run straight down the trail. There's a bathroom in the visitors' hut. Use it, then run back here. Don't go off the trail, you understand?" he demanded, trying to be quiet but his voice carried.

"Got it," she said, moving back and forth for effect.

He nodded, and she started to walk off quickly when another voice spoke up. "Are you going to the restroom?" It was a young woman with a little girl who looked about four years old. "My daughter has to go too. Can we follow you down the trail?"

It caught Cal off guard. She didn't have unlimited time, and this would slow her down. She would have to walk all the way down the trail. Cal was trapped. "Of course," she finally said with a smile, feeling Drunk Tommy's eyes on her.

"Thank you," the lady said to Cal and then turned to a man who was likely her husband and added, "You go ahead. We'll catch up."

Cal walked past Des, who mouthed *what the hell* as she walked past. What could she have done? Cal walked quickly, hearing the little girl chatting with her mom behind her.

"Could we slow down a little?" the lady asked behind her.

"I wish I could," Cal answered, "but I have to go."

"It's just that my daughter has tiny legs. It's hard for her to stay with you." The lady was almost pleading this time.

Cal rolled her eyes but totally understood the situation. It wasn't fair to punish these two innocents for her desperation. She took a deep breath and slowed her gait.

"Thank you. My name is Marie, and this is Reese. Can you say hello, honey?" she asked her daughter. The little girl was silent.

"I'm Cal. Where are y'all from?" she asked, keeping the conversation light, hoping she could pick the pace back up.

"Florida. My husband and I have always wanted to visit the Grand Canyon, so we brought little Reese. It's been such a nice trip so far. How about you?"

"I live in Sedona now, but I'm from Atlanta," Cal offered.

"Oh how nice to live in such a cool place. I love to see locals supporting other locals."

Cal said nothing. Instead, she looked at her watch and saw a few minutes had passed. She had to get away from Marie and Reese, but she didn't want to cause any alarm, and they were obviously nervous about walking alone. New plan. She would let them go to the bathroom first, then tell them to go on without her, hoping they wouldn't insist on waiting. This may at least get them to leave her so she could make a run for it. Marie could tell Tommy that she had told them to go ahead of her. She would have to hear poop jokes at the bar for a while, but that would be better than nothing.

Marie shared her life's story with Cal as they walked, everything from jobs to the birth story, which Cal could have done without. She didn't understand why new mothers had to divulge so much information about having a baby. It was almost like trauma victims who had to discuss their issues before getting over them. They arrived at the hut in about ten minutes, and she told them to go first. Marie was thankful and took Reese.

Cal waited outside, looking around. She decided the quickest way now was to cut straight to the right, hit the property border, and then work her way up. Eventually she could cut back across the pines to the trail, or at least she hoped she could. Cal wasn't exactly sure how large the property was.

Finally, after an eternity of tiny giggles and a reminder to wash her hands, Marie and her daughter exited the bathroom. "That isn't exactly the most hygienic place," Marie said.

Cal laughed out loud and wanted to retort, "Could have told you that," but she didn't. "Look, you two can go on ahead. My stomach isn't feeling good, so it'll be a while."

"Oh, we couldn't do that. It's okay, really. We'll wait. Honestly, this little one is pretty tired," Marie said, patting Reese on the top of her head.

"I insist, seriously. I heard the clearing at the end is breathtaking and magical. You'll miss it if you don't hurry with her. I run pretty fast, so I may even catch up," Cal said as she edged toward the hut.

"Well, uh." Marie looked down the path and back at Cal. "Are you sure?"

"I am so sure. Please, go ahead," Cal insisted.

"Okay, we'll see you in a few minutes. Thank you."

Cal walked over to the bathroom door and went inside for a minute, then peeked out to ensure they were gone. When the coast was clear, she ran as fast as she could, parallel to the road toward Sanchez Ranch. Once she got to the border, which was an electric fence for the cattle, she cut up through the pines. She was surprised by how many trees the ranch had. Cal assumed that most of the trees were on Tommy's property, but Officer Sanchez had quite a few of his own.

She imagined the Sanchez brothers and Tommy playing tag through the woods and wondered about their childhood. It would be fun to have neighbors to play with, yet they all seemed pitted against one another, except for Lucio and Tommy. They saw quite a bit of each other, and yet it was Officer Sanchez and Tommy whose stories connected.

The pine straw was thick along the border, and Cal

slipped a few times as she ran. It created an icelike effect on the ground. So far there was nothing to see, just trees and a clearing starting to come into view on the right. Cal could see the ranch house in the distance. The land wasn't as flat as she thought. Up on the butte, it was an optical illusion because everything looked on the same level except for the other buttes that rose up and died down suddenly. Cal was starting to breathe heavily. It had been a while since she had run this speed and distance, and the alcohol had taken its toll. She promised herself on the spot that she would drink less bourbon, knowing that she would likely forget that promise when night fell.

Cal picked up her stride, ducking under low-hanging pine branches. "Run," she told herself, pushing her arms up to gain speed. Ahead, she saw the trees thinning and the sun's golden light spilling onto a clearing. It was before her as quickly as she saw it, and she abruptly stopped. It was a garden out in the middle of nowhere. She bent down into the thick green. "What is this?" she asked out loud, running her fingers through the plants. "It could be carrots or maybe a spice?"

Cal knew nothing about gardening, being a city girl. No one was in sight, and the trees on the Sanchez Ranch side had created a buffer between the field and the cattle. She hadn't noticed that the fence had edged off to the right more, leaving this part to seem like Tommy's land. She continued walking through the field until she reached the other side where the trees thickened back up, and the fence was closer to her.

"How…odd. Why would he plant a garden so far from his house?" Cal looked around the field again and walked the row. It wasn't large, but it wasn't small either. The same plant was growing throughout, so it wasn't a variety of vegetables. It was strange and strange was what she was looking for, though she wasn't expecting it to be a plant. Cal took out her phone and took pictures of the plants and then walked out of the garden and took a shot of the entire plot. Her text tone went off. She looked down and saw it was from Des.

—Where are you? We are on our way back. You better get back here.—

Cal didn't know where "here" was; even if she ran through the pines, there was no guarantee she would make it to the group. And what if she came up behind them? There was only one option. She put her phone back in her pocket and booked it back the way she came. Cal had to make it back to the bathroom before the group finished the tour; it was the only possible explanation for her disappearance. Bathroom emergencies happened, and she had a witness.

She picked up her pace and started striking a little more through the trees, hoping to make a bit of a diagonal and cut off the perimeter she had run earlier. Her legs began to burn, and her chest felt heavy. Cal knew what was at stake and told her body to keep going. "Just a little farther," she chanted.

Like a cushion, the pine straw floor was quiet, and she heard tinkling around her. Cal thought of the story Drunk Tommy had told about the trees talking. She must be close to the trail. A flash of light from above got her attention. Up in the trees she saw wind chimes dangling and swaying in the wind with the trees. "That's how he does it. That little cheat."

Not that she could blame him. If you made money off magic and there was no such thing, you had to create something. Cal was almost lost in her thoughts when she heard the voices ahead and saw the movement. She had caught up to the group, and they were closing in on the trail entrance. Cal turned slightly to the left to stay behind the trees and continued to run. She could hear Tommy's voice echoing through the trees above the rest.

Cal saw a seafoam-colored structure ahead. Upon closer inspection, it was a trailer. Thinking this must be where he lived, she was careful to run behind it. Her lungs got a second wind, and she sped up. "I have to be close now."

Sure enough, the trees thinned back out and the hut was in view. She put her legs in high gear and sprinted to the bathroom door of the hut, shutting it quietly when she was safely inside, then waited. It wasn't long before she heard voices and laughter.

"Well, that's the end of the road, folks," Drunk Tommy said to rising applause. "I hope you enjoyed the Whispering Pines tour and heard the trees tell you something special. Don't forget to post your pictures online, tag us, and write a review on social media."

There was a jiggle of the handle, followed by a knock. "Oh, I'm sorry. I didn't realize anyone was in there," a voice said.

Cal thought quickly. "Yes, I'm sorry. I'll be out in a minute." She wanted to make sure that Tommy saw her emerge from the bathroom. Cal imagined a line forming outside the door and hoped it would draw his attention, but she didn't hear his voice. A text came through on her phone:

—*Des: Where are you????*—
—*Cal: In the bathroom*—
—*Des: Still? Did you actually have to go?*—

—Cal: No, I ran back here because I wasn't sure where you were. You have to get Tommy's attention over to the bathroom. He had to have noticed that I didn't rejoin the group.—

—Des: K—

About a minute later, she heard a commotion outside the bathroom. Des called through the door, "Hey, Cal, are you okay in there?"

She played along. "Yes, I'm okay. About to come out." Cal flushed the toilet and washed her hands, trying to make as much noise as possible. When she came out of the bathroom, three other tourists were waiting with Des over to the right.

Tommy stepped forward as Cal moved out of the way so the others could use the bathroom. "Damn, girl, did you fall in? In all my years I've given this tour, I've never had anyone miss over half of it to take a deuce." He laughed. He leaned in closer and said, "Tell me something…"

Cal held her breath and said a silent prayer to the pines. Her heart was beating quickly, even more so than when she was running.

"Did everything come out okay?" Tommy finished his question with a laugh.

Cal breathed out and laughed too. He couldn't resist a joke about going number two. She was happy he was a reliable idiot and said, "Yeah. Your magical trees are also magical laxatives."

"No extra charge for that," he said as Des and Cal walked off.

"Did you find it?" Des asked when they were closer to the car.

"Not here," Cal responded, quickening her step.

"Huh?"

"Just get in the car," she said, opening the door and slamming it shut. Cal wasn't sure what she had. The sooner they got out of there, the sooner she could figure it out.

Chapter Twenty-one

The whole process took them a couple of hours, so Cal was home before Grandma Ruth got too worried. Cal made her a sandwich and something for Des, but she was still too rattled to eat. When Cal and Des were settled in her room, she took out her phone and showed him the picture.

"It's a garden, Cal," Des said with disinterest. He took a big bite of the sandwich and glared at her. "You took a picture of a garden."

"It was a garden in the middle of nowhere between their properties. Isn't that odd? What kind of plant is it?" She handed the phone to Des, who zoomed in on the plant.

Des threw his head back and started to laugh. "No way, no way, no way," he repeated. "Oh man, Lucio isn't going to believe this."

"Won't believe what? What is it?" Cal asked, grabbing his arm and shaking it.

"You don't know what this is? Where'd you go to college?"

"Not sure why that matters. I didn't major in plants," she said, emphasizing the last word. "I swear if you don't tell me right now I'm going to—"

"It's weed. Marijuana."

It took a minute for her to fully realize the magnitude of the word. At first, she thought of the garden pest and wondered why anyone would get excited about something so trivial. Then it hit her. Pot.

"You're kidding me. Marcial Sanchez would never get mixed up in something like that? He must not know!"

"Hey, there's no reason to convince me, but I promise you he knows. There's no way something like this can be on his property without him knowing." Des zoomed onto the picture of the field, then scrolled around with his finger. "Look at this—it's right there, really out in the open."

"You can't tell anyone, Des. We don't know what this means. There are serious implications for something like this!"

"Yeah, and so is trying to bring down a man's business by dirtying his name. Cal, they started it. You have evidence right here that tells you why they tried to bring him down. Think of the visitors that climb up Belle Butte and that look down at this land. Before Courier built that spot, no one went up there. It was basically private property. You may not have noticed it before, but I bet the next time you take a tour up there, you'll see that field of pot, and anyone with a somewhat decent college experience will know what it is," he said, still giddy. "Damn, pot. Tommy doesn't seem smart enough to be in that business."

She remembered the nights she had smelled it on the street near The Vortex and around Sedona. Everyone seemed to ignore it, even Officer Sanchez. Her mind couldn't compute. "You have to promise right here, right now, not to say anything, Des. If Tommy or even Sanchez know that we were out there snooping, we don't know what they're capable of."

Cal hoped her words would calm down the obvious

adrenaline Des was feeling. He was almost jumpy. "I know the rules," he snapped. "This could be huge. Not only are they growing this stuff, but they must also be the dealers. I've heard people at the bar discussing how good pot is in Sedona. I always assumed it was just tourists bringing it in. How do we even have a climate suitable to grow it?"

"I don't know and I don't care. This just got real, and we have to do something with this information..." Cal's voice trailed off.

Des checked his watch, then grabbing the rest of the sandwich, jumped up. "Is it really five p.m.? I gotta get home and shower for work. Are you coming by the bar tonight?"

"Not sure," she said without looking up. "I need to get some things straight."

"Okay, well, I'll call you?" Des asked, walking to the door.

"Yeah, okay," Cal said dismissively. Once Des had cleared the room, she picked up her phone and called Jack.

"Hello?" Jack answered.

"Hey, do you have a second to talk?" Cal asked, a bit frantic.

"Sure, what's up?"

"It's not Mark Courier. He isn't the one," she said, her words starting and stopping like a telegram.

"What do you mean he isn't the one?"

"The story, the one we were writing. We thought it was about Mark Courier but we were wrong...I was wrong. I thought about the story and who the major players were. Two main witnesses, Tommy and Officer Sanchez, fed me most of my so-called facts and comments. So today Des and I went to Whispering Pines and snooped around."

"What do you mean you snooped around? Cal, what did you get yourself into?"

"I got myself into something bad, Jack. I found a garden, a small field of marijuana."

It was silent on the other end, and Cal could feel the invisible tension in the air between their phones. There was an audible breath. "I wish you hadn't done that," he finally said, his voice low.

Cal wasn't sure how to respond. Part of her agreed; she didn't want to know this information and wasn't sure what to do with it, but it was uncovered, bare for all to see. "Do we call the cops? The cops are Sanchez! Are they all in on it?"

Jack's voice was still low, almost inaudible. "You watch too many movies, Cal. It's less likely that it's an entire department, though I'm with you; not sure if I want to take that chance."

"So what do we do?" Cal asked. She didn't want to make a decision and didn't trust any decision she made would go as planned. Nothing had gone as planned to this point. Not only was Cal out of her league, but she was also hitting for the other team.

"I'm not sure if we can do anything, Cal," Jack said. "Who would we tell? Think about how this would affect everyone, affect the town, especially during tourist season. Let's be sensible here. Maybe we should chill out, hold our horses, and let it be for a while."

She couldn't believe what she was hearing. Did Jack want to bury the story? He was a journalist, an investigative reporter bound to the truth. Cal also thought Officer Sanchez was bound to honor, so her constructs of jobs and decency were crashing down around her. Was Jack willing to break the law to ensure the tourist season didn't end? She knew his business was failing at the magazine, and he admitted to being too gung-ho about the story surrounding Mark Courier. In fact, he was one of the first ones to really push the story to begin with.

A sinking feeling came over her, and she felt her arms and shoulders get heavy. Butterflies came back into her stomach, but they were different than the ones in the cabin that night with Des. These butterflies had claws and mouths that scratched away at her insides. Flashes of conversations and moments came into her mind, talks with Jack and Officer Sanchez and Tommy, each layering onto the other like waves on the shore, lapping away at her reasoning and leaving behind quicksand.

Is it possible? Could Jack be in on it? She didn't want to ask and wasn't sure how to without possibly hurting their relationship.

"Are you still there?" Jack asked.

She took a quiet breath and let it out slowly, hearing Grandma Ruth's words to listen to the whisper. "Yeah, I'm here. Just processing all of it." For now there was only one thing she could do. "I'm with you. We'll keep it on the down low until we know what to do."

"Good. I'm glad we're on the same page," Jack said, relief in his voice. "And it was just you and Des, right? Who went out there?"

Cal felt the butterflies, bloodying her insides again. She didn't like the question, and she hated herself for mentioning Des's name. "Yeah, just us," she said, trying to sound casual.

"Good," he said. "Send me those pics when you can,

and we'll deal with it together."

"Okay," she answered quickly, wanting to get off the phone.

"Let's talk again soon," Jack said calmly.

"Yes, definitely." Cal hit *end* on the call and curled into a ball on her bed.

Just a few hours ago, there was excitement in the mystery, and now it felt so real. This was not some Nancy Drew moment; this was real life. She felt trapped and didn't know where to turn. Des may be in danger, and she was the one to blame. If she had left it alone, just like Jack had suggested, it would have remained a mystery, and life would have gone on as before. Her phone was almost dead, so Cal quickly texted Des.

—Where are you right now?—

There was no response. He was probably in the shower or getting ready for work. Cal knew what she had to do. She opened a document on her computer and reviewed the details again, noting her conversations with people. The more she uncovered, the more she felt like a boiling pot with different ingredients being tossed in. Cal was the stew that was cooking and simmering, releasing the flavors, and no matter what it tasted like at the end, it would be of her creation.

Later in the evening she made Grandma Ruth dinner and sat quietly with her while the sun began to cast its red light onto the walls and other surfaces of the living room. Cal remembered a saying about sailors and the red sunset; it seemed like an omen. After dinner, her grandmother took a shower, and Cal put down the shades and readied her blankets on the chair; she wanted to make sure that her grandmother was comfortable and would sleep well tonight as Cal didn't know what the morning would bring. Grandma Ruth came into the living room and embraced her.

"I love you, Cally," she said, her arms wrapping tightly around Cal.

"I love you too," Cal said, inhaling the smell of lavender soap and hope wafting from her skin.

"Your heart is heavy, but I won't ask you to tell me. Whatever you found out this morning tempered you. I hope it was for the better." Grandma Ruth sat down as she spoke, easing her way into the chair. "Just remember to listen."

"I will." Cal gave her grandma a kiss. "I'm going out tonight. I won't be too late getting home."

"Okay," Grandma Ruth said, turning on the TV. "You know where I'll be," she added with a grin.

Cal left the room and looked at her phone. Seven p.m. and nothing from Des. She could still reach him before the bar got busy, so she headed out. Cal told her butterflies to stay away, that this was all drama, that she hadn't seen anything, and that life was as it always was in Sedona. It was tourist season, and people were bustling around, eating dinner, and finding entertainment for the night. Everything looked so ordinary.

As she neared The Vortex, she saw Officer Sanchez talking to a group of people. It was perfect timing to park and sneak in without being noticed, except there were no parking spots nearby. She decided on the alleyway between the bar and an attorney's office, which she thought was ironic. Trying not to draw attention, she pulled down the alley. There was a fence at the end of the alley with dumpsters against it, and then it cut to the left behind The Vortex. Cal parked and opened the door. She heard voices behind the bar, voices that were hushed and angry. The conversation was meant to be private, yet her ears yearned to hear. Cal left the jeep door slightly ajar, crept to the wall, and listened. She made out the voices of two men.

"You owe me, man."

"I owe you nothing. You already got your cut, kid. What do you think this is? A charity?"

"Tommy, you said if I sold out in two days, then you would give me that bonus, and I did it. I risked a lot."

It's Tommy, Cal thought.

"Do you know who you're dealing with, boy? I've been in this game for a long time. I've got eyes and ears all over this town, and any one of them could do what you did. You know, if your mama knew you were working for me, your life would already be over."

The boy let out a laugh. "You need me. When I get out of here, I'll sell stuff for you at school, make you some real money, not this tourist shit you wait on—" The voice cut off, and there was a sound of scuffling feet and a muted thump.

"You just don't get it, do you? I got people from all over the place peddling my goods. You think I need you?" There was a sound of breathlessness and a large spit that splatted on the ground. "I need you like a need I need a cavity. The next time you come back here, you better have sold twice that much before you ask for more money. That's how this works."

There was another thump, this time like a crash of wet clothes onto the ground. Cal turned around and walked off quickly to the front of the bar and into the light. She disappeared through the hole and straight inside. From there, she looked out the window and waited for someone to leave the alley. "Come on," she said to herself. "Come out of there." Time passed slowly, and she almost forgot where she was when a bump on the back nearly knocked her over.

"Oh, excuse me, miss," an unfamiliar voice said. Cal whirled around to see a stranger. She waved him off and turned back to the window. There was still nothing.

"Hey, you," Des's voice came over the crowd.

Cal knew she couldn't stand there all night without looking suspicious, so she walked over to the closest end of the bar. "We need to talk."

"Okay, what do we need to talk about?" he asked her, pouring a beer into a glass and giving it to a guy sitting in front of him.

"Do you have a break coming up?" she was feeling jumpy, her fingers tapping against the bar top.

Des came over to her and put his hand down on hers. "Not for another hour or so, why?"

"Jack's in on it, Des. I called him, and he's in on it," she whispered, leaning into his ear.

"In on it? You mean with the…?"

"Yes. He basically told me to bury the story. He gave me some bull about not wanting to ruin tourist season here."

"That's not bull, Cal. That's real. He may just be concerned about it."

"It was more than that. It was how he said it. Des, this is bigger than I thought. He knows you were with me."

"So? Do you really think those three are in it together? Think about that, Cal. How logical is that?"

"You're right—it isn't logical, which makes it scary. We don't know who's in on it. Jack mentioned that, which I think was meant to scare me away from telling anyone about it. He probably called Officer Sanchez and Tommy when I got off the phone with him. Then, when I pulled into the alley just now, I swear I heard a drug deal go down between Tommy and some kid."

"What kid?"

"I don't know! I was trying to wait it out to see, but no one came out of the alley."

"They probably used the back. I haven't seen Tommy tonight, but I'm sure he'll make an appearance. How about Officer Sanchez—is he out there?"

"Yeah, that's why I parked down the alleyway. I didn't want him to see my car. I'm freaking out, Des. We've already said too much right here. Have you told anyone about today?"

"No, no one. I went home, showered, grabbed food, and came here. We had to do inventory before tonight and—"

"And you didn't tell Lucio?"

"I didn't tell anyone."

Cal's head was on a swivel, taking in the scene. She didn't know what to expect, only to expect something.

Just then, Tommy entered the bar, a bright white cowboy hat shining like a beacon on his head with a black t-shirt half tucked into jeans and light-brown boots. "Well, howdy-do, my people," he said with a laugh, and half the bar cheered to see him.

Of course they cheer. He's got them somehow.

"Des," she whispered, keeping an eye on Tommy, watching the locals come up and give handshakes and high-fives to him like he was a local celebrity. She knew him as Drunk Tommy, as a joke, but most people didn't seem to mind him. Why not?

Des leaned forward to her. "What?"

"Why do the locals love Tommy? What's in it for them?"

"Not sure. He's a pain," Des answered.

"Seriously. Think about it. He's a loser, and we know that, but why do they not know that?"

"He's funny… sometimes and—"

"He's Robin Hood," she said.

Des laughed, and Cal put her hand over his mouth, looking back at Tommy, who was still talking to a group of people. "He steals from the tourists and gives to the locals. The pot. People know about it and want it to continue because Tommy is paying them. I bet he has dealers all over the place. I heard him in the alley with that kid and he said that. He has dealers all over the country. He makes a mint and pays his people. And I bet he isn't the only one. If Officer Sanchez is involved, he's also paying influential people. Jack may not be involved, but I bet he's getting paid somehow."

"Cal, this is crazy, and I mean farfetched crazy. You need to stop watching TV. This is real life, and stuff like this doesn't happen in real life." Des shut up quickly and looked up. Tommy was standing at the bar next to them.

He looked down at Cal. "I'm surprised to see you here."

"Why's that?" she asked, playing coy.

"You were in that bathroom for a long time. Tell me something—did that stomach of yours feel the healing of the pines?" Tommy turned his attention toward Des. "I'll take a triple whiskey, son."

Des walked off to grab the bottle, and Tommy sat beside Cal. Cal was still standing and edged away.

He pulled the front of his hat down and laughed. "You know, I was really looking forward to giving you that tour. I've often thought of taking you to that clearing where the magic happens to people and showing you my own magic."

"You're so gross. You know that, Tommy? Tell me something." She felt the question rise up in her, and she couldn't choke it down. It was like taking a pill without water. Her mouth was dry, and there was nothing to help lubricate it. She blurted out, "How long have you been growing that field of pot?"

Tommy peered from underneath the hat, eyes squinted. He reminded Cal of a cat who noticed its prey from afar, only she was the prey. A smile inched over his face. "Look at you," he said without moving his mouth. "Look. At. You."

Des put the drink down in front of Tommy and went down to help another customer. Cal wished he had stayed, but she felt safe that Tommy wouldn't make a scene in the bar. Tommy picked up the drink, took a long sip, and then put it back down.

He looked at the glass for a moment, then up at her. "I thought you were smart. I even told Officer Sanchez that you were smart, too smart. But you got no common sense. You wouldn't have gotten all wrapped up in this if you had. You're in too deep, and there's only one way out." He took another sip.

"You gonna kill me, Tommy?" she asked, trying to hide her fear behind a slight smile.

"Well"—he shifted on the stool— "sort of. You see, you have a decision to make here. You can either be a tourist or become a local. Tourists don't live with us long because they don't understand us. They come and spend a moment of their lives, and we give them a memory. Locals, well those are different animals. They endure the summer heat and the winter snow. They live through droughts and monsoons. They understand what it means to dig in and survive somewhere. Have you ever had to do that? You came here for your grandma."

Tommy stopped long enough to take a drink. "She was sickly when you got here, cancer, I think I heard it was." Cal nodded. "Now I hear she's doing better, even walking around more. Now ain't that a miracle? You seem to have friends here, some you'd probably even call family; it sounds to me like you're a cactus starting to take root. Are you catching my drift?"

Cal wasn't sure what Tommy's drift was, but what he said was right, as much as she didn't want to admit it. The thought had popped into her head multiple times over the last couple of weeks, yet the last twenty-four hours made her question it. Could she stay in Sedona for a long time? Did she even want to? The sleepy town that awoke with the kiss of the tourist was both cursed and blessed. And with the current situation, part of her wanted to load up the jeep and run. Yet, at that moment, something was drawing her in, some unseen force that made her nod in response to Tommy's question.

"Well, that's about as quiet as I've ever seen you." Tommy laughed.

"Can I get you anything?" Des was back in front of them.

"Yeah, I'll take a bourbon," Cal answered, her eyes still on Tommy's.

Tommy smiled. "Yep, I'll take another one. You got what it takes to be local. Yep, you drink like one, you have friends, hell, I think you even pay taxes, but you're missing something. You aren't on the inside yet. Do you want to be?"

His question hung in the air like a smell that was neither completely bad nor completely good but definitely noticeable.

"I live here, don't I?" Cal responded, hoping it was enough to warrant the rest of his sentence.

"Then you have to get on the inside. We can offer you what you really want. There's money, family, and a fair amount of protection. All you have to do is say the magic word." Tommy's smile was perfectly white, the lines of his face deep crevices against the tan skin.

"Are you asking me whether I want to be a part of your little illegal drug action?"

"I don't think I said anything about illegal drugs. You can think about it, and get back to me when you're ready, but don't take too long. People 'round here can be a little jumpy, and remember that part about being protective? That's real. I guess I'll see you soon." Tommy stood, started to walk away, but turned suddenly. "You missed the part of my tour where I mentioned the power of the whisper in this place. We're built on it: crystals, pines, plants, and potions. You're either part of us or you're against us."

This time he walked off through the crowd, disappearing with only his cowboy hat bobbing above the rest.

Tommy was a warlock; he had to be. Nothing else could explain his strange power over people. At this moment, Cal felt powerless.

"Hey, what did he say to you?" Des asked, pouring a drink. "It's crazy busy right now. I wanted to stand with you," he admitted.

"He wouldn't have talked if you were here. You're not a threat. You're a local, right?"

214

"In a sense, yeah, but my parents work at the resort. They aren't exactly the typical Sedona dwellers. My mom goes to church. The religion around here is a bit more...earthy," he joked, but it was forced.

"Which is why you didn't know about this. Do you think everyone does? Like Lucio, you think he knows?"

"If he didn't, I'd be surprised. He grew up on Sanchez Ranch, and this is Tommy's second home. He's definitely involved."

"Think about it. If Officer Sanchez is working with Tommy, and Lucio hates his brother, how would he know? Maybe this is why they dislike each other?"

"Doesn't track." Des leaned in. "The rivalry was over the bar. You know that, right?"

"No, I've never heard the story. Honestly, I think people assume that I know things."

"You're aware of the ranch, right? The Sanchez Ranch in all its glory has been in the family since the Civil War, and the cattle are prize-winning, like the best in the West from what I hear. People in Sedona have had this love-hate relationship with them for years. They don't give jobs to any of the people in Sedona, except for the family, but they provide some status. The brothers got a share of the ranch when their father passed away. Marcial is this upstanding citizen, all clean-cut and law-abiding, well at least what you knew of him until today."

Des paused to pour a draft of beer and hand it to one of the waitresses. He continued, "When he was younger, he was not. Lucio said that his father's death was a wake-up call to Marcial. He told Lucio he had to leave to prove he was worthy of the family legacy and promised he would get his shot one day. When he came back, police badge in hand, Lucio was ready. Marcial assured him his time would come, but he needed to establish himself in the community first. Lucio agreed to stay while Marcial got a job with the police department. As Lucio tells it, months turned into years, and he finally said enough was enough. He demanded that Marcial give him half of the inheritance so he could leave and pursue his dreams. Marcial refused, saying that it'd break up the ranch. Lucio threatened to sue his brother, but in the end he just left and got a loan from a local bank to fund this place."

"Wow. I mean, I can see Lucio's point. I think I'd be pretty upset too, but at the same time, if it was going to break up the ranch, that'd be bad too. Why didn't Marcial fund it himself? Or try to help him in some way?"

"Who knows? I only heard the story from Lucio. Perspective is a funny thing."

"Do you trust him? Lucio?"

"About as much as anyone trusts their boss of a few years. Why? What are you thinking?"

"I'm thinking after work we have a little talk with him. Maybe we can't say anything, but he can. If there's anyone motivated to tear this down, it would be him!"

"I guess it's worth a shot," Des said quickly as someone called for another drink.

Cal had to stay inside the bar until closing time. She couldn't risk leaving and getting stopped by Officer Sanchez. Someone finally vacated a stool beside her, and she slid onto it. It was going to be a long night.

Chapter Twenty-two

As if darkness sucked the life out of Sedona, the bar crowd dried up little by little. Cal realized she was a part of a game, one bigger than her; one that she neither fully understood nor wanted to play. Up until the last couple of weeks, her existence in Sedona had been a blink in time. She never thought of it as fertile ground to plant her roots. Hell, she barely had enough money to plant anything, yet the prospect of leaving town sent ripples of sadness through her veins. But why?

What about Sedona had captured her heart?

There was Des, the incredibly kind Des, who looked for the good in everyone, even if there was no good to be found. There was the miraculous improvement of Grandma Ruth, who was now up and about, back to her old self in many ways. There was, until today, Officer Sanchez and his family, who had welcomed her into their tribe. But then there was also Jenny at the market, Lucio, Jack, and everyone up at Belle Butte; Cal wasn't just a tourist anymore—she was a local. She knew their stories, and now she knew their dark side. It was a ridiculous time to get sentimental; she knew it. Why now? It was as if Tommy's words threatened her existence, not just in Sedona.

"It's closing time." Lucio slapped his hand down on the bar hard, making Cal jump.

"It's about time," she smirked, feeling her palms

moisten again. "I need to talk with you."

"We've talked more in the last few days than ever before. More questions?" Lucio laughed as he wiped down the bar with a rag.

"I want to know about the field." It was pointblank, straightforward, and Cal knew it would elicit a response if she waited long enough.

"We don't have fields here in Sedona," Lucio answered, continuing his work.

"You know what field I'm talking about, Lucio, the one that connects your family's land with Tommy's."

He scowled as his hand polished one spot on the bar vigorously. "That family is not my family."

"But they are your family. You're a Sanchez. You know about the marijuana; you know about their business. What's in it for you? Why haven't you reported them?"

"If you think it's that easy, you don't understand this place at all. I always knew you were nosy. I knew it from the first time I saw you. Anyone who's friends with Jack. If you think that anyone will stand up to Officer Marcial Sanchez, well—"

"I can't believe what I'm hearing!" she yelped. "After all that talk about hating your brother, you're loyal?"

"Loyalty has nothing to do with it. I'm just not stupid. Tommy was my friend, too. It's not like I'm not getting anything out of the deal."

"So, you're all corrupt, every one of you. It's the whole town versus Belle Butte?"

"What does Belle Butte have to do with anything?"

"Tommy wants them out. He knows you can see everything from up on the butte. I can only imagine the lengths he's gone to keep his little secret safe. Or maybe all of you have done things...There must be another reason. People have been hiking that butte forever, and it hasn't bothered them. They can screen the field. You don't have the whole story."

"I agree with that. But they want Belle Butte gone. If not for fear of discovery, then why?"

"I don't know what to tell you, Cal. I'd warn you to stay out of it, but it sounds like you're in too far. The thing is when you can't trust anyone, but you can trust everyone, you learn quickly to listen for the whole truth."

Part of her wanted to fight back, ask more questions, wrestle with the facts but she needed to get home. She couldn't think with the stench of the bar permeating her nostrils and the sounds of overserved tourists hollering in her ears.

*****

Cal got home around two in the morning, her mind as electric as the sky. In the distance, lightning flashed, warning the inhabitants that storms were on the way. The last couple of days had left her with more questions than answers, and she was starting to feel the unseen pressure of time. There had to be something that connected the pieces. Why was the entire town on Tommy's side? How could they be involved in such an underground business? Why was Belle Butte still the enemy even though it was bringing money into the town? Why was Tommy against Belle Butte? Could it be as simple as needing to hide his operation?

She fell asleep to the questions, letting them drag her into darkness and dreamed of the last time she saw her parents driving off after dropping her at her grandparents' house. She imagined a car smashing into theirs, leaving them dead in a twist of metal, the smell of gasoline, followed by an explosion that blew plumes of smoke into the sky. With a gasp, Cal woke up and looked at the clock. It was just past six a.m.

Closing her eyes was out of the question, so she opened her laptop and the article she had written for Jack appeared on the screen. Cal read it, admiring her use of diction and syntax, and then realized its one-sided nature. It focused entirely on the few facts she had gleaned about Mark Courier but was missing the motive.

While she was convinced he was not hiding anything underground, she wondered why he was nervous enough to come to her house in the middle of the night to plead his case. His business would have been hurt by the accusations, but surely as soon as the truth came to light, all would be forgiven. Lucio had also said that the fields Tommy and Officer Sanchez had cultivated were hidden enough to where hikers on the butte wouldn't have noticed. Why would Tommy be worried?

It all seemed personal. Mark Courier and Tommy were the trump cards, yet what made them so? They couldn't be more different. Mark was sophisticated, intelligent, well-traveled, and a businessman. Tommy was a local and, well, a drug dealer and peddler of nonsense. Why were they foes? Was it purely the proximity of their land?

Cal sat back in bed, resting her head against the wall and rubbing her eyes. She needed coffee but didn't want to risk waking Grandma Ruth. "Jack," she said aloud. Cal picked up her phone and messaged him.

—Hey, you owe me. I want you to find out if there is a connection between Tommy and Mark Courier. I have

a feeling there is something we don't know.—

She hit send and laid her head against the wall. The phone vibrated a minute later.

—*Are you serious?*—

Cal didn't want to dignify the text with a response but knew she needed Jack's research skills. There were only so many social media and database searches she could do. Jack was well-connected, and though she wasn't fully sure she could trust him, it was better than going at this alone.

—*Yes. I could be grasping at straws...*—

Cal waited as the ellipsis bubble blinked on the screen.

—*Alright, I guess I owe you. I'll see what I can find out.*—

With that, Cal was satisfied and got dressed for the day. She had a full work schedule at Belle Butte and getting there early wouldn't hurt. Plus, maybe it was time to ask a few questions to those loyal to Mark Courier.

****

On the drive up from Sedona, she could sense the change in the air, the smell that only rain creates in the desert. Though the sky was mostly blue, patches of white floated in from a distance. She meant to look at the weather before coming to work but forgot.

Cal vacated her jeep at the same time Nia did.

"Whoa, long time no see, townie." Nia said as she shut her car door.

Cal couldn't help but notice the unkempt nature of Nia's clothing: wrinkled, stretched, as if they had spent time crumpled on the floor.

"Have you been home lately?" Cal remarked.

"Let's just say I've been spending a little time

elsewhere." She smiled radiantly. "It has never been this good, Cal. Mark is so much more present here. I think he's really taken up with this place as if it were in his blood. Thank you, Belle Butte!"

"Wow, I'm glad you two are—"

"In love! I am one hundred percent, totally in love!" Nia crowed.

Cal had been so preoccupied with what happened over the weekend that she hadn't thought about the drama of Belle Butte. It felt more like a reality show than the real-life mess with the likes of Tommy and Officer Sanchez. Her stomach sank as she looked over the edge of the butte toward what was Tommy's land and the Sanchez Ranch. Sure enough, she couldn't see anything. It was as if the field were invisible.

Nia broke the silence. "Listen to me going on and on. How was your weekend? Do anything crazy?"

"You know, just…hung out."

As much as Cal wanted to divulge the weekend's chaos to someone, she knew Nia was not that person. She still wasn't sure who to trust. Mark had laid his intentions bare the other night. It was Tommy and Officer Sanchez who were leaning toward villainy. Too many questions needed to be investigated before she could answer Tommy without losing her anchor, her home.

"Nia, you've known Mark for a long time, right?"

"Yeah, I mean, a few years. Like I said the other night, we worked together in Vegas. I met his father a couple of times."

"Did you ever meet the rest of his family?"

"I don't think he has a 'rest of the family' to meet. I mean, his father is still alive and a piece of work, but I believe his mother died a while ago. He doesn't talk about her much."

"No brothers or sisters?" Cal didn't want to be pushy, but all she could find online about Mark Courier was business related. This was the one area of his life that seemed off-limits to social media.

"Nope, none of those. Come to think of it, his mother must have passed a long time ago. When he tells me anything about his past, it's always connected to his father. He must have had a lonely childhood," Nia said reflectively, as if she had just considered his lack of mother as another reason to love Mark.

"The lack of parents can be a lonely feeling," Cal whispered, then shook her head.

****

Cal lost herself in the work of the day, giving multiple tours, cleaning the bathroom, and wiping down the cabin. It was after five when Jack's message buzzed on her phone.

—*The only connection I see is that Mark Courier's mother lived in Sedona for a while. In fact, the address is Whispering Pines.*—

Cal read the message twice before responding.

—*How is that possible? Hasn't his family lived there forever?*—

She waited as the ellipsis bubble flashed on the screen. "Come on, type faster," she said aloud.

—*Yeah, generations. I think you might have your answer, Cal.*—

"Holy shit!" she exclaimed. "It can't be, can it? How could we have missed it?" Cal dropped the phone into her pocket and grabbed her stuff. She could not bear to keep this find to herself.

Chapter Twenty-three

"It's funny how you imagine what someone looks like and then—"

"And then they're so much more handsome than you thought? Yeah, I get that a lot, brother. Is that why you're here, to connect to your other half? Well shit, son. I'm surprised."

"Oh, I've been by, Tommy. I've been by a few times in my life. When I was a boy, my dad brought me here and showed me the life my mother once lived before she met him. She hated this place out loud, but then she would talk about how magical it was, how easy it was to disappear and hide."

"She got that disappearing thing down." Tommy, laid back in his chair, laughed. "I'd sure as hell like to see you get to the point. I have things to do."

"I've made some mistakes in my life. I guess we all have. I think I took after Mom more than I would have liked to."

"I'll say an amen on that one."

"I came here to make up for those."

"Oh yes, the baptismal waters of Belle Butte. Can't even imagine how much money you've poured into that piece-of-shit rock. I'm not really sure how you've gotten away with it. But you know, I'm a man who understands how to use the land to one's advantage. Tell me something—how long are you going to store that radioactive shit down in those rocks? You may have fooled that girl, but you sure as hell haven't fooled me. We're cut from the same cloth, only I don't shit where I eat."

"Tommy, that's the difference between you and me. You still think this place is worth a damn. This is a drive-by freak show! Between talking trees and rocks, you attract hippies and spiritual nuts. They don't put money in your pockets, not really. Resorts, spas, and places like mine bring the clientele that will usher Sedona into the modern era. Don't you see? My name will go down in history here while yours will die with your little trees."

"Is this before or after we become the next Chernobyl?"

"I'm not a nuclear power plant, Tommy. I'm not creating the waste."

"You're just storing it for people who do."

"Something like that. You can learn something from me, you know. It's called diversifying your portfolio."

"And what happens if your little diversity gets into the water?"

"Suddenly you care about the land?"

"I've always cared about the land. I live off that land. That land is what sustains this place. That's what we are."

"That's good, really good. I'm going to add that to my website. Oh, speaking of. I think I'm going to hire Cal for that website-editing job; she could use the money, and she's a loyal employee."

"Well, I don't know if I agree with you there. I don't think her allegiance can be bought."

"Maybe, but it wouldn't be good for you if it were. If my little operation goes down, so will yours. I know everything about your land and that good ol' Officer Sanchez. Your little business is impressive, honestly. However, if you send a bunch of agencies to investigate me, they'll surely find what you've hidden in those pines. Do you really want to take that chance, Tommy? We could help each other, you know. We could be the brothers we were meant to be."

"Do you know much about the tribal presence here in Sedona, brother?"

"Just the basics."

"Huh, the basics. Okay," Tommy snorted. "There was this one tribe, the Hopi people, who were part of this land. Interesting tribe, the Hopis. They were peacemakers, which is funny considering they're now completely surrounded by the Navajo Reservation a few hours from here. Like many tribes, they were highly spiritual people, believed that people existed because of the stars and that one day the 'star people' would come back and rescue them from this world. A bunch of alien bullshit if you ask me, but there's one thing that struck me about them. They believe that you will reap what you sow. You don't understand this place, and you can stare me down with judgment, but I was born and raised here. This place is home, and my family has sown and reaped this land for generations—"

"You forget, Tommy, it's our family. Hey, I'm not here to start something with you. I'm here to give you a chance to be part of something bigger than you are. All of the big business here is on my side. They want to see Sedona become more than a side trip that niche tourists take. They want to see class, five-star tourists who come and enjoy everything this place offers. Don't you want that for yourself? For your 'generations'?"

Tommy sat, staring at Mark Courier. He hated everything he stood for. He hated his mother for choosing a life that looked like Mark. He wanted to lunge forward, take him to the ground, and show him what homegrown Sedona looked like. But the air was unstable, the earth beneath his feet unsettled, and the conversation had opened his eyes. Mark Courier was seeking more than a brotherly agreement; he was using their mother as leverage to shut him up. And why would Tommy need to be shut up?

He took a swig of beer but kept an eye on his brother. "You're afraid of me." Tommy let the words sit in the air and waited for Mark to fully digest them.

Mark shifted in his chair but kept his face straight and unaffected. "Now why would I be afraid of you?"

Tommy was impressed. "Because you need me! You're starting to realize that the people here aren't a bunch of idiots. Is that why you shipped all of your people in from California or wherever the hell they came from?"

"Oh, Tommy, you're shortsighted, aren't you? I came here as a courtesy—that's all."

"Did you? Or did you realize that people in Sedona are a family and look out for each other no matter what kind of money they have?"

"I don't know what you're inferring." Mark stood up from the chair and took a step toward the stairs. "Whether you like it or not, this is happening, and your land is part of it."

"My land is part of it because you can't ensure what you've hidden in that butte will remain that way. You can't secure it. You have no control over it and need assurance when it goes to shit. You need me and my land, the only place in miles that would be impacted by your nuclear spill."

"Nothing will spill. It's foolproof. If you sign these papers, you'll receive more money than any business you could start." Mark pulled a wad of papers from his back pocket and dropped them on the porch. Tommy sat, eyes unmoving from Mark's. "Keep your businesses; do what you'd like; I don't care. Sign the papers and make even more money—that's all I'm offering. Drop your witch hunt, shut your town up, and we'll all live in harmony, wealthier than ever."

Tommy leaned down, grabbed the papers, and nodded toward Mark. It was an acknowledgment, nothing more. Mark seemed to take it as such and moved down the porch stairs toward his car. "I'll give you forty-eight hours to make your decision. If I don't hear from you, I'll have to move on to plan B," Mark said as he got into his car. "I'd rather not see my brother in federal prison," he added as he shut the door.

Tommy sat still and drank the rest of his beer in one shot, throwing the empty can at the car as it drove off.

The sun was starting to set over the pines, leaving specks of gold across the dirt and patches of weeds around the trailer. Through the pines, Tommy could see the bones of the new homestead that were rotting, a skeleton of the past that would soon cease if a storm picked up enough wind speed, and there was one brewing in the distance, rumbling. Above that was Belle Butte, with its shark-fin protrusion postured to strike. There was no easy way to face this foe, and with that he walked to his truck.

****

The Vortex on a Monday night without tourists was

quiet. Everyone who was smashed the night before wouldn't dare come in again unless it was just a terrible Monday. However, during tourist season, Monday night was an extension of the weekend, every barstool full and every high top spilling over with glasses.

Tommy walked straight to the end of the bar and glared at Des.

"What can I get you, Tommy?" Des was always smiling.

"Double whiskey, no water."

Tommy swiped his hand up his forehead and under his hat, his father's hat. It was still a dusty-white color, though sweat through the years had created a ring design along the rim from much wear, like the inside of a pine tree trunk. Age always leaves a mark.

"Here you go." Des slid the drink to Tommy.

Tommy slammed the drink back, leaning his head toward the ceiling. As it fell, his eyes settled on Cal at the other end of the bar, talking to Des. She looked at Tommy with a half-cocked smile and tipped her drink toward him. The last time he had seen her, there was panic in those eyes. He was doing the threatening, he was in control, but that smile, that one right there, was not one of unease. She wasn't scared at all. Cal stood up and started walking in his direction. Tommy didn't take his eyes off hers.

"I was hoping you'd show tonight," Cal said, sliding beside him.

"I've waited a long time to hear you say that." Tommy smiled, tipping his hat. "Tell me something— what did I do to get such a sweet hello?"

"It's not what you did"—Cal leaned in and whispered— "it's who you are." She moved away and nodded to Des; he brought her another drink and hovered.

"What the hell is that supposed to mean?"

"Don't play dumb, Tommy. I mean, I know you're dumb, but this…this is just too good! I didn't know I had been set up as a tug-of-war between brothers." Cal's words dripped from her lips, a verbal victory.

Tommy nodded and looked down at his empty glass and back to Cal. "It doesn't change anything," he finally said, knowing his words were a lie. It changed everything. Tommy was no longer in control of his deck of cards. Before today he still had a play, a royal flush of opportunity to remove Mark Courier from the picture. Until today, Cal had been his ticket to remove the threat. All she had to do was send in the article, leave the actual town out of it, and let the cards fall where they may. No other names would be involved; everyone would be safe. She didn't understand the game; she didn't understand family; she didn't understand home.

Des must have filled up Tommy's drink because it was brimming with two more shots of whiskey when his eyes met the glass again.

"It changes everything," Cal responded. "Don't you get that? It's brotherly rivalry. You don't want him here because it puts your business at risk. Do you ever consider other people? Are you truly this selfish? What happened to the 'can't we all just get along' cliché?"

Tommy's face flushed, and he hurled his face toward her. "Oh, I get much more than you, much more." He stuck his finger in her face and tried to control his volume. "You think you know the whole story, but you know nothing. This isn't about some brotherly rivalry; this is about more than that. This is about legacy; this is about the legacy left before us. It's about the land, the trees, the water, the buttes, the canyons, the tribes, and the people…you can't just appear and understand it all. Once you're rooted, it flows through you; it speaks to you; it lives in you. You will never get that because you're not part of that. You work up there on that butte with someone who could give two shits about what we are, who we are, and you think you have it all figured out. I feel bad for you, Cal, tumbleweeding along. You're just dry roots, rot, dust in the wind. We don't need you anymore. *Get out!*" Tommy yelled.

The bar was silent, every face turned toward Tommy and Cal. He could see Cal's eyes starting to water, red flushing her cheeks, a slight shake of her hands as she removed them from her glass. Noise returned to the bar, but Tommy's eyes were once again unmoving.

"If it's really more than that," Cal said, her voice quivering, "then you deal with your own mess. I'm out." She stood up and walked away.

"Hey, Cal!" Des shouted. "Wait up."

The words fell hard on Tommy, much harder than he anticipated. There was a weight that he hadn't felt in a long time: responsibility. It was time to take matters into his own hands.

Chapter Twenty-four

"Wait up, Cal!"

"No, I'm done," she said. "I felt like I had him, and now I feel like an ass. So what if they're brothers; what does that really prove? What was I thinking?" She collapsed on the curb, her hands cradling her head.

Des' arm came around her, holding her against his chest. "It proves that there's more to the story, Cal. You shouldn't have been in the middle of it." He lifted her chin up with a single finger. "You probably know more about Drunk Tommy than anyone in this town. He isn't going to mess with you anymore."

"What he said in there…"

She wasn't sure what she was feeling. It was a terrible mix of guilt and confusion, as if she had solved a crime and realized that the criminal wasn't all that bad. The last two conversations with Tommy had revealed more about him than she had seen. Yes, he was a ridiculous human being, an absolute drunk, a pot farmer and dealer, and an overall pain in the ass. Still, now there was another layer, a layer that was proving much stronger than the pathetic facade. While he shamed his family's name and let his actual business go a bit, Sedona meant something to him. The people, the land, and even the magic played into each part of his life. Why did he start growing pot? And why was he now so against his brother? If he were genuinely jealous of him or hated him, why wouldn't he tell people they were related? Why hide that?

"What did he say?" Des asked.

"Tommy is the one that told me about Mark hiding something under Belle Butte," Cal blurted out as she stood.

"What?"

"Tommy told me about that. He wanted me to find out and write that article to shut them down, knowing the possible risk to him. When I was up at the butte today, I could barely see Tommy's property. I truly doubt anyone would notice the field. If I had written the article, he would have been out of the picture and safe from anyone nosing around his property. But I didn't…" Cal waited and stared at Des.

"Okay…"

"Because Mark stopped me. That night he came to my house, he told me everything, well almost everything. He gave me a sob story—but left out the part about his estranged brother. I asked myself so many times why he would have come in the middle of the night to bare all on my front porch. He was guilty, Des."

"He got away with it then. You put the gag order on Jack and walked away."

"But I didn't, did I? I continued to dig. We went to Tommy's, found out the secret, called him out, and his response?"

"He invited you in." Des narrowed his eyes.

"Yeah. He wanted me as an ally, knowing I was working at Belle Butte and Mark didn't fire me, which was also weird. They're both hiding something, both afraid of the other. What do you think Mark has in those tanks?"

"I'm guessing you don't want me to say water." Des sneered.

"We have to find out. I'm going up there."

"Tonight? Cal, you're crazy. There's a storm, a big one, one the news is saying will flood the canyons. We may be unable to make it down from there if we go up."

"I can deal with a little rain. The worst that could happen is I get fired," she said, walking toward the jeep.

Des ran behind her. "Or arrested! You can't just break in."

"Can't break in if I have the key." Cal shook her keys in the air and opened her jeep door.

Des opened the passenger-side door. "I don't like this. I'm coming with you."

"You sure? You could get arrested."

"Oh, I'm coming."

Night had fallen on the desert, and a drizzle bathed the butte in clouds and mist. Only a few road lights were leading up to the butte. Cal planned their break-in as they drove, thinking through the camera placements and alarm system. The path of least resistance would be the back door, but she would need the main-building keys. All she had were the keys to the cabin and the locker room.

"What's the plan here? I'm not going in blind." Des had been hitting his hands on his legs making beats since they started driving. His anxiety was palpable.

"The cabin. Clark and Nia could possibly have keys in their lockers. We can pry them open, snag the keys, and get in through the back door."

"And if we aren't lucky?"

"Let's not think about that."

The parking lot was well lit, but the rain was coming

down steadily now, leaving puddles in the dirt as they approached Belle Butte. Cal parked to the side of the road, and they hiked around the periphery in case someone else was there, though no other cars were in sight.

"The last time we came to this cabin we almost—"

"And then we did kiss, so we don't have to talk about what almost happened," Cal interrupted with a whisper. She heard Des chuckle behind her.

"Do you hear that?" Des was turned toward the butte, looking up as a flash of lightning lit up the space around them. "Sounds like water."

"It probably is. Remember the waterfall?" It was the first time Cal had thought about the supernatural waterfall in weeks. "The rain must be filtering through the rocks. This is the first big rain since the company was built."

They quickly made their way to the cabin, unlocked the door, and started for the locker room. Cal stopped to grab a toolbox from the closet.

The lights came on immediately as they entered the locker room.

"Shouldn't we turn those off?" Des asked with a deep breath.

"Geez, Des, nervous enough? Why are you breathing so hard?"

"Could it be because we're breaking laws? Have you ever done this before?" Des asked as Cal fumbled with a screwdriver against the metal.

"Loads of times. I spend most of my weeknights breaking into lockers." The screwdriver slipped from Cal's hands and bounced on the tile.

Des picked it up. "This is one of those fancy lockers.

You need a key code."

"And do you happen to know Clark's key code?" Cal shot back.

"Nope, but I bet I can guess it." Des put the screwdriver down, took out his phone, and turned on the flashlight. He held it close to the four-digit lock, cleared the wheel, and slowly clicked through each number. He finished with a *voila* as he opened the locker.

"How did you do that?" Cal asked, astonished.

"I wasn't always a bartender, Cal."

The locker was in disarray, complete with Clark's uniform, sunglasses, loose change, and bandanas. They took the clothes and shook them, hoping the keys would appear on the ground.

"Dammit, Clark." Cal brushed her hands through her hair and kicked the clothing on the ground. "I guess we try Nia's locker…she may have a key—"

"Or," Des interrupted, "I could try picking the lock."

"No offense, but up until tonight, I thought you were the cleanest bartender I'd ever met, and now that little bubble has popped. You can pick real locks, too?"

"I haven't done it in a while, but I probably can. But if there's an alarm, it'll sound."

"It would sound even if there were a key. As long as we get to the cave, I don't care if we get caught. If we get caught, they get caught."

Cal shoved everything back into Clark's locker, and Des removed a couple of tools from the box. The rain was falling harder, splashing down the side of Belle Butte and making ruts in the dirt toward the main building. They splashed to the back door; Des went to work immediately.

"This is a nice lock, very new and stiff."

"Thanks for the commentary, but can you pull this off? What was that?"

Cal and Des froze, rain streaming down their faces in the darkness. "Crunching and splashing," she whispered. "Did you hear it?"

"Could be an animal," Des answered.

"Whatever it was stopped moving. Should I go look around the corner?" Cal motioned toward the side of the building where the light from the parking lot streamed onto the ground, sharp and fluorescent.

"Are you crazy?" Des returned to work on the lock, quietly moving two objects inside the hole with his ear pressed to the knob.

"Are you almost done?" Cal's voice was low and urgent, her eyes darting around the back side of the cave mouth. Narrow Gap was black at night, looking like a mouth gaping open. Lightning flashed red and violent against the rocks, sending a thundering roar echoing through Belle Butte.

"Geez," Des said calmly. "I haven't seen a storm like this since I was a kid! *Aha!*"

With that, Des turned the doorknob and pulled the door; cool air rushed into their faces.

"You're a genius." Cal grabbed Des's face and kissed his lips quickly before stepping in.

"Well, I have a couple of tricks up my sleeve."

"Get in here!"

Cal started to close the door when she felt a force blocking its path. "What the hell?" she whispered and peeked through the crack. A hand, an arm, a shoulder, a face in the shadows braced the door from closing.

"Boo," said a voice in the night. A distinct smell of whiskey and beer drifted into the building and lay stagnant.

Cal opened the door, letting him step into the room. "Tommy, what are you doing here?"

"I'm guessing you know the answer to that question." Tommy took his hat and shook the rain from the brim before sliding it back on his head. "Try another."

"Okay, what the hell are you doing here, Tommy? Did you follow us?" Cal said a little louder; the sound echoed through the large room, competing with the beating of the rain against the roof and windows.

"Do we have to talk about this here?" Des's voice was much softer. "We may not hear an alarm, but someone else might. Let's just get on with it. This weather isn't playing games."

Outside, the parking lot was a steady flow of water, the downpour creating a water slide off the side of the butte.

"I always knew you were smart." Tommy laughed.

Cal glared at Tommy and took the elevator key from Christy's desk drawer. The three of them disappeared down the shaft without a word. When the door opened, they were in the first cave.

"There's nothing here," Tommy said.

"Would you keep your voice down, Tommy? It's a cave, probably not stable, considering what it's built on." Cal pointed to the maintenance hole. "The canisters are down there."

Her stomach was starting to burn, lit on fire from the lack of food and the presence of alcohol. She replayed the conversation with Mark in her head, heard his explanations, and wondered if all of this was for naught as she slipped into the yellow suit. *Why would they need these then?* If the canisters were full of red water, were they afraid of contaminating it? Did that make sense, or was she that naïve?

They took turns stepping down the hole. They reached the next door and heard the rush of water below.

"Wow, this is amazing," Des said, nearly inaudible against the sound of whitewater, which was much louder than Cal remembered.

"It's higher than the other day when I came here." There was only a tiny patch of sand now; the water had taken over the cave. "How is that possible?"

"You still don't believe in the magic of this place, do ya?" Tommy laughed. "Oh ye of little faith." He walked to the water's edge, removed his gloves and face mask, cupped his palm, filled it with water, and washed his face. "This was a holy place, a sanctuary for the Hopi tribe. Your boss up there, my brother, didn't dig this out; he stole it, perverted it. It wasn't a lucky guess; it was calculated."

"What does that mean?" Cal moved closer to him, eyes narrowing.

"He must have staked this place out for a long time, done his research. He needed a spot that people didn't know about that was safe. I doubt anyone knew this place existed except maybe some local tribespeople. But he didn't hire anyone local, or"—he nodded in Cal's direction— "not really local."

Cal felt a pang of sadness. She didn't understand why it hurt not to fit in, especially into Drunk Tommy's world. Why did she care so much? But wasn't that her motive? To prove that she fit someplace. Wasn't that why she was here?

"Only the problem is, the water can't be controlled.

It never could. It flows underground here in Sedona. Now, where are the canisters?"

"They're right"—Cal turned to the alcove where they sat a few days ago, but they were gone—"what the? They were here! All of them, stacked high and deep right here!" The place where she pointed was no longer sand. It had been replaced by water, voracious and hungrily eating away at the side of the cave, sending whitewater in all directions.

"I believe you," Tommy said, dropping his head.

"Where would they have gone?" Des asked. "They couldn't just disappear."

"Not disappeared," Tommy responded. "Hopefully, they were moved." He crouched beside her. "He knows we know. We're too close."

"Does that mean he'll leave?" Cal said.

"Hell no. They are here, someplace. He may have already sunk them down in the water somewhere, or the water swept them away. They aren't far."

"Then how are we going to prove it? Without those canisters, we have nothing." Des crossed over behind them.

"Not nothing." Tommy returned to the door, putting his gloves and headgear back on.

"So, we're leaving now? That's it? We come out of this with a loss?" Cal ran up to Tommy and put a hand on his shoulder. "I want to believe you, I do, Tommy. I want to believe that somewhere in you is the truth. That you didn't make all this up. But right now all I see is nothing. Mark's story checks out because he told me those canisters would ship with water to be bottled. Where are they? Huh?" Cal took her hand off Tommy's shoulder and waited for him to turn around. She wanted him to face her, to say anything that would help make sense of this.

"I've got nothing." Tommy's voice was quiet, sullen.

With that, he went through the door and up the maintenance hole, Des and Cal close behind him. They emerged into the top cave and stopped. Mark Courier stood statuesque before them, the light dull around him. Water was beginning to crawl down the cave walls, sending the light dancing against it, shimmering.

"I love technology." He laughed, sending a ripple of sound booming from the walls. "And you knew! You knew there were cameras and alarms, and you still came. I like that."

She removed her suit and walked toward him. "Where are they?"

"Excuse me?" Mark took a step back from Cal.

"You know what I'm talking about. Where did you put the canisters?"

"Oh, yes. The 'water,'" he answered, putting air quotes around *water*. "Well, we put those away. I had a feeling my big brother here might be poking around at some point."

"Yeah, you really do know me." Tommy dropped his suit and glided his cowboy hat back onto his head. "This family reunion has been nice, but I need a drink."

"Hold on there." Mark stepped in front of Tommy and put his hand out. "You aren't going anywhere."

"I believed you," Cal said with a growl.

"Did you? I don't think you did. It looks like you believe him." Mark pointed at Tommy and laughed again. "I wasn't expecting that—I have to be honest. I suppose people can be dragged down by their surroundings, but you seem so bright, Cal. You've got so much going for you. You want to be an editor, right? You want to provide a life for yourself and your grandmother, right?" Mark moved closer to Cal and dropped his voice. "I can give that to you. You can live wherever you want and do your dream job. Work for my company."

Cal looked at Mark and then over to Tommy; both had given her a similar choice. Both offered her a chance to live and thrive, to give Grandma Ruth a chance, only the stakes were higher. She would have to ignore the pit in her stomach and the moral and ethical dilemma that had surfaced over the last couple of weeks.

Could she ignore Mark's possible radioactive den under the butte in exchange for a new job and security? Could she be a part of Tommy's undercover operation, drugs filtering throughout the desert thanks to his fields? Why was she the object of their battle, a trophy to be won? Whether she liked it or not, if there was radioactive waste under the butte, Mark would poison the land just as he had done in Mexico, and that was worse than Tommy's illegal operation. At least he wasn't destroying anything, and the town was behind him. Even still, her spirit was unsettled. She could feel the water beneath her feet, the current pushing the liquid rapidly, roaring and lapping, yet her feet were dry. A lump rose in her throat as she felt three sets of eyes bore into her head. The pressure was building. Where was the release?

Cal closed her eyes and caught flashes of the last couple of weeks in her head, bits of lies and truth, moments of laughter and confusion, the ebb and flow of life. She saw Grandma Ruth rejuvenated, living and breathing. Cal felt her spirit expanding into the desert, howling at the moon, throbbing red against the hills. She was no longer a tumbleweed. She had roots, and this was her home. No one was going to take that away.

"I don't need either of you," she responded dryly and smiled. "This has nothing to do with me. You have nothing to do with me. If you two want to draw guns for this land, that's your business. What side do I pick? The one that saves Sedona."

Before Mark could breathe, Tommy lunged forward, knocking him to his back. Des and Cal ran to the side and edged toward the elevator, watching as Tommy threw a punch, landing his fist against Mark's face. Mark kicked Tommy back and scrambled to his feet, throwing his shoulder into Tommy, who was still reeling from the kick. Tommy fell to the ground and inched backward, grabbing one of the suits off the ground. Mark grabbed Tommy's collar and brought him to his feet, only to be met with Tommy's hands, each clasping an arm of the suit and twisting it around Mark's neck. Mark struggled against the fabric, kicking his feet until his knees collapsed in the dirt.

"Tommy, don't!" Cal yelled, running forward.

"Let him go!" Des chimed in, but Tommy pulled the arms hard, and Mark's face turned purple.

Cal stepped closer, moving her hand to Tommy's. "If you do this, it's over for you, Tommy. It will be murder, and this place will keep going. Killing him won't fix what he's done."

Tommy looked at her, the wild animal starting to retract back into his body. The cave began to quake. He released his hands, and Mark fell to the ground, gasping for air.

"We need to get out of here," Des said quietly. "It's not safe."

Tommy reached down, put Mark's arm around his shoulder, and dragged him to the elevator. No one spoke as they rose to the surface, the elevator shaking slightly as they ascended.

"Son of a bitch," Tommy exclaimed as the door opened. The rain had turned into a deluge, engulfing the building, making the ground move around them. Tommy dropped Mark, who fell to his knees and remained while Tommy backed into the room, looking out the windows.

Above them, the butte rose toward the sky, their view shrouded by the rush of water running down against the windows. It looked as if the building were surrounded by a waterfall, gushing and gurgling.

"Will this building hold up?" Tommy asked Cal.

"He said it would. Mark bragged that it was everything proof," Cal answered, shaking her head.

"It's not just that," Des added. "The water is underneath us. At this rate, we'll be swept away from all sides. Or we'll sink…"

"That's comforting." Cal poked around her pocket for her phone. "No signal. How about you?"

Des took his phone out too. "No."

"Son of a bitch!" Tommy exclaimed again and moved quickly to Mark, who was coming to on the ground. "You did this. You came in here, created this monster piece of shit, and didn't even think of the consequences. It was a holy place, and you destroyed it. How much of that radioactive shit is down there?" There was a loud rumble above them, around them.

Mark coughed, then laughed. "Enough to destroy your precious pines."

Tommy kicked Mark in the face, knocking him again to the ground. "We've got to get out of here,"

Tommy urged, the rain around them pounding, prodding, pleading to get in.

Cal pointed toward the side of the butte, barely visible in the darkness. "If we can just make it through Narrow Gap, it's our only chance."

"Go inside another cave? Are you crazy?" Des shook his head. "Nah, I'll take my chances."

"Tommy's right, Des," Cal said. "We can't stay here, and we wouldn't make it to the car, and even if we could, we would get swept off the road. The cave is safe. The water doesn't run in there like you think, it…filters or something. We'll be safe if we can get there."

"What about Courier? We can't just leave him here to drown."

"I'll carry him. He's my burden," Tommy said, low and steady, then stooped again to place Mark's arm around his shoulder.

Cal didn't understand. It wasn't that she wished Mark dead, but she didn't get why Tommy was suddenly full of valor. Mark's dream was already over, and Tommy's was too. Why care about him now?

"Let's go!" Tommy shouted at Cal, and the three of them and Mark, who was propped up on Tommy's shoulder, went to the back door.

At first, it didn't budge, the weight of the water pressing against it. Des and Cal leaned into it again and pushed hard. The door gave enough to send the water gushing into the building and allow them out. Rain streamed across their faces, and their ankles were immediately submerged. They moved slowly and carefully, inching toward the cabin, which looked like it had already shifted down the hill.

Cal remembered Clark saying that it never belonged

there and would never withstand the power of the butte. They angled up toward Narrow Gap, hanging onto the railings against the rock. The constant pull of the water made it impossible to speed their advance. Cal tried to keep her eyes forward, the parking lot's lights below them flickering against the rain. She slipped twice, gripping the railing with both hands to stabilize against the mud and water. Inside, the cave was dry and dark; the power had gone out.

"What now?" Des asked, shaking water off his 'fro.

"We wait." Cal looked over at Tommy, who had propped himself against a cave wall with Mark. She couldn't tell if they looked like brothers. It was even harder to tell now that their faces were swollen from the fight. Tommy was aged, skin wrinkled from the sun, but his eyes held light.

"Even when it isn't raining, you can hear the water running through the rocks." Cal kept her eyes on Tommy, who was staring out the mouth of Narrow Gap. "Clark compared it to veins when he brought me here for the first time. I think about Grandma Ruth and how much stronger she's gotten since we moved here. It's like she plugged into something that charged her, like a battery. Not that I believe in all that mystical stuff." Cal laughed.

"But you do." Tommy turned his face, and Cal caught a slight smile forming thinly. "I think we all do sometimes. When my mom left all those years ago, it rained like this. It rained so hard I couldn't tell whether I was crying or the sky was. It flooded every damn bit of our land, blew a bunch of pines down. It seemed like it took us forever to clean up that mess."

"You miss her," Cal stated.

"Not anymore. She never loved this place. That's

more obvious now than it ever was." He bumped into Mark's shoulder and looked at him. "I guess she got the upper hand. The die has been cast, and our fields and forests will be destroyed."

"Maybe not, Tommy. Maybe those containers are secure." Cal tried to sound convincing but even she felt the loss of hope in her statement.

"Then it's a matter of time." Tommy leaned his head back against the cave wall. "I've made a lot of mistakes in my life. I'm a drunk, been arrested, hell, I grow the best pot in Arizona...I wanted to feel the magic of this place again, to believe that it's still here."

Below them, the cracking and popping of the building sounded violent through the rain. Des got up and looked down from the entrance. "I've never seen anything like this, not in real life."

"I guess we made the gods mad." Tommy laughed. Mark coughed next to him, and he leaned forward. "There you are, brother. I thought that last shot may have knocked you out for good," Tommy said.

"Where are we?" Mark said slowly, coughing again.

"Narrow Gap," Cal answered, walking over and crouching in front of him. "You're just in time for the show," she added, pointing toward the entrance where Des was still watching, the cracking sounds getting louder.

Cal stood up and joined Des. The roof of the main building was already sagging, and the water had created a trench around the building, digging out the foundation with its relentless power.

"Looks like quicksand," Des said.

"It is. Won't be long now." Cal caught Des's eye and grabbed his hand. "If we leave here alive, I think I owe you a drink."

Des laughed. "I think you owe me a date."

"I'll take that." Cal turned around and watched Tommy and Mark slumped against the wall. "What are we going to do with them?"

"If we ignore them, maybe they'll go away," Des joked in a whisper.

"I wish. At least the threat seems neutralized."

"Is it? We didn't find the canisters, and I don't know about you, but I don't think Mark will tell the truth about what was down in that cave."

"Maybe not, but he won't be able to rebuild, and there won't be a place for him to store it. He'll leave—"

"And get away with it again. Cal, can you live with that?"

"Jack can get that article printed. The EPA will come out and test it."

"Do you really think Tommy's plan will work? It was a scare tactic. He knows that it wouldn't be enough to bring in the forces. It would have to be more than that." Des looked down. Another loud pop and the roof caved in, sending vibrations through Narrow Gap.

"What the hell was that?" Tommy stood up and looked out in time to see the back wall cave in.

"There it is, the sweet sound of a dream dying," Tommy's voice sounded both victorious and sad.

His eyes crept up to the horizon beyond the building. There wasn't much to see, just darkness and rain, but Cal knew what he sought. Down below was his dream, also dying before him. They stood there for a long time in silence, watching the building eventually plunge into the dark hole of the cave below, listening to the water rush around them until, little by little, the rain let up.

Chapter Twenty-five

Cal pulled up to the prison and stepped out of her jeep. Her new pair of red high-tops gleamed in the sunlight. It was her first time visiting a place like this, and she was immediately nervous. Tommy's phone call came out of nowhere a week before; her curiosity was piqued.

"Place your phone, keys, well, everything, right here," an older officer directed her when she entered the door.

"It's important," Tommy had said on the phone. "Just come out here, and I'll make it worth your time."

If the same conversation had occurred two months before, she would have yelled, "Hell no," and hung up the phone, but she had witnessed a change in Tommy.

After the night on Belle Butte, Tommy had called the police and turned himself in. He told them about his marijuana franchise and was arrested. During the trial, he pled guilty and got a hefty prison sentence of five years. The state destroyed the field, or what was left after the storm. Tommy made it clear that his neighbors were unaware of what he was growing.

Officer Sanchez kept his sterling reputation by helping to lead the investigation into Belle Butte, starting with the illegal building permits on the land itself and eventually the contamination of the underground river. The land was not unscathed; many animals and plants died from the chemicals and people got sick. The town was shut down until it was determined safe. Mark Courier was arrested but his bond was paid. Currently he was awaiting trial at his home in California.

"I'm here to see Tommy Roth," Cal said across the counter.

She was taken down a hallway and into a room with several tables. Men in orange jumpsuits sat across from their loved ones. Cal wondered what she was doing there. Again, she felt like she didn't belong.

"Tell me something," a voice came from behind her as she sat down. "Did you ever think you'd come to see me in prison?"

"I always thought it was a good place for you," Cal snapped, and Tommy sat down in front of her.

It was only the second time she had seen him without his cowboy hat. His hair had been cut, and he had stubble on his face. He looked better than he had in the past.

"Prison is treating you well." Cal nodded in his direction.

"That almost sounded like a pickup line." Tommy laughed.

"You wish." Cal rolled her eyes.

"What I wouldn't do for a double whiskey right now."

"The Vortex isn't the same without you."

"I don't doubt that one bit. The king left the building." He snorted and leaned down. "And how about you? What are you up to now that the world has turned upside down?"

Cal took a deep breath. "I watched the place where I worked sink into a massive hole, so I've pretty much been out of a job. Jack's given me as much work as possible, but he will be closing up shop. There isn't anything out there for someone like me, at least not in Sedona."

"How about your grandma? How's she?"

"It's a miracle, really. She's in full remission and getting stronger. In fact, we've had to come up with a schedule for who uses the car since she started volunteering at the local food shelter. Grandma Ruth has always been tough but beating cancer has given her a new *raison d'etre*. Alice said she's never seen such a recovery, as if the cancer had just disappeared."

Tommy looked down with a small smile. "Sedona will do that to ya."

The look on his face broke Cal a little. Seeing Tommy there, atoning for his sins, taking the fall for everything was almost more than she could bear. She wanted to say something, anything, but no words came.

"Here's the thing," Tommy finally said. "Whispering Pines is just sittin' out there, probably grown over as shit right now because I ain't there. Those feds destroyed the field and probably most of that property along Sanchez Ranch. I need someone to live out there and put in some work. I'm not saying it will be easy, and it won't make you a millionaire or anything, but it might put some money in your pocket."

Tommy stopped and looked up. Cal stared into his eyes; tears welled up, gravity begging to take them down her cheeks. She felt the water rush around her again, saw the life she had led over the last year, and wanted so badly to hug him or say something of worth.

"I'll be in here for a while, and even when I get out, who knows what the future holds. It would be nice seeing

Whispering Pines back to its former glory, the way my granddaddy created it. Think you could do that, Cal?"

"Tommy, I don't know what to say?"

"Well, hell, girl. That would be the first time you were ever speechless."

Cal laughed, sniffed, and wiped the tears from her eyes.

"Now my trailer is a piece of shit, but you can probably clean it up or something. My family has some money that I can give you access to. The feds took all my money. I left the keys for you at the front, even my truck keys, cuz your jeep can't haul stuff around on that property."

"Tommy, I—"

"I know, I know, and stop cryin'. I can't do nothin' with a cryin' girl. You got to be tough, like those pines, like everything else that grows out in the desert. You're no city girl now. You're a desert girl."

"Time's up!" one of the guards yelled.

"I guess that's my cue. I expect that when I get out, you'll have done right by my family's name," Tommy said as he stood up.

Cal also rose and opened her hand to him. He took it and they shook. She felt the thumping of his heart through his palm, the pumping of blood through his body. "I promise."

She stopped at the desk on the way out and collected her things, and with them was a bag. Cal opened it as she stepped outside: Tommy's cowboy hat and a ring of keys greeted her. She grasped the top of the hat, dusted it with her other hand, glided her curly 'fro back, and placed it on her head.

People aren't all good or all bad; they're just people.

Maybe the world would be better without a man like Tommy, or perhaps the world was full of them. But today, at this moment, Cal was thankful for him.

"Huh," Cal said aloud as she touched the brim of her new hat, "feels right at home."

A word about the author…

Kerry Fryar Freeman resides in Chapel Hill, NC with her husband and three children. Her stories are set in real places that are best known for their curious quirks and endearing characters.

She writes a blog called "Books and Bevies" where featured authors, from New York Times Bestsellers to self-published, pair their books with beverages. She can also be found at KerryFryarFreeman.com and followed on Twitter @KerryFFreeman and Instagram@Books_and_Bevies.

Printed in the USA
CPSIA information can be obtained
at www.ICGtesting.com
CBHW062313230124
3713CB00012B/884

9 781509 250974